Praise for the

For *Life and Other Shortcomings*

✳ Winner: 2020 International Book Award
✳ Winner: 2020 American Fiction Award
✳ Winner: 2021 IBPA Benjamin Franklin Award
✳ Winning Finalist: 2020 Best Book Award
✳ Winning Finalist: 2020 BkMk Press Fiction Award
Included in 2020's Best Beach Reads by *Parade*

"Featuring 12 stories about women in various cities and eras, each share a connection to one another. And you're along for the journey as they reveal certain truths about the female experience. It's an anthem, and also a cry for a change."
—*Parade*, "20 Classic and New Books About Feminism"

"A compelling collection that captures the mystery and menace beneath love and family life."
—*Kirkus Reviews*

"I'm in love with this book. It is just so good. It's real and definitely something that makes you feel like you've been heard and you have a friend."
—**Ann Garvin**, Founder of Tall Poppy Writers and *USA Today* best-selling author of *I Thought You Said This Would Work*, *I Like You Just Fine When You're Not Around*, *The Dog Year*, and *On Maggie's Watch*

"Pitch perfect and very haunting, *Life and Other Shortcomings* is a true delight. Adjmi's interlocking stories are as funny as they are tragic. Her characters are so real and relatable, you'll find yourself rooting for them, even as they get into trouble. Adjmi is a great new talent."
—**Alison Espach**, author of *Notes on Your Sudden Disappearance*

"Corie Adjmi has a flair for dramatizing scenes. She homes in on the killer moment, and her dialogue is so honest that I was cringing at times . . . It is just so vivid. "
—**Susan Breen**, author of *The Fiction Class*

"Corie Adjmi's stories are sharply written, unsparing, and spot-on. With wisdom and humanity, *Life and Other Shortcomings* plumbs the mysteries of adult life: the menacing underside of love, the protean nature of grief, and the baffling difficulty of staying true to ourselves and the things we value most. Assured in her storytelling, Adjmi writes with force and perception. Her stories are a must-read."

—**Elyssa Friedland,** author of *The Most Likely Club* and *Last Summer at the Golden Hotel*

"Among the women of these stories are dutiful housewives, devoutly religious women, insecure teenagers, and many other colorful characters. Pop culture references peppered throughout—including nostalgic callbacks to Dr.Scholl's sandals, Swanson's Frozen Dinners, Star Trek, and The Brady Bunch—only add to the realism and heart of the book. These stories are full of drama, humor, descriptive language, and insight, and they make for a very enjoyable read. Adjmi subtly, but so perceptively, unfolds the characters' private fears, hopes, and dreams, zeroing in on how a single experience or event can change a life."

—**Jewish Book Council**

"Twelve accounts bear witness to the female experience, and how the choices we make look differently depending on when and where we live. As a whole, the collection illustrates the influence of patriarchy, especially so before the #MeToo movement."

—*Travel + Leisure*

"Corie Adjmi's Life and Other Shortcomings is a slice of life literary work full of lessons that need to be shared today. Juxtaposing the present with the past, the book reveals a web of interconnected stories meant to relate to women›s everyday lives. These stories are so honest and relatable, it hurts."

—*Readers' Favorite*

"We're all familiar with the happy parts of relationships, we've been raised on them, but *Life and Other Shortcomings* gets into the nitty-gritty of what comes over time."

—**Paperback Paris**

"All that glitters is not gold in Corie Adjmi's wonderful short story collection *Life and Other Shortcomings*. Adjmi exposes the fear, envy, and yearning that simmer just beneath the surface of her characters' beautiful lives. Her writing is both elegant and powerful. I was hooked from the first page to the last."

—**Ellen Sussman**, *New York Times* best-selling author of four novels, *A Wedding in Provence*, *The Paradise Guest House*, *French Lessons* and *On a Night Like This*

"For fans of *Three Women* by Lisa Taddeo, Amazon's *Modern Love*, and HBO's *Mrs. Fletcher*, *Life and Other Shortcomings* is both a cautionary tale and a captivating window into women's lives. An honest, incisive, and compelling portrayal of the female experience."

—**Beyond the Bookends**

"Corie Adjmi's linked short stories tell of the heartaches and difficulties of growing up—physically and spiritually—as a woman in a patriarchal society. Wonderful writing!"

—**Francoise Brodsky**, Director Shakespeare & Co

"When you're tired of binge-watching Netflix, this collection is an honest cautionary tale about the female experience."

—*Brit + Co*

"Twelve stories highlight very different women and their journeys. Take a peek into these women's lives and into their relationships."

—**Frolic Media**

"Take a break from reality and relax with a great new book."

—**BuzzFeed**

"Honest portrayal of women in a patriarchal world."

—**Bookstr**

"Poignant, laugh-out-loud funny, and unnerving all at once, *Life and Other Shortcomings* is the one you've been waiting for. This collection is replete with emotionally charged, compassionate, true tolife characters. Stories come together to create layer over layer of veiled emotional and psychological complexity."

—**Nicole Dweck**, author of *The Debt of Tamar*

For *The Marriage Box* (2022):

"This book was real and authentic, giving the reader a stunning storyline and a unique cast of characters. There is so much growth and change within this story and it is so well written . . . I would highly recommend this book to anyone."
—**Readers Favorite**, 5 STARS

"*The Marriage Box* is a brilliant coming of age story that moves swiftly between the worlds of New Orleans and the Syrian Jewish community in NY. Our heroine, Casey, is flawed, kind and so vivid. We fall in love with her as she grapples to balance her need for independence with the comforts and constraints of tradition. I can't remember when I last enjoyed a story so much: I laughed, I cried, I learnt, and couldn't wait to turn the page to find out what Casey was going to do next. *The Marriage Box* is an absolute delight!"
—**Ariana Neumann**, *New York Times* best-selling author of *When Time Stopped* and National Jewish Book Award and Dayton Literary Peace Prize winner

"*The Marriage Box* is a wonderfully delightful page-turner that takes a deep dive into the intricacies of the Syrian Jewish community in New York. With humor, insight, and grace, Adjmi examines the plight of a spit-fire teenager who struggles to find where she fits in the world. As Casey Cohen journeys from wild teen to 18-year-old married woman, she will win every last reader's heart with her witty commentary, down-to-earth attitude, and courageous spunk. An unquestionable joyride from start to finish. This book is a must-read!"
—**Jacqueline Friedland**, *USA Today* best-selling author of *He Gets That From Me*

"A nuanced look at one woman's conflicted desire to break free from a regimented life."
—*Kirkus Reviews*

THE
MARRIAGE
BOX

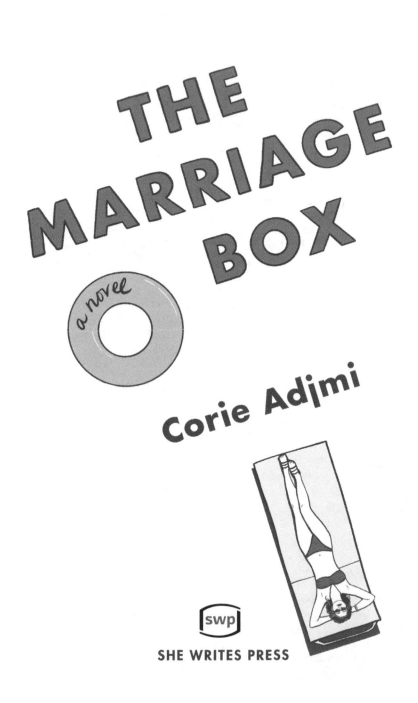

THE MARRIAGE BOX

a novel

Corie Adjmi

swp

SHE WRITES PRESS

Published 2022
Printed in the United States of America
Print ISBN 978-1-64742-079-6
E-ISBN 978-1-64742-080-2
Library of Congress Control Number: 2022904035

For information, address:
She Writes Press
1569 Solano Ave #546
Berkeley, CA 94707

Interior design by Tabitha Lahr

She Writes Press is a division of SparkPoint Studio, LLC.

To my children and grandchildren. This book is for you. Stories enlighten, they inform, they entertain. They cultivate empathy, raise questions, and foster change. Use your voices. Create your own narrative. Dream big. I love you.

Prologue

The night started out like every Syrian Jewish wedding. The florist pinned white orchids around the chuppah. Caterers folded yarmulkes into black half-moons. A photographer snapped our picture: me—eighteen years old, in a high-neck, long-sleeved, Victorian-style wedding gown, nails polished Rebel Red—and Tracey, my cousin and best friend, in off-white satin, neckline plunging enough to make people stare.

"Casey, you don't have to do this, you know," Tracey said.

While I'd spent the summer shopping for my trousseau and planning my wedding, Tracey had spent the summer getting ready for college, where she'd barhop and dodge unwanted pregnancies. Now and then, she'd study. She couldn't understand why I was adhering to my family's expectations— marrying a Syrian Jew, shopping at Tiffany's for wine and water glasses, contentedly testing chicken and eggplant recipes dashed with allspice.

"Smile," the photographer instructed.

Tracey looped her arm around my back. "You might as well smile now while you're still happy." We posed in front of a six-foot golden Jewish star. "Why can't you just live with him like every other normal American girl? This isn't 1882 Aleppo. It's 1982 America."

"This isn't America," I said. "It's Brooklyn."

In the few years since my family had moved from New Orleans, returning to our roots in Brooklyn, I'd learned the hard way there were rules. A teenage girl was taught to dress for seduction but was forbidden to have premarital sex. She couldn't date until she was sixteen but had to be married by eighteen. And she certainly couldn't live with a man unless she was his wife.

o   o   o

"And what's with your dress?" Tracey went on. "Why'd you pick something so virginal?" She used her fingers to form a halo over her head and smiled, posing for the camera. Hands on her hips, she looked at me. "You're doing exactly what you swore you wouldn't do. You said you didn't want to be like our mothers, who went straight from their father's house into their husband's. You said you didn't want to be like other Syrian girls who got married before they were of legal drinking age, before they had a driver's license."

"I have my license," I said, turning from Tracey.

The guests from New Orleans scoped out the Brooklyn synagogue like they were stepping on foreign soil. They'd never been to an Orthodox Syrian wedding, and you could tell from their faces, their foreheads crinkled, they were having a hard time accepting the idea of an eighteen-year-old getting married. Plus, the whole affair was kind of like *Fiddler on the Roof* spiked with *Lifestyles of the Rich and Famous*, a party for eight hundred people where every woman in the room, regardless of age or religiosity, wore a skintight dress (size two) and Christian Dior stilettos—dolled up like Barbie with long black hair.

I was an exception with light hair and fair skin, forever sticking out. "A blonde," my mother always said as if I were a foreign object, "in this house. Unbelievable."

Tracey stood by my side. "This is like *The Twilight Zone.* I can't believe you're getting married. 'Sadie, Sadie, married lady,'" Tracey sang the Barbra Streisand lyric as a tall waiter in a black tuxedo walked by. He smiled at her.

Tracey cupped her hand over her mouth. "He's cute," she whispered.

"He is."

Tracey wagged a finger at me. "Uh-uh. There'll be no more of that, young lady."

"Bye-bye to the good old days," I said, realizing I didn't know how to behave around cute single boys anymore.

Tracey smiled at our handsome waiter and took two shots of arak off his silver tray. She handed me one. "Drink up," she said. "You're going to need this."

"I want to get married. I want to do this," I remember telling Tracey.

But memory, like love, is fickle. It's true, I thought my life would unfold like a romance novel, one scintillatingly evocative chapter after another. When you're eighteen, you think your dreams are undeniable truths. At least I did. I had no clue my brain was still developing or that during my first year of marriage, I'd grow an inch.

New Orleans, 1980

On the morning of our move, I stay in bed studying the details of my New Orleans room so I can remember them later when my family gets to Brooklyn. At night, my curtain rods create shadows long as Pinocchio's lying nose, and the wallpaper—too young for me at sixteen—is printed with little girls wearing bonnets and carrying umbrellas, strolling this way and that with no apparent direction at all. I step out of bed, curling my toes into the carpet, plush as a Jazz Fest lawn. I dress, not caring what I look like.

On my way to the kitchen, I take in the sight of our pool table—and etch it, too, in my memory. Will I remember the green top where my brother, Sam, and I sat and sprawled and played? The deep pockets? All the glistening balls? Or would I only recall how my father had the pool table delivered to our house without telling my mother, and how it sat anchored in our den like a large ship.

The kitchen pantry is nearly empty. Preparing for our move, my mother let everything run out. No more Oreos, Pop-Tarts, Frosted Flakes, or Trix. All that is left is half a box of Captain Crunch. I sit down at the dinette table and pour chocolate milk thick as velvet into a bowl. Cereal bobs like a bunch of baby yellow life rafts.

"I have to fix things, Elsie," I say to the cow pictured on the carton. "There's got to be a way to make things right." I drink the last bit of milk, carry the empty bowl to the sink, and let my hands linger under warm, soapy water.

Through the window, I spot my parents in our driveway jostling luggage, loading our car. When they finish, my father slams the trunk shut. He splays a road map across the hood, and my parents huddle over it. It is barely light outside and my mother is already dressed. Perfectly fit, she wears a crop top and low-riding jean shorts. I slip a hand under my tee shirt and with a finger trace the scar on my stomach. Not wanting anyone to see it, and humiliated about how I got it, I would never wear an outfit like my mother's.

The plan is that my father and I will drive from New Orleans to New Jersey, where we will spend the summer in a rented house. My mother and Sam are traveling by plane. I wanted to go with them, but my father, still mad about what I've done and not wanting me out of his sight, said, "Cassandra, you're with me."

While I never liked the sound of my full name, when my father said it then, so full of disenchantment, it felt particularly off-putting.

We leave New Orleans just after dawn. My mother and Sam stand, as if in a police lineup, watching as my father backs our black Cadillac with cherry-red leather seats out of our driveway. Tears well in my eyes as we pass our magnolia tree. It's overgrown and blocks much of our house. My father wanted to transplant it in our backyard but didn't because Mr. McKinley, our gardener, suggested we leave well enough alone. Magnolias have a hard time adapting.

We drive down Canal Boulevard, a street that sways as if jazz beats below it. At a red light on Harrison Avenue, I glance at the library I spent hours in—learning the Dewey decimal system and flipping through the card catalog, trying to locate

my summer reading books—and my mind floods with memories of Tracey. Playing king of the raft, riding our bikes for
Snow Balls, sleepovers, gymnastics, watercolor painting, and
hook rug classes. Even the time we got a week of detention
for leaving school during lunch now feels like a fond memory.

An orange sun threatens to rise in the distance, and I cry as
my father speeds across the I-10. Wordlessly, we travel through
Louisiana and Mississippi, stopping for gas whenever we run low.

Gone with the Wind rests on my lap. I never thought of
myself as someone who'd take things that didn't belong to me,
but with all that's happened, it doesn't seem to matter anymore.
So, on the last day of classes, I stole the novel from our high
school library.

It's not that I'm an avid reader. I just wanted something
to connect me to the South and to my Franklin Prep classmates who are smart—real smart—ferocious readers, winners
of national essay contests and state science fairs.

Franklin Prep is considered to be one of the best schools
in the city, but I never tried to get good grades. Maybe it's
because my mother didn't care. "Just get Cs," she'd say. "Just
get by." But Franklin Prep is a college preparatory school,
and that distinction was key. Plus, the girls in my class were
basically hairless with tiny pug noses, while I have hair on my
arms, above my top lip, and on my big toes.

My father turns on the radio. His purse is wedged between
his thigh and the car door. Without taking his eyes off the road,
he unzips it. He plops a piece of Bubblicious shaped like a tiny
pink brick into his mouth.

I thought my father carrying a purse was the most humiliating thing ever until the day he picked me up after school on
his red motorcycle, wearing a shiny silver helmet and dark sunglasses. Mr. Catonio, the headmaster, was out front, standing
under the American flag, and he studied my father as if he'd
encountered an alien from another planet.

My father raises the volume on the radio when Queen's "Another One Bites the Dust" comes on. He drums on the dash and sings out loud.

Are you happy, are you satisfied?

o o o

When I told Tracey we were moving, even though we hadn't talked for weeks because of what had happened between us, she said, "Who moves junior year? Nobody. Nobody moves junior year of high school. Tell them."

But since my parents believe everything that has gone wrong in New Orleans is my fault, they aren't interested in my opinion. They want to move back to the community where they both grew up. Back to a world that is safe and controlled.

Stuck in some kind of weird time warp, Syrians follow Orthodox traditions, and my parents want that now, so instead of returning to a prep school in September, I'm enrolled in a yeshivah, a religious school, where boys and girls learn in separate classrooms.

Every day, Sam will have to pray, thanking God he is male, and I will have to wear a skirt long enough to cover my knees. Tracey is going to freak out when she finds out that a girl's virginity is still valued like some kind of precious prize.

My father swerves, avoiding roadkill, and *Gone with the Wind* falls to the car floor with a thud. I pick it up and place it back on my lap. Outside the sun hides behind clouds, and I study license plates. In what seems to be never-ending time, I see plates from Tennessee, Arkansas, Colorado. Even California. People from everywhere travel like free birds across our country.

Air conditioning blows on my arms and legs, and I get goosebumps. Bringing my knees to my chest, I slide the vent closed.

"Are you cold?" my father asks, adjusting the temperature.

"I'm fine," I say.

This is the first thoughtful thing he's said to me in weeks. Stretching, I rest my feet atop a box on the car floor. It contains knee-high purple boots, the ones Grandma Rose sent from New York.

"Isn't that just like your grandmother," my mother said when the package arrived in the mail. "Not a practical bone in her body. Who cares if it's one hundred degrees in New Orleans? Every girl must have plum-colored boots." She lifted them from the box and looked at them up close. "I have to admit, they're stunning," she said.

Later that night, alone in my room, I tried them on, prancing around in a bra and panties, modeling the boots in front of the full-length mirror behind my locked door. At Franklin Prep, the kids in my class wore Lacoste and corduroy. I thought I'd never wear purple boots. *Ever.* Turns out, teenagers have little say in their own lives, and who could have predicted I'd be leaving behind my preppie school, moving to New York, and bringing the boots with me.

My father changes the radio station, and Diana Ross sings "Upside Down." He taps a single finger against the steering wheel and blows a pink bubble.

We still have a long way to go. Exhausted, all I want to do is sleep. I try to adjust my seat for more legroom but can't. The back is crammed with cartons and bags full of our belongings: our family photo albums, my mother's jewelry, my father's trophies—and his .38 caliber Smith and Wesson.

The gun is in a box, jammed in a corner. Not wanting me to touch it during our journey, my father pointed it out, which was totally unnecessary because I always knew where he kept it.

We are not the kind of family to own a gun—most Jews don't—and my mother didn't want my father taking it with us to New York. She'd read a story in the newspaper: A woman had flown in from out of town to surprise her boyfriend on his birthday. She hid in his closet, and the birthday boy, not expecting anyone in his apartment, shot at the noise, accidentally killing her.

But my father had been unwavering. "New York is dangerous," I overheard him telling my mother. "This is the eighties. It's not like when we were growing up." He agreed to keep the gun unloaded. But for our own safety, he wouldn't leave it behind.

Not wanting to think about violence, yeshivah, or this dumb move, I sandwich *Gone with the Wind* between my head and the window and close my eyes.

New Orleans, 1976

I probably wouldn't have ended up in Brooklyn if it wasn't for my father's gun. He didn't even start out wanting it, but the year of the bicentennial, the year I turned twelve, his brother, Uncle Bobby, finagled a police badge from the mayor of New Orleans and had been showing off, claiming it was a lifesaver. It had come in handy—saved him a couple of speeding tickets—and my father wanted one too. After that, one thing just kind of led to another. Maybe that's how everything in life happens.

The NOPD badge transformed my father into some kind of superhero. Fearless while at his souvenir store in the French Quarter, almost daily, he pinned shoplifters against the wall.

"He's out of control," my mother said to her sister, Aunt Susie, while offering her milk for her coffee in our kitchen.

Aunt Susie is Uncle Bobby's wife and Tracey's mother. Sisters married brothers. Tracey and I call ourselves double first cousins, all our relatives the same, and we love telling people this family fact and watching their disbelief.

My mother poured coffee for herself and did not add milk. She sat down next to Aunt Susie. "He's a big fish in a small pond," my mother said, insulting my father and the city of New Orleans simultaneously.

My mother never liked New Orleans and had no idea she would end up living there. My father was set to work for her father, Grandpa David, in New York, but my father and Grandpa David didn't get along. Plus there was opportunity for him in New Orleans, where his father, Grandpa Sam, lived. According to family lore, Grandpa Sam was supposed to be just passing through New Orleans after coming from Aleppo, but he fell in love with "back of town"—raw, smoky basements and jazz music. He found work peddling silk stockings to ladies of the night and eventually opened a store on Royal Street, where he sold souvenirs. Seduced by all the glittery Southern decadence, he treated my Syrian grandmother badly after marrying her and taking her away from her close-knit family in Brooklyn. They had five children, my father being the youngest, before my grandmother Cynthia moved back to Brooklyn, taking my father, at five, with her. So even though my father adored community life, he needed to make a living, and the family business was in New Orleans.

After a few robberies in our neighborhood, my father came to believe his badge wasn't enough. "What am I gonna do, flash it at a burglar?" No, he needed something more. That's when he came home with his gun. He extended his arms, revealing it to me and Sam. It shined smooth as an eight-ball.

"I can't deal with this insanity," my mother said, sweeping her long black hair away from her face. "What kind of crazy city is this? You're not a cop, Steven. Are you?" She put her hands on her hips. "Are you a cop and I don't know it?" And probably because she saw *Live and Let Die* that summer, she added in a British accent, "Maybe you're Bond. James Bond."

"Very funny, Sharon." He turned from her and restored his gun to its brown leather case, fastening the safety strap around it.

o o o

That summer women's liberation was in full swing, and my mother wanted to be a part of it. She thought it was important she get a job. Aunt Susie questioned my mother's decision to enter the workplace, reminding her that she still had two children to raise.

My mother and Aunt Susie had conceived days apart, and Tracey and I were supposed to be born back-to-back, practically twins. I was due first, but Tracey came out three weeks early, beating me into the world.

My mother said Aunt Susie was making a big deal out of nothing. "You act like I'm abandoning my kids."

Aunt Susie just looked at her.

"Stop it, Susie," my mother said.

The next day, she put an ad for a housekeeper in the *Times-Picayune*, and a woman from Guatemala showed up for an interview. Her name was Nellie, and she followed my mother to the yellow velvet couch in our living room, telling her how she'd come to America craving a better life and how she'd left her family behind. She said she wanted to live with us and that we could be her family.

My mother hired her immediately. I watched from the doorway as Nellie unpacked her bags in our guest bedroom. "You can come in," she said, not looking at me. I sat down at the foot of Nellie's bed while she set a statue of Jesus Christ on her dresser. I had never seen a statue like that before, and Nellie must have suspected I was curious about it because she turned and glared at me. "These are my things," she said, struggling to speak English. "Don't ever let me see you touching my things."

Within a few days, my mother secured a job at Net Set in the Lakeside Mall, and she wore her work uniform, a white tennis skirt with an appliquéd yellow ball on the pocket, with pride. As further proof of her commitment to the women's movement, my mother gave up her standing appointments at the John Jay Salon, cut her Cher-length hair short, and joined a new culture of women who thought, *Why bother?* My father was furious and viewed this act as deliberate and hostile.

"It's my hair," my mother said.

"I'm aware of that, Sharon. But I have to look at you."

My father believed American women had gone too far and that it was a mistake to think looks didn't matter. He had his own idea of beauty, a Syrian man's expectation, and he was always saying that at the very least she could put lipstick on before he came home from work.

The tension between my parents was high that summer. Things would start out fine and somehow end in disaster.

o o o

One hot New Orleans day, my father suggested we go swimming. In the deep end, Sam did a cannon ball. I did a jackknife. My father dove and glided through the water.

"Let's see who can hold their breath the longest," my father said when he came up for air.

The three of us formed a circle and dunked. I came up first, then Sam. My father stayed under. After what felt like a long time, he rose to the surface but floated facedown. I tapped his shoulder and he didn't budge. Sam grabbed his arm. "Daddy, the game's over."

"Help!" I cried. "Help!"

My father sprang up with a roar and dug his fingers into my ribs.

"Stop it!" I screamed.

He fastened my arms together, holding me tight, and put his face close to mine, scratching my cheek with his dark sideburns. "You're my hostage," he said in a sinister voice. "I'll never let you go."

"What's going on out here?" my mother asked, opening the sliding door. "You know I hate teasing."

"We're just playing," my father said. "Come join us."

She was wearing a black bikini, and she closed the door behind her.

"*Ooh là là*," my father said, staring. And my mother blushed from his flirting.

My father stepped out of the pool and wrapped a towel around his toned waist. He slid his bedroom door open, put on the radio, and turned up the volume. We had central air conditioning, and never careless, a genuine supporter of the Give a Hoot, Don't Pollute campaign, my mother asked him to close the door. My father wanted to hear the music and said it would be fine to leave it open for a few minutes. He smiled, took hold of her hand, and lifted her from the lounge chair. George Harrison's "Give Me Love" played in the background. Standing behind her, he danced and held her arms out to the side like wings of an airplane. His towel fell as he wiggled his red Speedo bathing suit against her. "Give me love, give me love, give me peace on earth," he sang.

I sat dripping near the edge of the pool. My mother remained rigid, motioning at me with her chin.

"It's okay, Sharon." He spun her around and smiled. "Give me love," he sang as if there had never been a disparaging moment between them, as if he could simply move forward from this minute on in pure marital glee. "Let's have another baby."

"What? Are you crazy?"

He let go of her hands and stepped back. "Why is that crazy?"

"I just got a job. I'm just starting to live." She sat back down, stretched her legs out on the lounge, and lifted her *Good Housekeeping* magazine. When she didn't look up, my father walked away.

Even though my mother needed to keep my father at a safe distance, she didn't want to push him too far away, so for the rest of the day she was attentive and kind. She made both tuna fish and egg salad for lunch and served mayonnaise on a plate instead of out of the jar. We sat outside at our round table under an umbrella. Wearing a black lace cover-up over her bikini, my mother held tongs and smiled. "Salad?" Her red lipstick shimmered.

"No, thank you," my father said, not looking at her. "I'm not hungry."

My mother turned her attention to me as if unaffected by his response. "Tuna or egg?" she asked.

My parents were at it again, this game of theirs. I might as well have been invisible.

After lunch, my mother went inside and took Sam with her. "It's too hot," she said, shutting the sliding door.

My father let his legs dangle off the edge of the diving board and dragged his big toe through the water. I sat next to him, my blonde hair in braids, my legs skinny as a chicken's. Side by side, our reflections rippled below. Neither one of us said a word. And then just like that my father snapped out of it, stood up on the diving board, held his fist to his mouth like a microphone, and sang, "When you were young and your heart was an open book, you used to say, live and let live. . . ." And he danced, putting on a show, before he dove back into the water.

Just then our gardener, Mr. McKinley, unlatched the gate. He had his son with him, who was about my age. He was Black and I thought he was cute. Wearing my yellow bikini, I ran from one end of the pool to the other, and the flaps on my bathing suit fluttered like petals in the wind. This was when I still wore bikinis, before the scar on my stomach, before everything went bad.

I jumped into the pool with my fingers closed around my nose, knowing the gardener's son was watching. I swam toward him. Sweat dripped from his cheeks. His eyes were dark pools of hope.

"Daddy," I whispered. "It's really hot. Do you think we could let that boy swim with us?" At that time in New Orleans it was unlikely to see Blacks and whites mingling, but my father did the unexpected.

"Sure, we can." He climbed the pool steps and motioned for Mr. McKinley to cut the motor. "How'd your boy like to swim? It's awfully hot out."

Mr. McKinley looked stunned. "He won't be bothering y'all none?"

"Of course not," my father said, drying off.

Beyond the patio, Mr. McKinley pushed his lawn mower over our grass while his son stripped off his tee shirt and, still wearing his long shorts, treaded carefully into the shallow end. My father laid a towel across a lounge and slathered on Bain de Soleil.

"What's your name?" I asked the boy.

"Quentin," he said, holding on to the side of the pool. "But everyone calls me Q."

"Should I call you Q?"

He nodded, moving toward the deep end, reaching hand over hand, as if reaching for a dream.

"Want to race?"

"Can't," he said.

"Why not?"

"Can't swim."

This information was mind-boggling, and typical of how I gathered knowledge about people and the world, a series of spontaneous, jarring incidents piled one on top of another like dirty dishes in a sink. Until then, I hadn't realized that not everyone went to day camp and learned to do the backstroke, the sidestroke, and the American crawl.

Q circled the pool's perimeter, clinging to the edge.

"Want me to teach you how to float?" I asked.

He shook his head, his body rigid as a wrought-iron fence.

"Come on. Try at least," I said, showing him how. I thought that if I could float, he could float too.

He closed his eyes and let his legs come off the pool bottom. Water rushed over his face, entering his nose and mouth, and he sprang up gurgling. Instinctively, I moved toward him to help and saw water gleaming on his dark skin. He was a *boy*. He was a Black boy. I stepped back, acknowledging the distance between us.

We were quiet for some time before he sat next to me on the pool steps.

"Sorry," I said.

Without looking at me, he asked, "Want to be my girl?"

I didn't want to hurt his feelings but didn't know what to say. I wondered what Tracey would do, so I put myself inside her skin and imagined I was her.

"I already have a boyfriend," I said quickly so that he might believe it was true. The light in his eyes dimmed, and I wondered if he knew I was lying.

He climbed the pool steps, wrapped his shirt around his neck, and helped Mr. McKinley load their truck. On tiptoes, I peered over the fence. My heart clenched as I watched them pull away.

○   ○   ○

Over time, I saw there was a pecking order. Occasionally, messages were covert, like when my parents dressed up for a costume party and my father was the winemaker and my mother was the grape. Or when he was Professor Higgins and she was Eliza Doolittle.

Other times, the lessons were blatant. Like the night someone tried to break into our house through my parents' bedroom window. It happened just a few weeks after my father brought home his gun, days after swimming with Q. In many ways, it kicked off the long string of events that led to our move. Sam and I had been in the den watching *The Six Million Dollar Man* when my mother ran in to get us.

Back in their bedroom, my mother whispered, "Be careful, Steven." Usually, she needed my father to lift the pink velvet loveseat so Nellie could vacuum under it, but that night she moved it with ease. She pinned Sam and me against the wall, the loveseat our barricade.

"Stay down," my father said as he edged his way to the window. He pressed his back to the wall. Elbows bent, he anchored the gun in front of his chest and waited.

The prowler lifted the window. The alarm rang. My adrenaline soared and I went numb, picturing the worst. My father leaned out his bedroom window, aimed the gun down the unlit path, and pulled the trigger. The sound was deafening.

I covered my ears with my hands and hoped my father missed. He slammed the window shut and locked it. "You're safe," he said.

My mother turned on the lights and hurried to her connecting bathroom. I stayed close while she reached in her medicine cabinet for Valium, cupped her hands under running water, and gulped down tiny blue pills. She rubbed at smudged mascara under her eyes and positioned her face close to the mirror. "We've got to get out of this godforsaken city."

"I can't believe I pulled the trigger," my father said, putting on his white terrycloth robe.

"Do you think you hit him?" my mother asked, her hand on his shoulder.

"No. But that's not the point. I could've."

We headed to the den, and my father placed his gun on the pool table. He poured himself a scotch, took a swig, and reached for the telephone. My mother and Sam collapsed on the couch, but I stood near the pool table and studied the gun.

"Step away, Casey," my father said. "You're not allowed to touch it. *Ever.* You hear me?"

In no time, two policemen arrived. "Good evening, sir."

"Come in, gentlemen," my father said, directing them to the yellow velvet couch in our living room. "Someone tried to break in through my bedroom window," he said, sitting across from them.

I stared at their shiny silver badges and the guns in their holsters as they informed us that there had been a few robberies in our neighborhood lately. "On Topaz Street, Amethyst, and Crystal."

"What a gem of a city," my mother said, perched at the edge of her chair.

"Sharon. This isn't the time." My father looked at one cop and then the other. "I tried to shoot him."

"That's good," the cop sitting closest to my father said.

"That's good?"

"Yes. You know, the man who is suspected of these break-ins is Black. The law allows you to shoot if you're defending yourself inside your home."

"But he wasn't in my home. He never got past the window."

The cop leaned forward and stared into my father's eyes as if he were too stupid to understand. "Sir, we would've dragged his dead Black ass into the house."

In the middle of the night I woke with fright wondering what would've happened if my parents hadn't been home. My fear was not only in getting hurt, or dying, but in coming back again. Coming back into this world as someone else, and it could be anyone depending on the luck of the draw, because I believed it was about luck or turn taking. One time you got to be a white girl living in a brick house with your parents, but then it was your turn to be someone less privileged. Young, I trembled under the weight of my covers, leveled by all that injustice, and felt with unbearable force the burden of being powerless, truly powerless, simply because you were who you were.

Alabama, 1980

My father pulls into a gas station, and I wake with a stiff neck. WELCOME TO ALABAMA, a sign says. My father opens his car window, and I feel nauseated from the smell of gasoline.

"What can I get you, sir?" the attendant asks.

"Fill 'er up," my father says.

A woman in a black convertible drives up next to us.

"That's self-serve, ma'am." The attendant motions with his chin. "But I'd be happy to help you when I'm finished with this gentleman."

The woman steps out of her car, her long legs tan. She struggles with the nozzle. "I'm in a terrible rush. How do you work this damn thing?"

My father gets out of our car and approaches her. "Allow me."

"Aren't you a doll," she says as my father inserts the gas pump into her tank.

Her cheeks are shiny and tight; she seems almost plastic.

"Self-serve, in these heels? Ridiculous," she says. "Don't know what I would have done without you." She rests a hand on my father's back, and I recognize her Lee Press-On Nails from the time Tracey and I went to K&B and bought a box. It was unbelievable how those ten glossy nails worked like magic, *presto*—we were dazzling, desirable creatures.

When the woman asked my father for help, I didn't do anything. When she touched my father's back, I still didn't do anything. But when she says, "Aren't you funny," dragging out each syllable as if we have all the time in the world to chat and get to know one another, I snap. Half asleep and totally miserable, I call from our car, "Oh, yeah, he's hysterical. I've been laughing all day. Tell her about yeshivah, Dad. And how we're going to keep Shabbat. Tell her where we're headed. Because that's really funny."

The woman's arm snaps off my father's back as if it's on a spring. She gets into her car and drives away.

"What was that about?" my father asks as he pulls away from the gas station.

I don't answer.

Staring straight ahead, he says, "Your mother is wonderful. I wouldn't trade her for the world. But you know," he continues, as if I should understand, "she has a cup of coffee and half a cantaloupe every morning without fail. I'm not like that. If I eat apples too often, I get in the mood for strawberries. And there's no harm done in reading the menu as long as you eat at home."

Gross.

"Where we are going is good, Casey. You'll see." He sits up taller and takes a deep breath. "There is community. Community is important. Belonging to something is important. We gave up Syrian ways a long time ago, and it was a mistake. Look at what can happen. Casey, I'm talking to you," my father says, stepping on the gas.

Pulling my visor down, I hold back tears and stare at myself in the tiny mirror, my eyes rimmed red. Cars and road and trees fall farther and farther behind. Everything I have known—my best friend, my school, my life—falls farther behind.

I look at my father. He's singing KC and The Sunshine Band's "That's the Way I Like It" as if he doesn't have a care in the world.

Once, years ago on vacation in Florida, I strolled with my father along the beach, while Sam and my mother sat on a towel in the sand.

"Don't stop to feel the water or you'll chicken out," my father said. And before I could decide what to do, he scooped me up into a tight embrace and galloped into the sea. A huge wave crashed over our heads, knocking me from his arms. I stood, spit salt water, and rubbed my eyes.

"Don't be a baby," he warned.

"I won't."

He smiled. "You're a real trouper. Thought you might cry."

"Never," I said.

We broke the waves for hours that day, just the two of us. Now and then, we blew kisses to Sam and my mother on the beach.

o   o   o

The sun slips behind a cloud. The sky turns dark. It drizzles, first softly, then harder and harder, until it rains—a fierce downpour—the noise of innumerable fists pounding on the glass. The windshield wipers swoosh back and forth.

"I can't see a thing," my father says, studying our surroundings. "Can I change lanes?"

I look around. "I can't see either," I say.

"Put on your seat belt," he says, flipping on the hazard lights. And taking a chance, he veers toward the shoulder. When he stops, we sit in silence. Rain pummels.

"You okay?" he asks.

"Really?" I say, my eyes narrowing.

"Casey, don't start."

"So why ask if you don't want to know?"

My father shrugs.

"I want to go to college. I'm going to be an artist."

"Casey."

"Aunt Susie told me about the Marriage Box. I'm not going in it, no way. I'm not a show dog. And I'm not getting married."

My constant, wild anger is all new, and my father isn't used to it. When I was young, I'd do whatever he wanted. I turn away from him and stare out the window. "American Pie" comes on the radio and I mouth the words.

New Orleans, 1976

After the shooting, a letter saying my father was a hero and a Good Samaritan, the kind of citizen every city needs, was hand-delivered to our house. The chief of police signed the letter and jotted his home phone number below his signature, adding a personal note, something about how if my father ever needed anything, the New Orleans police department would be happy to oblige in order to repay him for his bravery. My father believed it was a favor he'd never use.

For weeks after the break-in, my parents were on edge. My mother was particularly disturbed, and she certainly didn't need another reason to hate New Orleans, so in order to ease her anxiety, my father surprised her with a trip to New York. She hadn't been back to see her Syrian friends in over a year, and her best friend, Irene, was making her son's Bar Mitzvah party at Studio 54.

The night before their trip, I sat on her bed. Watching as she packed her clothes, I felt increasing panic due to the attempted robbery, but also because Nellie would be left in charge.

"I don't want you to go," I said.

"Don't start now, Casey. You're not a baby and I deserve this vacation. I haven't been to New York in ages."

"It's not fair."

"Not everything is fair," she said. She twirled like a can-can dancer. The fringes on her black dress swung out. "What do you think of this?"

"It's beautiful," I said, making myself comfortable on her bed.

"I think I'll wear this to the party." She pivoted, checking herself out in the full-length mirror, lifting one leg and then the other, balancing like a flamingo, scrutinizing first the black strappy sandal on her right foot and then the pump on her left. "Which one?" she asked.

I pointed to the strappy sandal. Girly and fun, I wished it could always be like this with my mother. When she needed another piece of luggage from the attic, my father went to get it. Sometimes I went up with him, but that night he went alone. When we heard a thud, my mother and I ran to see what happened, and we found my father dangling from the living room ceiling, his legs scissoring. Bits of plaster crumbled to the floor. "Daddy, hold on," I cried.

"What happened?" my mother asked.

Struggling, he lifted himself up and sat on a beam. He looked down on us. "What does it look like happened?"

"Looks like you fell," my mother said, giggling.

"I could've killed myself, Sharon. Very nice."

"What?"

"I fall and you laugh."

"You're okay, Steven."

"I'm coming down."

"Are you going to use the stairs this time?"

o o o

The following morning, I stood sullen at the door and watched my father lug suitcases to the curb. My parents waved and blew kisses as their cab pulled away.

Around ten, William, our family handyman, came by to patch the hole in our ceiling. Whistling, he hauled a ladder to the living room. White paint speckled his Afro and his frayed blue jeans. "Good Lord," he chuckled. "Your father sure knows how to make a mess of things." His smile was broad, and I stared at his glistening gold tooth. "Mr. Steve," he said, shaking his head back and forth, "dangling from the ceiling." He stared at the hole, scoping out the damage. "He must've been mad as hell."

"He was," I said.

William climbed the ladder, and curious, I stared at his long black fingers and the white half-moons on his nail beds.

"Whatcha gonna do today, Miss Casey?"

"I don't know," I said.

"It's a beautiful day. Sun's shining bright." He climbed down the ladder. "You should get some air. Ain't gonna stay this nice out forever, you know. You gotta enjoy it while you can."

"Maybe later," I said.

"I'll get this hole fixed up in no time. Want to help?"

"Sure," I said, swept up by the invitation. I'd always been drawn to William, and I wondered if he knew about the robbery, if he understood what the police could do to someone like him.

He turned on his portable radio and sang "Love and Happiness." "Come on," he said, including me. "We have work to do." He laughed, shaking his head as he strolled out the back door. "Mr. Steve, dangling from the ceiling. What a hoot." We stood in front of his truck, and he clipped a tool belt around my waist.

By noon, William's work was done, and I wanted to go to Tracey's house. Nellie said I had to eat lunch first.

This is what I can tell you about Nellie: She was hooked on *The Edge of Night* and Tom Jones. She had a mole on her cheek that looked like a bug, and when she smiled, it sort of crawled across her face. Even though Nellie was the meanest person

I knew, she taught me to pray: "Dear God," I'd start, every night before going to bed. While she watched Carol Burnett, I plucked gray hairs from her head, and when I was sick, she placed alcohol-soaked cotton balls that burned like fire in the pit of my underarms until the fever broke or I fell asleep. She knew how to respond to weakness, but when I stood up for myself, she knocked me down fast.

Nellie poured me a glass of milk knowing I hated it. "Maybe you can get away with not drinking milk when your mother's home, but you won't get away with that while I'm here," she said, putting the glass in front of me.

The smell made me gag.

"You're not leaving until you finish it," she said, strolling to the refrigerator.

Nellie would never treat Sam that way. She adored him and had no shame about lying to strangers, saying that Sam was indeed hers.

When I told my mother that Nellie had pulled my hair, she said it must've been an accident. At some point, I stopped telling my mother the bad things Nellie did to me because Nellie had warned me that if I tattled, my mother would fire her, and then she'd have to leave our house and go back to Guatemala. You'd think that's what I would've wanted, but for a long time, it wasn't. I believed, even though she sometimes hurt me, she loved me too.

"I can't drink it," I said, staring at the glass of milk.

"Then you're not going out." Two pieces of Wonder bread popped from the toaster. "Do you know there are starving children in the world?"

I nodded.

"Ungrateful."

I held my breath and took a sip of milk. Gagging, I pushed the glass away and it accidentally fell over. Milk spilled everywhere, dripped off the table, and formed a puddle on the floor.

Nellie came up behind me and grabbed the back of my neck, pushing my head down, smashing my cheek to the table, and it hurt.

"Who do you think you are?"

I thought I might throw up, but I was terrified of what she'd do to me if I did. Tears streamed down my face.

"Look at this mess. Go get cleaned up," she said.

In my room, I wept, hating Nellie and wanting my mother. Feeling sorry for myself, I wiped my tears. A spider crawled across my windowsill. With an arts and crafts scissor, I snipped at its back leg, which was delicate and thin as a single eyelash. It limped, and a spot of blood stained its path. I dropped the scissor, horrified.

o   o   o

Tracey rode her bike over. She wore a halter top and jean shorts. We were at the age where childhood and adolescence intersect: when you are not one or the other, but some form of both.

We closed the drapes in my room and plopped on my bed. Tracey was in a talkative mood, and I could tell she wanted to make me feel better. She went on and on about what a bitch Nellie was for making me drink milk. I didn't have the nerve to call Nellie a bitch, even in the privacy of my own room, but I was glad Tracey did.

As Tracey talked, I stared at her, mesmerized by how beautiful she was. Her older sister, Cathy, didn't care about looks how Tracey did. Cathy dressed like a hippie, didn't believe in makeup, and was completely comfortable with her long frizzy hair. Aunt Susie cringed every time Cathy came home with another vintage blouse, and it killed her that day after day, Cathy wore the same camouflage pants. But she was a straight-A student, and Uncle Bobby took credit for her smarts. Between Cathy's successes and her brother Big Sam's failures, most of Uncle Bobby's attention was spoken for. Tracey learned at an early age that if she was going to get any attention at all, it was going to be from Aunt Susie. So, she used her good looks to make Aunt Susie proud. And to get boys to like her.

"When we grow up, we'll move to New York City," Tracey said, trying to make me feel better. She placed a pillow behind her head. "I'll be a model. You'll be an artist. We'll live together."

She dreamed and planned for us, and after some time, I did feel better. I wanted to thank her for coming over by making it worth her while, so I mentioned my father's gun. Her face lit up when I told her I knew where he kept it.

We got Sam to distract Nellie, which at first wasn't easy because he was addicted to TV. He knew every word to every commercial, singing, "Two all-beef patties, special sauce, lettuce, cheese, pickles, onions, on a sesame seed bun," as if it were a nursery rhyme. But he was intrigued by the idea of seeing my father's gun up close. Following our instructions, he spilled Hawaiian Punch on his shirt and then summoned Nellie. While she busied herself with Sam's stained shirt in the laundry room, we sneaked into my mother's bedroom and locked the door. "It's up there," I said, pointing to the top shelf in my father's closet.

"Well, what are you waiting for?" Tracey asked.

I lugged my mother's vanity chair to the closet, stood on tiptoes, and reached for the gun.

"Listen," Sam said. "Nellie's calling us."

I jumped off the chair, my hands shaking.

"Calm down," Tracey said to me. She grabbed hold of Sam's shoulders and looked him in the eye. "You can handle this."

I put the chair back in its proper place, and Tracey and I scurried inside the closet.

Nellie banged on the door. "What are you doing in there?" she screamed. "Why is this door locked?"

"Can't a guy get a little privacy around here?" Sam shouted back. "I had to go to the bathroom."

"Open this door," Nellie said.

"Okay. Okay."

Nellie pushed the door open, and it smashed against the wall. "Why didn't you use *your* bathroom?"

"Casey was in it," Sam said, and I was impressed with how he could lie.

"Where is Casey?"

"How should I know? A person can't even go to the bathroom in peace around here." He stormed out and disappeared down the hall. Nellie followed him.

"Nice work," Tracey said, patting Sam's back when he returned.

Moving quickly, I dragged the chair over to the closet and again reached for the gun. The leather case was smooth under my hand. As I drew it toward me, something fell from the shelf. A video called *Deep Throat*. Tracey bent to pick it up.

Focused on the gun, Sam didn't see the video, and I wanted to keep it that way. In a voice that mandated urgency, I told him to check on Nellie and make sure we were safe. Tracey and I faced each other—me with a gun in my hands, and her—with an X-rated video in hers.

"My parents have stuff like this," she whispered. "It's no big deal. Let's watch it," she said, stashing it under her shirt.

We showed Sam the gun, its power deferred.

o o o

Tracey's house wasn't like mine. Ours was an orange brick ranch; hers was white and sprawled like a plantation. Black shutters framed the windows, and giant wrought-iron lanterns gleamed on either side of her front door. Aunt Susie referred to her house as a lunatic asylum, and I loved going there. Tracey and I would sit at the dinette table and listen to Aunt Susie blab on and on about the jerk who cut her off on Canal Boulevard, the weather and how it made her hair frizz, and Uncle Bobby and what a pain in her ass he was, insisting on fresh-squeezed orange juice every morning. My aunt and uncle reminded me of that game, "rock, paper, scissors." Aunt Susie was paper, a fluttering free spirit who attracted all with her charm. Uncle Bobby was the scissor cutting into her whenever he could.

The ceiling in Aunt Susie's room was two stories high. Tracey locked the door.

"How do you know your mother won't come home?"

"Relax, will you?" Tracey tossed *Deep Throat* on her mother's bed. "She won't be here for hours. She's at some fancy luncheon in the French Quarter."

I twirled my mood ring around my finger. "And your dad? What about your dad?" While I didn't want Aunt Susie to find us in her room, I was more scared of Uncle Bobby.

"He's not home either. Don't worry so much."

We pulled heavy navy velvet across thick poles, closing their regal drapes.

Tracey opened Uncle Bobby's night table drawer. "Look, my parents have lots of these." She grabbed a video from the top of the pile, slid it into their VCR machine, and hopped on her parents' bed, patting the mattress, inviting me to sit next to her. Jazz music played in the background, and a woman appeared on screen. She wore a skintight red dress, and her blonde hair was sprayed into an up-do, not loose like my mother's or Aunt Susie's. On a plaid couch, she sat alone and lit a cigarette. She placed the pack of cigarettes on a glass coffee table and laid a Bic on top. A man joined her on the couch, and he also lit up. They talked, but I was too anxious to concentrate on what they were saying, so I just watched the woman smoke, paying attention as she let the ash grow impossibly long, giving me time to play a game in my head, betting if the ash would fall, singing to myself, *Ashes, ashes, they all fall down*. But the woman knew what she was doing and always managed to flick the ash, long and dark, into the ashtray before it fell.

Just as I began to relax, she stubbed the butt, extinguishing the flame, and she unbuttoned her shirt. The man unhooked her black lace bra, and her flesh expanded like Pillsbury Pop and Fresh dough. He put his face in between her breasts, his sideburns bushy as woolly caterpillars, and she moaned.

I covered my face with my hands. "This is gross."

Tracey laughed at me and then sprawled her body across the bed, oohing and aahing, imitating the woman on the video.

At that point, I didn't know a lot about sex. My father once read to me from a book called *Where Did I Come From?* and there were pictures of a man and a woman naked. I was uncomfortable and couldn't concentrate, but my father continued reading with resolve as if he were a college professor simply lecturing important facts before a final.

After reading, my father tested me. "What does the woman have?"

"The egg," I said, proudly.

"And the man, what does he have?"

I couldn't remember and didn't want him to think that reading to me had been a waste of time. "The bacon?"

"That's funny," my father said. "Oh, God, that's really funny," he said, laughing and holding his belly.

o o o

Big Sam pounded on the door. "Tracey, are you in there?"

I jumped up and ran to the television, my arms stretched wide. Tracey stayed where she was, planted in the center of her parents' king-size bed, and screamed, "Go away, Big Sam."

Big Sam turned six the month my brother Sam was born, and in order to minimize confusion and distinguish one Sam from another, everyone called him Big Sam.

"You better open this door if you know what's good for you," he said. Tracey hopped off the bed and headed for the door.

"What are you doing?"

"I'm going to let him in."

"Are you crazy?" I sprang to the door, blocking it.

"What's the big deal? Casey, you're such a prude."

"A what?"

"A prude. You're so uptight."

But I was scared of Big Sam. I'd seen him chase Cathy with a kitchen scissor, detaining her until she begged for mercy. I'd seen him fight with Uncle Bobby, deliberately inciting his temper, watching it build like contempt, as he questioned and disregarded what Uncle Bobby attempted to teach him. And one night, when Uncle Bobby asked Big Sam to quiet down at the dinner table and Sam wouldn't, Uncle Bobby's cheeks had gotten red hot. He'd clenched his fingers around the edge of the table, thrown his chair back, and chased Big Sam up the stairs. Cornering him, he hit him with his belt as if he could actually beat Big Sam into submission. It was nothing, we were told, that any self-respecting father wouldn't do. Big Sam retaliated, getting back at his parents, and the rest of the world, any way he could. But mostly, he dealt sarcasm the way he dealt drugs.

Tracey pushed me aside and opened the door. Big Sam strutted across the blue carpet like a naval officer on deck. "Look at you," he said to me. "What are you watching?"

"Nothing," I said, not looking at him.

"Oh, you're watching something."

On the television screen, the man unzipped his pants. I turned my face, ashamed.

"You like this, don't you?"

"No, I don't."

"No, I don't," he mimicked. The TV flickered behind him. He pushed me down on the bed and straddled my stomach. With one hand he pinned both arms above my head and put his face close to mine. "I won't tickle you," he said, worming his finger closer and closer to my armpit, "if you don't move. Not a muscle." He paused. "You have to trust me, Casey. Do you trust me?"

"Get off me, Big Sam."

"You don't trust me, do you?" He brought his finger closer to my underarm.

Tracey headed to the bathroom. "Just tell him you trust him, Casey."

"I trust you," I yelled, so scared I thought I might pee.

"Okay. Then I'm gonna let go of your arms, and if you don't move, I won't tickle you." He released his grasp, and I was careful not to flinch.

"Good girl," he said, smirking. "You do trust me. You're a good listener. Too bad you're an awful judge of character," and he dug his nails into my skin, tickling me until I couldn't breathe. His big hands moved over my body, touching me in places no one had ever touched before. I bucked and clawed and grabbed the patches of hair under his arms. He jerked back. "Feisty, aren't you?" He pinned me again and looked me dead in the eye. "Little Miss Goody Two Shoes isn't so good, is she?"

Just as Tracey came back, Big Sam grabbed *Deep Throat* from the bed and held it above his head.

"Give it to me," I said, jumping up, trying to get it.

"Casey," he teased with a slow drawl. "All in good time. Tracey, tell her to calm down, will you?" He headed for the door and then stopped. He turned to us. "If you want it, you're going to have to work for it. And for your information," he said to Tracey, "Hawkeye's coming over."

Tracey had a huge crush on Hawkeye. Hawkeye's real name was Earl, but when he and Big Sam became friends, Big

Sam said, "No way I'm hanging out with a guy named Earl. You need a cool name, man. Hawkeye. I like Hawkeye."

According to school gossip, Hawkeye was a druggie, famous for rolling monster joints before most kids rolled out of bed. There was a rumor he popped pills, colorful as confetti, and snorted coke off his history textbook in the Franklin Prep hallway near his locker. At the time, Hawkeye didn't interest me. I liked his little brother, Morgan. But to Tracey, Hawkeye was everything.

o   o   o

Tracey and I crept up the stairs and down the hall. We knocked on Big Sam's bedroom door and waited for him to open it. When he did, Big Sam smirked, shirtless. He arched his back and extended his arms above his head, *Deep Throat* in hand. "Come on in, girls, the party's in here." Big Sam shut his door and latched the hook, locking it. Posters of David Bowie covered his walls and "Fame" boomed through four black speakers big as coffins. His plaid drapes were closed, and the only light in the room came from a lava lamp on his night table, a blob of blue floating, aimlessly, a giant jellyfish in the sea.

"Here's the deal," Big Sam said. "You want this video? Both of you have to massage my back for five minutes each." He placed the video on the top shelf of his bookcase.

I didn't want to touch Big Sam, but I had to get that video back. My mother would know it was gone in no time. She was meticulous, everything always in the exact same place. We tested her once, Sam and I. We hid an ashtray. One with an orange-and-red design like peacock feathers. It was a game. How long would it take? We timed her. She looked around. One, two, three, four, five. Five seconds and my mother knew what was missing from our whole house. I wasn't like that. Someone could take down the Shaun Cassidy poster I'd tacked to the wall in front of my bed, the one I stared at every night before falling asleep, and I wouldn't notice.

I couldn't even think about what would happen if my parents discovered I'd gone for their gun and stolen their X-rated video instead. I had to make sure they never found out, and whatever it took, I had to get that video back. Tracey grabbed my hand, pulling me toward the center of Big Sam's room. "Come on," she said.

o   o   o

Big Sam dove on his bed, and I kept my eye on the video. The blue light of the lava lamp waved over his smooth back, and his muscular arms glistened above his head. "Climb on," he said, and Tracey straddled Big Sam, sitting on his behind. When the digital clock showed 2:03, Tracey began to massage his back. I watched as her fingers pinched his skin. Big Sam closed his eyes. "Lower. Harder. To the left," he groaned. "That's good."

At 2:08, Tracey hopped off his bed. "Your turn," she said to me.

Big Sam sang to the music, "All night, he wants the young American."

Wishing I never took the video from my parents' room, I sat on Big Sam. He was not hairy like my father. I touched his bare back, feeling his hot skin against mine. Uneasy, I kneaded his flesh with my fingers, acquainting myself with this unfamiliar territory. In the blue darkness, I imagined my mood ring turned black.

When five minutes were over, Tracey turned on the light. Big Sam sat up, his hair messy and wild. Tracey and I stood like beauty pageant contestants in front of him. "Well, I could just give you two the video and that would be that," Big Sam said. "Or I could keep it." He swelled with grandiosity as he weighed his options. "I think I'm going to keep it," he said. "At least until Hawkeye gets here."

"No way," I said. "That's not fair."

Big Sam ignored me and strutted over to a rack of weights. A dumbbell in each hand, he lay on a bench and did presses. Exhaling, he lifted them. Inhaling, he sucked up all the air.

There was a knock at the door.

"Open up, man. It's me," Hawkeye said from the hallway.

Big Sam put the weights down and opened his door. "You're just in time," he said.

Hawkeye wore sunglasses, always trying to cover how one eye was different than the other. Not in a bad way; it was kind of like how no two mountains are the same. He sauntered across Big Sam's room and raised two barbells over his head with ease as if he were lifting Q-tips. "In time for what?"

"Truth or Dare," Big Sam said. "You see, these girls want that video." He pointed to *Deep Throat* on the shelf.

Hawkeye dropped the weights at his feet and stood. "That's cool."

"I'm in," Tracey said, willing to do anything for Hawkeye's attention.

"If we play, can we get the video back?" I asked.

"Deal," Big Sam said. "Ladies first."

We sat in a circle on the floor, and Tracey started. "Hawkeye, Truth or Dare?"

"Dare."

And wasting no time, she pointed a finger to her lips and said, "Kiss me."

My mouth hung open so wide that if any of them looked my way, they would've seen all six of my silver fillings. Over the last few months, Tracey had begun to change. She'd bought three different kinds of black mascara, each with a special wand, and she carried them in her purse—one for curling lashes, one for lengthening, and one for thickening—and just like that she could make herself look older, more mature, glamorous.

I wasn't that advanced yet. I was still applying plain old Vaseline to my lashes and wearing beige training bras, while she had lace lingerie in as many colors as there were flavors at Baskin-Robbins.

Hawkeye leaned forward, still wearing his sunglasses, and kissed Tracey smack on her mouth. Tracey hesitated a minute, savoring this small victory, then gazed at Hawkeye. "Your turn."

Hawkeye looked at me. "Truth or Dare?"

There was no way I was going to pick dare after that, so I picked truth.

"What's the furthest you've gone with a boy?" Hawkeye asked, smirking.

"Well," I said, grateful for this relatively easy question, "Brett, my new neighbor, and I rode our bikes to Lakewood South."

Big Sam, Tracey, and Hawkeye laughed so hard I thought they might throw up. Big Sam hurled his body to the floor, stretching himself out on the carpet, kicking his legs. His laughter got louder and louder while Tracey couldn't catch her breath.

"No. No," Hawkeye said, doubled over. "I meant the furthest you've gone sexually."

Heat filled my body, traveling to my cheeks as if my head was on fire. My response was all the information they needed. Dying to move on, I asked Big Sam, "Truth or Dare?"

"Dare."

"You have to drink a mixture," I said.

"What are we, in second grade?"

Enjoying this moment of power, I kept talking. "A raw egg, a tablespoon of sour cream, a teaspoon of ketchup, eight splashes of Tabasco, half a cup of white vinegar, a tablespoon of salt, and . . ."

"I think that's enough," Big Sam said.

"I'm not done."

"Whoa," Tracey and Hawkeye said at the same time. And Big Sam let me finish.

"A quarter cup of oil."

"That's disgusting. And childish."

"Too bad, Big Sam. You have to do it," Tracey said.

"Okay," Big Sam said, unwilling to lose. We followed him to the kitchen. Big Sam prepared the mixture without much fuss and drank it down fast. He started to gag as he slammed the empty glass down on the counter, and his coughing soon morphed into choking. He turned white and then ran to the bathroom. Behind the closed door, we heard him barfing. It sounded like everything he'd ever eaten his entire life was being dispensed into that toilet bowl. When Big Sam finally came out of the bathroom, pale and drained, he said, "Okay, you want to play tough? You got it. Truth or Dare, Tracey?"

And not wanting to look like a wimp, Tracey said, "Dare."

"Do a show. A striptease."

"That's cool," Hawkeye said.

"I don't care. I'll do it. Come to my room," Tracey said, leading the way.

Big Sam and Hawkeye followed. I pulled on Tracey's arm and whispered in her ear, "Are you crazy? What are you doing?"

Tracey's room was all pink: pink wallpaper, pink curtains, pink sheets. She turned on the radio and "American Pie" came on. Hawkeye, Big Sam, and I sat on the edge of her bed, while Tracey closed the drapes and shut the lights. Through the space in between the drawn curtains, slivers of sunlight shined across the carpet like shards of glass. Tracey stood in the center of the room, and while the slow part played, she swayed back and forth, her bare feet planted on her pink shag. Cool as a cucumber, Tracey moved to the music, and when the tempo picked up, she danced faster and showed a smidgeon of her purple strapless bra.

When we were young, Tracey and I would spend the day in the French Quarter near my father's store, wandering up and down Bourbon Street, repeatedly passing the bar where Chris Owens, a stripper with celebrity status, worked. Curious, we'd peek in the half-open door, getting a glimpse of her topless, limber body curling around a pole. Tracey incorporated some of her moves, and I cringed as she stripped off her tube top and swung it from a finger. Slowly she unbuttoned her shorts, revealing matching purple panties, and I hoped she'd stop there. Tracey plucked a finial from her canopy bed and used it as a microphone as she sang to the music, "This'll be the day that I die."

She slipped off her shorts, and in her purple bra and panties, crawled sexily across her mattress, bunching the comforter in her fists. It was clear from their popping eyeballs Big Sam and Hawkeye were impressed. A bikini would've been equally exposing, but this was different somehow, and her raw confidence was disconcerting. When the song ended, Big Sam and Hawkeye whooped and hollered while Tracey beamed and put her clothes back on.

"Okay, Big Sam," Tracey said, getting to choose who went next. "Back to you. Truth or dare?"

"Dare," Big Sam said.

Tracey pretended to be thinking, acted as if we hadn't wanted to know the answer to this question forever. The stakes were high, and Tracey knew that Big Sam wouldn't chicken out. "I dare you to show us your stash."

"My stash? Who do you think you are, Police Woman?"

"Just show it to us, Sam. I'm not stupid. I know what you do."

"I didn't say you were stupid. In fact"—Big Sam paused— "after the show you just put on, you deserve an answer."

"I don't know, man," Hawkeye said, his voice a growl.

"Hawkeye," Big Sam said, putting his arm around him, "you have to trust. These girls would never tell. Their lives depend on it."

Goosebumps appeared on my arms and legs, spreading like my fear.

Back in Big Sam's room, he locked the door with the hook. Blue light saturated the room, filling it completely, as if air had color.

"Just remember," Big Sam said, "what you see here stays here." He strolled to the bookcase and reached for a Mardi Gras mask piñata. Strips of tissue paper, gold, purple, and green, adorned the mask and concealed how the piñata had been cut open in the back. He lifted the flap, turned the piñata upside down, and shook out Razzles, Jaw Breakers, Sweetarts, Lemonheads, and a number of plastic baggies full of white powder.

I knew the powder was a drug and that it was illegal. But I didn't know more than that.

"Don't get mad! Get Glad!" Big Sam said, mocking the commercial. He held a handful of baggies. "I'm the Glad Man." Baggies striped the carpet like a dashed line on an endless highway.

Tracey reached her arm out, and Big Sam grabbed her wrist.

"Oh, no. No touching," he said. "These babies are worth a lot of money." He untwisted a red tie on a baggie and, with his pinky, scooped up a fingertip full of white powder. He dumped the tiny mound on the bottom shelf of his bookcase, and with his driver's license, split the mass into two lines. From his night table drawer, Big Sam took a crisp dollar bill and rolled it tightly into a stiff straw. He held one end of the straw at his left nostril, and the other end was near the powder. He pressed a finger to his nose, sealing off his right nostril, and inhaled deeply, snorting until the powder disappeared. Just as he was about to do the other side, we heard a car pull into the driveway. All four of us ran to the window. Uncle Bobby slammed the car door shut and headed for the house. Before Big Sam could clean up, Hawkeye stepped in. "Not so fast," he said. And he snorted the other line through the straw just as Big Sam had.

"Anybody home?" Uncle Bobby called.

Big Sam turned on his bedroom light and scooped up the candy in large handfuls. He placed the baggies inside the piñata one by one and put the piñata back on the shelf as if it were a harmless memento.

By the time Uncle Bobby knocked on Big Sam's bedroom door, we looked like a couple of regular kids just hanging out.

"Well, if it isn't the life of the party," Big Sam said, patting his father's back.

Uncle Bobby tisked his tongue. "Don't be a wise guy."

"I'm not, Dad. I hear you're a ball at parties."

I wished Big Sam would stop provoking Uncle Bobby.

"I'm serious, Dad." His shoulder jerked to his ear. "Who's more fun than you?"

Uncle Bobby loosened his tie and craned his neck. "Well, it's true," he said, considering what Big Sam said. "I do get invited to a lot of parties."

Big Sam grinned as if he'd spent all afternoon fishing and finally hooked the big one. "There's a long river in Africa," he said, reeling Uncle Bobby in.

"Yes, there is," Uncle Bobby said, not sure where Big Sam was going.

"It's called De Nile."

Uncle Bobby flicked Big Sam's cheek. "Okay, Mr. Smart Ass, you can eat dinner in your room by yourself tonight."

Big Sam saluted. "Yes, sir."

When Uncle Bobby left, Big Sam said, "Hold on. The game's not over." He looked at me, his pupils black seeds of revenge. "Casey, Truth or Dare?"

I was still humiliated from picking truth earlier and looking babyish in front of them, so I picked dare. Big Sam shut off the light and took a candle the size of a coffee can from his bookshelf.

I stepped back.

"Come sit down," Big Sam said, patting the carpet. He

placed the candle on the floor next to me, struck a match, and lit the wick.

"Lie down," Big Sam said, looking directly into my eyes.

I shook my head, petrified of what Big Sam had in store for me.

"We can't lose now," Tracey said.

Big Sam glanced at the video on the top shelf. "Hawkeye, I guess you and me will be watching *Deep Throat* tonight."

"Okay, okay," I said. I lay down, and Big Sam strolled to his closet. He lifted a wire hanger from a pole. Tracey and Hawkeye sat on either side of me, watching. Big Sam twisted the hook of the hanger, shaping it into an S. "For Sam," he said. Taking his time, he heated the S in the candle flame as if he were roasting a marshmallow. I jumped up when Big Sam brought the hanger close.

"Casey," he said in a deep voice, "this will be our bond, something to remember this day by. Think of it like blood brothers or ear piercing, a ceremonial connection."

"Is it going to hurt?"

"Well, it won't tickle. But when I'm done, game over. I'll give you the video."

"I don't believe you."

"I swear," Big Sam said, the hanger back in the flame.

"I'll make sure," Hawkeye said, linking his eyes with mine.

I glanced at Tracey, hoping she'd come to my rescue, but she just sat there. There was no choice. I needed the video and wanted the game to be over.

It happened fast. Hawkeye pinned my arms down and Big Sam pressed the hanger onto my belly, the S searing into my skin, excruciating. Without holding back, not caring that Uncle Bobby might hear me, I screamed louder than I'd ever screamed in my life, and I think I scared Big Sam, because he stopped. I sat up and looked at my stomach. The S swirled like a monster hurricane, my belly button the eye.

Big Sam handed me the video and smacked Tracey on her butt. "Y'all get out of here now," he said, "before we all get into trouble."

o   o   o

Holding back tears, I went to the bathroom and locked the door. Tracey knocked but I wouldn't let her in. Once, when I made a cake for Sam's birthday, my finger accidentally touched the oven rack, and Nellie put toothpaste on the burn, which eased the pain. In the bathroom, I applied toothpaste to this new burn. The old mark on my finger had faded, but if you looked closely, you could still make out its shape. Tears welled in my eyes. I wondered how long this scar would last. Maybe forever.

o   o   o

By the time I got home, Nellie was in the den, busy eyeing Tom Jones on TV, and Sam was in his room probably watching Star Trek. I needed to put the video back, so I sneaked into my mother's room with it tucked way up high under my shirt.

Usually, I liked spending time in my mother's room when she was in it and relished it almost as much when she wasn't. I felt safe there, protected by the four walls of her room like a baby bird in its shell. But that night, I felt betrayed by everyone close to me. Furious, I wanted to rip the comforter from my mother's bed, overturn her drawers—spewing scarves, bras, and her negligees.

I put *Deep Throat* back on the top shelf of the closet next to the gun, letting in the fact that my parents were the kind of people who watched X-rated videos.

They weren't the only ones with secrets.

New Jersey, 1980

The first thing my father does when we get to New Jersey is look for a safe place to store his gun. Our rented house is furnished—ugly, Early American—and my father hides it behind boxes of Bubblicious in his dark wood nightstand drawer, camouflaging it under a pile of tee shirts.

The second thing my father does is join Getaway Beach Club, where members of the Syrian community come together to mingle. Grandfathers play backgammon and gin rummy, intoxicated with camaraderie and tradition, while their wives gossip and dole out *ejje* sandwiches. Young parents watch their children swim, and teenage girls, wanting to get married, gather in the Marriage Box.

The Marriage Box is a roped-off section behind the pool where young girls lounge on display in animal-print bikinis adorned with fringe or spotted with sequins. They pose in flattering positions, lying on their backs to keep their stomachs flat, flaunting their freshly waxed tan legs, hoping to attract their *naseeb*, their God-given intended.

In order to stay away from the Marriage Box, I get a job as a waitress at the snack bar. Serving hot dogs, French fries, and Coca Cola works out well. There is solace in refilling napkin holders, saltshakers, and ketchup bottles.

My second day on the job, I offer two men menus. They don't bother to look up.

"I'll have a hot dog," one of the men says. "Sauerkraut. Mustard. Make it well done."

I don't say anything.

"You got that?" he asks, slipping his sunglasses down to the tip of his nose. He peers over them. "Hey, aren't you Steven and Sharon Cohen's daughter?"

The other guy smacks him on his shoulder. "What are you talking about? She's not Syrian." He stares at my cut-off jean shorts and sneakers.

I know I don't look Syrian. Grandma Rose, who speaks Yiddish, calls me her Little Shiksa. "You're *honey*," she always says, comparing me to Cathy, who is milk white, and Tracey, who is olive. That's how Grandma speaks. Purses, leather jackets, and shoes are canary yellow, emerald green, and robin's-egg blue.

I look up from my pad. "Yes, Steven and Sharon are my parents."

"What are you doing working here? This place isn't for you," the guy with the sunglasses says.

"I like my job," I say, respectfully.

"How old are you?"

"Sixteen."

"But this is not right for a sixteen-year-old Syrian girl. You need to be home taking your pretty pills. Isn't that right?" he says to his friend. "She needs to be taking her pretty pills."

I stand stunned, shocked by the words coming out of his mouth. *Is he for real?*

At Franklin Prep, we were taught women could *do* anything, *be* anything. Once during a dance recital, I wore a crayfish costume, and I twirled and twisted and flew across the Franklin Prep stage while my mother took pictures. Standing in front of this man, I wanted that back—the ability to move my body freely across a stage and through life, limbs swaying in all directions like a tree on a windy day—feet tapping like rain, heart pounding, thumping, beating like thunder.

Then again, later that day, I told my mother I wanted to be a dancer when I grew up, and as she removed bobby pins from my hair and untangled the crayfish headpiece, she said, "Casey, don't get carried away. Why does everybody have to get so carried away?"

The man's arrogance bothers me, but I don't say anything because I need my job, I need the money. I'm saving up for college and a plane ticket back to New Orleans, both things my parents are giving me a hard time about. They want me settled in community life, not flitting all over the world.

The man unfolds a wad of cash from a money clip and hands me a ten-dollar bill. "You have a beautiful smile," he says.

I hold the money tight. I've made too many mistakes already. I can't afford to make more. All I have to do, I assure myself, is keep my mouth shut. And smile.

After walking away from the two men, I slip the ten-dollar bill into my sneaker, feeling satisfied that this hard-earned money will bring me one step closer to my goal, which is to get as far away as possible from the Marriage Box.

New Orleans, 1976

For a week after we played Truth or Dare, I wore long, loose shirts so the mark on my stomach wouldn't show and nothing would rub against it. To mask the pain, I took Tylenol every four hours and hid in my room, drawing and marking a calendar, counting the days until my parents came home.

The wound healed slowly, first reddening, then blistering, and finally getting infected. Since my parents were away and I couldn't tell Nellie, I went to Mrs. Graf, our school nurse. She was Morgan and Hawkeye's mother, and everyone at school knew the only reason they could afford Franklin Prep was because Mrs. Graf had faculty privileges and reduced tuition.

I lifted my shirt and told Mrs. Graf I'd been baking in a halter top and leaned onto a hot tray. She marveled at the shape of the burn, an "S," but if she had questions, she didn't ask. She used a Q-tip and applied Neosporin, taped a gauze patch over the burn, and sent me on my way.

Tracey ran up to me in the hallway and jutted her chin toward my belly. "You okay?"

"Now you ask?"

"What does that mean?"

"Nothing," I said, but what I really wanted to say was *Why didn't you stop them?* I was feeling sorry for myself even though I didn't have a right to complain. After all, I'd watched her strip and then listened to Big Sam brag to Hawkeye, *Look at my baby sister go.*

In time, things settled down. My parents returned from New York, my wound scabbed and healed, and my problems went back to being typical teen-girl troubles, like having to deal with my frizzy hair in brutal humidity. When parted down the middle, it framed my face in a triangle. In an attempt to control it, my mother suggested an Afro. "Everyone in New York has one. I'll get one too."

Before I knew it, I was facing myself in the oval mirror at John Jay's Beauty Salon. John Jay himself combed my wet hair in front of my face, and it dangled below my chin. He snipped above my eyes, and I stared as twelve inches of hair fell to the floor in a clump. For the next few months, until my hair grew out, everyone thought I was a boy.

"How could you?" I asked my mother one night.

"How could I what?"

"I look like a boy."

"How was I supposed to know you wouldn't like it?"

My mother wasn't going to take responsibility for the mistake. She liked her hair short and didn't understand that what worked for her might not necessarily work for me.

I was having the same problem with Tracey. Once in a while, she'd get Hawkeye to meet her at the levee, and she'd plead with me to accompany her. I liked her asking me, so forgetting my pride, I'd go with her, only to be left watching them make out.

Shrinking, I'd turn away.

Tracey thought nothing of this. "If the situation was reversed, I'd do it for you," she said. "That's what friends are for."

But we both knew the situation would never be reversed.

o o o

The next time I saw Mrs. Graf, she was giving a presentation in our classroom. She wore a white lab coat and came to teach us about germs and the common cold. She gave us tips, one being that we should wash our hands with plenty of soap and warm water for as long as it took to sing "Happy Birthday" twice. A few months later, Mrs. Graf gave a lecture on lice and shared guidelines for prevention. My hair was finally growing out, so I listened carefully.

It was around that time that the rumors about her started. Everyone at school was saying how Mrs. Graf smoked pot and took prescription pills just for fun. I didn't believe the gossip. Mrs. Graf seemed nice. Morgan was in my class, and it was obvious she adored him. He was her baby boy—a straight-A student, a talented musician, and a budding artist. To Mrs. Graf, he was a star, while Hawkeye was dirt.

I understood how Mrs. Graf felt about Morgan because I'd had a crush on him for as long as I could remember, and while I couldn't always be certain, I thought he liked me too. He'd asked me to spend the night one time in kindergarten and wrote me over fifty Valentine's Day cards in fifth grade. *Roses are red, violets are blue, you are a loser and a dog too.* While the words weren't nice, the sheer number of cards convinced me. Red and white envelopes, big and small, filled the paper pouch taped to the front of my desk. Everyone else's pouch was near empty, while mine overflowed, full. He'd put in a lot of time.

Franklin Prep had many ways of asking *How popular are you?* And on Valentine's Day it was determined by how many carnations you received. That year, Tracey got eight. I got one. Plenty of girls in my class got none.

My carnation was red and the card was blank. Anonymous.

"Looks like you have a secret admirer," Tracey said, securing her bouquet with a rubber band.

o o o

When Morgan volunteered to work on the Save the Children fundraiser, designing the main bulletin board, I did too. Tracey said she thought it was weird that a middle school boy liked art, but I didn't.

Morgan brought a radio into the art room and played rock music, drumming on the radiator under a sun-soaked window. I watched as he ripped paper instead of cutting it, preferring a ragged edge to a straight one. When we cleaned our paint brushes in the sink, his hand grazed mine and my body shook. The fact that he hardly spoke made everything more exciting when he did. "That's good," he said, pointing to a flower I'd drawn. Each and every word was a gauge of how much he liked me.

In the hallway, I stood on a chair and reached to staple a crepe-paper bee to the upper part of the bulletin board. I was careful not to stretch too high so my shirt wouldn't lift and reveal the scar on my stomach. I couldn't think of anything more humiliating than Morgan finding out about my parents' X-rated video or that I'd played Truth or Dare with Hawkeye and Big Sam. Everything was connected. One story leading to another.

o   o   o

When I got my period for the first time, I wasn't surprised. Mrs. Graf had given us girls a lecture. I called down the hall to my mother, who was watching TV in the den.

"I'll come at a commercial," she yelled back.

Nellie showed up instead. Standing outside the locked bathroom door, she asked what was wrong.

"Nothing," I answered, not wanting to tell her, having a vision of the way things should be. I wanted my mother to be the first to know. But my mother wasn't as sentimental, and as far as she was concerned, if Nellie could handle *it*, whatever *it* might be, why not?

"You can tell me," Nellie said, knocking on the door. "Open up, Casey. Let me in."

But I wouldn't open the door. Instead, I took a bath and washed my hair. As my fingertips scrubbed my scalp, my eyes closed, water cascading from the faucet, Nellie used a butter knife to unlock the bathroom door. Since playing Truth or Dare, I'd been extra careful about hiding my body, worried that if Nellie saw my scar, she'd tell my mother. Big Sam would get into huge trouble, and just thinking about Uncle Bobby's rage, and my father's, scared me. At all costs, my parents couldn't find out about me touching the gun and taking their video. They'd be livid.

When I opened my eyes, Nellie was standing over me. I wasn't sure how long she'd been there or if she'd had time to see my scar. I brought my knees to my chest fast. "Get out!" I screamed. "Get out."

o   o   o

The night of the Bacchus Ball, I stood next to my mother at her vanity table while she glued fake lashes to her lids and dabbed perfume on her wrists. Nellie entered carrying the shirt she'd just ironed for my father. It hung on a wire hanger just like the one Big Sam had used, and I touched my stomach, replaying that horrid day in my mind.

My father came out of the shower and leaned against the frame of the dressing room door, talking to my mother, a towel wrapped around his waist. Nellie looked away, blushing. When she left the room, my mother said to my father, "Maybe you shouldn't walk around like that. Nellie seemed uncomfortable."

I'd been feeling threatened for weeks. I knew what had to be done.

"No," I said, "Nellie likes seeing Daddy like that. The other day when he walked by in his underwear, she whispered, *Qué guapo.*"

My mother allowed this information to sink in. A chunk of false eyelashes dropped from her lid and clung to her cheek.

"*Guapo*," I said. "It means 'handsome' in Spanish."

"I know what it means," my mother said, staring at herself in the mirror. She used a tweezer and reattached the lash to her lid. Dressed in an emerald-green gown, she went to the ball, and fired Nellie in the morning.

From the doorway, I watched Nellie pack her bags. She lifted her Jesus Christ statue from the dresser and wedged it in her suitcase, cushioning it between pink rollers. I was surprised to find myself getting choked up, recalling the good times when my parents went out and she'd play Joe Cocker's "You Are So Beautiful" on the record player, and we'd exercise on the green carpet in the living room, our legs scissoring above our heads. In the kitchen, we'd sing "Let the Sunshine In," and sometimes we'd paint by numbers, sitting side by side at the dinette table, or color in books the size of posters. Girls from all over the world. Some wore clogs and held tulips, some were wrapped in kimonos and carried fans, others were dressed in thick fur, standing next to igloos.

I said goodbye to Nellie near the back door, feeling a confusing mix of emotions, a brew of guilt and sadness and also relief. To this day, I'm not sure if I knew my mother would fire Nellie, but with her gone, my secret was safe.

"Adios," Nellie said, bending down to kiss my cheek. "Such a black heart," she whispered in my ear.

I ran from her and found my mother in the den ambling around the pool table. The screen door slammed shut. I darted to the window and watched Nellie as she walked away. For the first time since our pool table arrived, my mother racked the balls into a triangle. A stick in her hand, she twisted a cube of blue chalk on its tip. "Is she gone?"

"Yes."

"Good," she said.

And she hit the red ball into the corner pocket.

New Orleans, 1979

My chances of becoming a Franklin Prep varsity cheerleader were slim, but somehow winning that spot in high school had become the most important thing in the world to me. I dreamed that once I put on that green-and-white uniform and swayed my pom-poms in the air, I'd finally belong.

On the day of tryouts, I practiced my routine one last time in the locker-room mirror before heading to the Franklin Prep auditorium. In the entrance foyer, there were gilded portraits of our school's founders, and the theater itself was like a real Broadway playhouse, equipped with professional lighting and adorned with heavy dark green velvet curtains. Backstage, sixty freshman girls applied lip gloss, brushed their hair, and waited for their number to be called.

When it was my turn, I smiled broadly and crossed the stage. I'd practiced nonstop for weeks in front of the wall-to-wall mirror in my bathroom, scrutinizing my every move: the position of my arms, the tilt of my head, the height of my jump. I had a strong voice, a big smile, and tons of energy. I could kick my leg over the top of my head and do a full split, but it was still a long shot because everyone knew becoming a cheerleader was part beauty contest, part popularity contest.

Tracey didn't want to be a cheerleader, and it bothered her that I did. "How can you stand it?" she asked, folding a piece of Big Red into her mouth. "All those varsity wannabees, such phonies. So prim and proper. It's all that plaid," she said, putting a second piece of gum in her mouth. "You can't be spontaneous wearing plaid." Tracey wore low-cut blouses, the lace on her bra showing. She didn't have good grades or school spirit; she had cleavage.

"And you're going to have to go to games every Friday and Saturday night all through high school."

I didn't care. I wanted different things than she did.

The three winners were to be announced after school in the senior courtyard, and the thought of entering that forbidden terrain added to my excitement. Tracey and I often peeked into the courtyard, beyond the magnolia tree, where twelfth graders swapped class notes, lounged on benches, and against school rules, dared to kiss. We fantasized about the day we'd be allowed in. Tracey came with me to hear who'd won, pretending to be supportive, but I knew she just wanted access to the courtyard.

Don Hinkle, the football quarterback, stood on a wrought-iron bench, towering over the crowd at six feet two and 185 pounds. He wore a white Lacoste shirt, khaki pants, and Docksiders. He looked perfect. Kim Blair, the reigning head cheerleader and that year's Homecoming Queen, stood next to him, in uniform, and she looked perfect too—blonde hair, high ponytail, ivory girl skin, legs athletic and strong.

"I have the winners," Don shouted, and the student body gathered around him. He unfolded a piece of paper.

"Alice White," Don yelled. Everyone clapped and whooped. Alice was talented and a good choice.

"Okay, y'all. I need your attention. Quiet down," Don said. There was silence and I reached for Tracey's hand. "Elizabeth Hicks," Don announced. Elizabeth was the most beautiful and popular girl in our grade. The crowd roared. Tracey yanked her hand away. "You're killing me," she said.

"I'm sorry. I'm just nervous. What if I don't make it?"

Tracey didn't answer. She'd never lost anything in her entire life. She couldn't possibly understand what this meant to me.

Again, Don asked everyone to settle down. The suspense was torturous. This was my last chance.

"Casey Cohen," he yelled.

I jumped up and down, clapping and screaming, knowing that this was the beginning, the very first moment of my brand-new life. I couldn't believe it, and I could tell by the look on Tracey's face she was more shocked than I was. She never thought I'd make it.

o o o

After school, I found my mother leaning against the refrigerator, drinking Tab in our kitchen. I told her the news.

"You must be very excited," she said.

"I am."

She put the can down near the stove and slung her purse over her shoulder.

"Where are you going?" I asked her.

"The grocery store. My life is a series of errands." She turned to face me. "Don't cheerleaders have lots of practices after school?"

"Yeah, I guess they do."

"How do you expect to get back and forth?"

I shrugged. "I don't know."

"Don't you think you should have thought about that before you tried out?"

o o o

The following month, Tracey got her driver's license. At first, she was happy chauffeuring me around, so getting to games and practices wasn't a problem. In fact, it was the oppo-site. Tracey loved rolling the car windows all the way down and smoking cigarette after cigarette with Elvis Costello's "Alison" blasting through the speakers. But when the novelty wore off, Tracey didn't want to drive me to games anymore. And my mother didn't either. Plus, Tracey was annoyed I was busy every Friday and Saturday night and not available to accom-pany her to Fat Harry's, a New Orleans bar where all the high school kids hung out. Being underage at a bar in New Orleans wasn't unusual; in fact most everybody at Fat Harry's was, and I wouldn't know until I moved to New York that go-cups filled with alcohol were illegal.

Tracey made a habit of getting drunk and doing whatever she could to make Hawkeye notice her. Carrying a blow-dryer in her purse, she'd style her bangs obsessively in between classes or in the Fat Harry's bathroom, determined to keep them straight despite relentless and severe humidity. Her con-tempt for Franklin Prep was palpable and grew stronger every day. She barely studied and wouldn't do anything athletic because she refused to sweat. Dressed in my green-and-white uniform, I was the symbol of all she abhorred.

After weeks of begging, alternating between Tracey and my mother, to be picked up after a game or practice, I was kind of worn out. Stranded one day in my cheerleading uniform, I waited, and waited, and waited for Tracey to show up, which she might or might not do. I was sitting on a bench below the American flag when Hawkeye screeched to a stop in his jalopy. He screamed out the passenger window, "Hey, need a ride?"

Tracey still had a wild crush on Hawkeye and called his house regularly, doing hang-ups, just to hear his baritone voice. Once, she climbed through his bedroom window while he was sleeping and stole a picture of him, shirtless.

I'd always been intimidated by Hawkeye and felt my body tense.

"Get in," he said.

"No thanks," I called back. "I'm good."

"You sure? I don't mind."

A few minutes later, admitting Tracey wasn't coming and desperate for a ride, I got into Hawkeye's car. It was the color of a jalapeño and smelled like something spicy. Hawkeye had always been cute but now he was even cuter. His face was chiseled like a Greek sculpture, and he'd grown more muscular. He made a U-turn.

"I live that way," I said, pointing in the opposite direction.

Without looking at me, Hawkeye asked, "You know how to drive?"

"No, not yet."

"Well, what are you waiting for?" He pulled to the curb. "Come here, I'll teach you." He patted the seat next to him.

"No, no, it's okay," I said. "My dad said he'd teach me. And I'm signed up for driver's ed."

"Don't take driver's ed. Those people are idiots. You're going to drive around in one of those cars that go five miles an hour with a gigantic yellow sign on the roof that says Student Driver. It might as well say Loser. Come here." He tapped the seat. "I'll teach you."

Still, I hesitated.

"Come on, I don't have all day." Hawkeye lifted his sunglasses an inch off his nose, his left eye drooping, an everlasting wink.

I scooted over next to him, and we sat side by side in the driver's seat, my bare leg touching his. He placed his hands on mine, and together we turned the wheel. At first, I sat rigid as he worked the gas pedal and the brake, but as I got comfortable, he let me try. "You're a natural," he said.

Hawkeye was usually so tough around me, wanting to impress Big Sam and Tracey. It was nice to see him soften, and sitting next to him felt mysteriously normal.

Intermittently, he called out instructions as I drove on Jefferson Avenue and State Street. I turned on St. Charles. "I'll take it from here," Hawkeye said. I got into the passenger's seat, and Hawkeye headed to the Butterfly, a section of Audubon Park notoriously reserved for high school seniors.

"I have to get home, Hawkeye. My parents are going to wonder where I am."

"Relax a minute, will you?" He parked the car and reached into the back seat, grabbing a six-pack. I knew what seniors did at the Butterfly when the sun went down, and even though I didn't drink, when he handed me a can, I took it.

"Welcome to the Butterfly," Hawkeye said, smiling. He held his beer out and tapped it against mine. "You're in the big leagues now."

"It's really no big deal," I said. "Tracey's been here a million times."

"That girl," he said, shaking his head.

"What?"

"She thinks she's so cool." He gulped down his beer and crushed the can in one hand.

"Isn't she?"

"She's got nothing on you."

"I have to go home," I said, feeling myself blush. "It's getting late."

Hawkeye got out of the car and strolled to the trunk. He lifted three piñatas—a lion, an alligator, and an elephant—and placed them one by one in the back seat. They were decorated with tissue paper bright as a million rainbows.

I waited in the car and watched Hawkeye carry the alligator piñata to the front door of an ivory-colored brick ranch, delivering it like a pizza. He made three stops, and in between each, he told me about his family's piñata business: how his mother arranged sales, how he delivered, and how his brother, Morgan, custom-made each piñata.

Remembering the Mardi Gras piñata in Big Sam's room, it didn't take long for me to figure out Hawkeye was dealing drugs. I wasn't sure if Hawkeye wanted me to know what he was doing or if he thought I was too stupid to put two and two together. Wanting to seem cool, I didn't say anything but felt an urgency to get home. Even though I hadn't actually done anything wrong, it seemed like I had: a betrayal to my best friend and to my crush, a deadly sensation that I'd been in the wrong place at the wrong time.

The following Friday night, Tracey bumped into Hawkeye at Fat Harry's. "Come over tomorrow," he told her. "And bring your little friend."

New Orleans, 1979

Air conditioning hummed in a window. Hawkeye shooed his cats, Tiger and Spooky, off a springless couch, and Tracey and I sat bare-legged on lumpy cushions covered in knotty fabric.

"How y'all doing?" Hawkeye asked, sitting on a wood chair. He wore a tank top and folded his exposed arms across his broad chest.

"We're good," Tracey said, her bangs feathered perfectly.

Hawkeye smiled. "We have this place to ourselves tonight."

Tracey smiled. "Where are your parents?"

Leaning forward, Hawkeye lifted a pack of cigarettes off the coffee table and pulled a lighter from his back pocket. He lit up, inhaled, then exhaled. Smoke coiled around his face, veiling him in some sort of dreamlike illusion. "Can't tell you where my father is," he said. "Haven't seen him in three years. And my mother, the school nurse? The healer of all things evil? She and my stepfather, cop of the year, have gone fishing."

Everyone at school thought Hawkeye was damaged. He got drunk at a party once and told a story about how when he was little, Mrs. Graf cut his fingernails and snipped off the tip of his finger with the clipper. *Oh, I'm so sorry, honey*, she said. But according to Hawkeye, she wasn't. He also said that for years, she gave him daily allergy shots he didn't need, showing as much empathy for his discomfort as she might a pin cushion.

Behind him, over the gas fireplace, there were family photographs: Morgan and Hawkeye wearing holsters and holding guns in matching cowboy Halloween costumes; one of Mrs. Graf, from many years before in her nurse's uniform, a collared white dress, her hair in a bob, smiling and waving like Jackie O; and another of Hawkeye and Morgan's real father hugging his two young boys—one on each knee.

Hawkeye asked if we wanted anything to drink. Tracey said she'd have a beer, so I said I'd have one too. I didn't really drink, except for that one time with Hawkeye at the Butterfly, but everyone I knew had been drinking for a while already. It was time.

"Morgan," Hawkeye called over his shoulder, "bring a couple of beers, will you?"

Morgan entered carrying a six-pack of Bud. His black tee shirt said The Who. I couldn't believe I was finally getting to hang out with him.

"Hey," he said, meeting my gaze.

"Hi," I said, lowering my eyes, afraid they'd reveal too much. I looked down at the beer cans he placed on the coffee table.

"How about some music, Little Brother," Hawkeye said.

Morgan walked to the other end of the room, near where a *Dark Side of the Moon* poster hung, taped to the wall. There was a tear at the bottom, and the edges curled. A *Cars* album played on the stereo. Morgan threw his head back, gulping beer while lyrics, "my best friend's girl," blared. He sat on the floor, propped his can on the carpet next to him, and flipped through albums showing us: Tom Petty and the Heartbreakers, Supertramp, Michael Jackson's *Off the Wall*.

"Want this next?" Morgan called out from across the room, lifting Pink Floyd.

"Sure," Hawkeye said, resting a Bud on his thigh. He tossed his sunglasses onto the coffee table.

"Beer's so filling," Tracey said, standing. "I need to use the bathroom." She took her purse from the couch and hung it on her shoulder. Her blow-dryer stuck out.

Left alone with Hawkeye, I felt jittery and the silence wasn't helping. "Beer's good," I said, trying to start a conversation as "Another Brick in the Wall" played.

I'd asked Tracey on the way over to their house if she was sure Morgan would be there, and she said, "Of course Morgan will be there. Why else would Hawkeye invite you to come?"

Tracey didn't know that Hawkeye had given me a ride home from school, that we'd stopped at the Butterfly, or anything else.

"You see Big Sam much?" I asked.

"Not much," Hawkeye said, and he leaned back on his chair, a total balancing act. "He does his thing. I do mine."

"I heard he has to go to summer school."

"That's not happening," Hawkeye said. He reached for another cigarette and found the package empty. He crushed it into a ball and threw it amongst the beer cans on the table.

"For sure," I said, shaking my head as if I agreed. Without Tracey and Morgan nearby, I didn't know what I was doing there.

Hawkeye chugged a beer and crumpled the hollow can. "Hey, Morgan," he called over his shoulder. "Make the music louder, will you?" He leaned in toward me, resting his elbows on his knees. "That's my little brother," he said, pointing his chin at Morgan. "He's innocent."

"You think?"

"I know. And I want to keep it that way," he said. His voice was deep and threatening. He smirked and put his sunglasses back on. Fear rose in me. I wanted to get away from him. Our secrets bonded us, whether I wanted them to or not.

When I stood, Tracey was next to me, and I could tell she'd blown her bangs.

"I have to go to the bathroom too," I said.

The beer had gone to my head, and I had to concentrate hard in order not to stumble as I walked down a poorly lit hallway. I opened a door, mistaking it for a bathroom, only to discover countless colorful piñatas lining the shelves. I wondered how Morgan had no idea what his family was up to.

Back in the living room, I stood near the couch and reached for another beer. I chugged it fast and crunched the empty can in my hand like Hawkeye had.

"Whoa," Tracey said. "What got into you?"

Emboldened from beer, I sat with Morgan on the carpet as he put an album on the record player. "You know which band this is?" he asked.

It felt like some kind of test, one I wasn't willing to fail, so I nodded and hoped he wouldn't find out I was lying. As soon as I got a chance, I glanced at the album cover on the floor. America. Morgan drummed on his thighs to "Sister Golden Hair."

o   o   o

Over the next few weeks, Morgan took me to Red Lobster, The Boot, and of course Fat Harry's. We hung out at the levee, drawing and talking, and at first, dating Morgan was everything I dreamed it would be. I did whatever I could to be the perfect girlfriend. I took time getting ready, always wanting to look my best, and I'd eat soggy, cold French fries before ever complaining to him. He was on his best behavior too. Whenever I teased, reminding him how mean he'd been to me over the years, he just laughed and said he only did that stuff because he liked me. Said he didn't know what else to do.

One night, at Fat Harry's, Morgan kept looking into my eyes and leaning in close, leaving Tracey out. She was having a hard time because Hawkeye was ignoring her. Earlier in the week, she'd smuggled beer into the school courtyard for him and stolen a joint from Big Sam's room. Hawkeye simply drank the beer, smoked the joint, and left.

"You're too easy," I told Tracey. "Some guys only want what they can't have."

It wasn't helping that Morgan was giving me so much attention. She wasn't used to boys preferring me, and this was an awkward situation for both of us. So, at Fat Harry's when she said she had to go to the bathroom and asked me to go with her, even though I didn't want to, I went.

Tracey stood in front of the bathroom mirror and applied lip gloss. "You and Morgan seem to be hitting it off."

"Yeah, I guess," I said. I was unable to keep my mouth from smiling. "He's so cute."

"He used to be cuter."

I didn't let Tracey get to me. Delirious, life seemed perfect. I thought nothing could knock us down.

o   o   o

A few days later, during cheerleading practice, I forced a split and pulled a muscle. I changed into track shorts and left practice early. Morgan picked me up in the Graf jalopy. Even though it was technically the family car, Hawkeye never let him drive it.

"How'd you get the car?" I asked. "You never get it."

Morgan flexed his muscles.

Laughing, I traced the contour of his arm with the flat of my hand. There were so many things I liked about Morgan, but I liked his arms best.

"Hawkeye got a brand-new car. This baby's all mine now."

"Cool. What's that about?" I asked, pointing to the ash-tray. It was filled with soil and a few straggly green shoots.

"Hawkeye did that. It's pot."

"And your mom's okay with it?" I asked.

"It's medicinal," he said. "My mom gets intense migraines."

"But why grow it in a car?"

"My stepfather's a cop. It's Hawkeye's way of disrespecting the law. He'd love to get pulled over."

"I wouldn't."

Morgan drove to the Butterfly. On the way, we listened to the radio, and he told me how members of Santana formed Journey, that Eric Clapton played with the Yardbirds and formed Cream before creating Derek and the Dominos. He kept drumsticks in the glove compartment and, at red lights, drummed on the steering wheel. On the back seat, there was a sketchpad and pencils. Later, under an oak tree, we sat in the shade and drew.

"Want to come over?" Morgan asked.

"Sure," I said.

The humidity outside was fierce, and inside Morgan's house was damp as a rainforest. The windowpanes were covered with moisture, and the air felt clammy. There were plants everywhere in terra-cotta pots, ceramic ashtrays, coffee mugs, and Cool Whip containers. On the windowsills, along the fireplace mantle, and on bookcase shelves. In plain sight, on the coffee table, there was a manual: *Beginner's Guide to Growing Weed at Home*, featuring straightforward advice for designing indoor cannabis gardens, choosing seed varieties, planting, pot harvesting, storage, and more.

Mrs. Graf was in the kitchen boiling water. I hadn't seen her around school in a while, and she looked different. She usually wore her hair in a tight bun, but now it was loose and messy, dangling around her sunken face like Spanish moss. "Hey there, Casey," she said. "Welcome." A cigarette seesawed between her lips, her eyes vacant.

"Hi, Mrs. Graf," I said. Her disheveled appearance was disturbing, and the pot growing everywhere had me feeling uneasy. I reminded myself that she was an adult, a nurse, and she must know what she was doing. *Medicinal*, Morgan had said. She poured boiling water into a mug and sat at the dinette table, which was cluttered with Philadelphia cream cheese containers filled with soil. Some of them budded.

"If y'all want anything, help yourself, you hear? I'm going out," she said, smoke swirling from the lit cigarette in the ashtray.

Morgan led me down a hall. We passed a closed door with a sign that said ENTER AT YOUR OWN RISK. "Hawkeye's room," Morgan pointed.

There was an enclosed porch. Jumbo egg cartons lined shelves under sunny windows. They were also filled with soil, hundreds of shoots beginning. On a dark wood table, there was colored tissue paper, glue, and scissors.

"Sit down," Morgan said, pointing to a chair at the table. "I'll be right back. I'm going to show you how I make piñatas."

I didn't want to have anything to do with Morgan's piñatas, but I couldn't tell him that, so I kept my mouth shut, and as I waited for him to return, I tapped my feet, nervously, thinking about how if my mother knew where I was, she'd kill me. It was funny how she'd be all over it if an ashtray had gone missing, but the whereabouts of her daughter? Clueless.

Hawkeye stood at the door, shirtless, wearing sunglasses. "What are you doing here?"

"Morgan said he's going to show me how to make piñatas. He really has no idea, does he?"

Hawkeye sat in a chair next to me. "He's a good kid," he said, his face too close to mine. He put his hand on my bare thigh. A burning sensation ran through my body.

Morgan walked in with two frosted Pop-Tarts, and Hawkeye pulled his arm back. He stood and left the room.

Warm Pop-Tart icing was sticky on my fingers, and I licked it off. Morgan and I sat side by side, cutting tissue paper strips and listening to Led Zeppelin, "Feather in the Wind."

I knew what I was doing was wrong, but I didn't stop; I just kept cutting. I wanted to tell Morgan that Hawkeye was using the piñatas to deliver cocaine, but when I thought about Hawkeye's warning, I didn't.

It was getting dark, and just as Morgan was about to bring me home, Big Sam banged on the enclosed porch window. Morgan let him in and Big Sam blew past him, causing Morgan to fumble over a chair. Hawkeye heard the commotion and stood at the door.

"You've got to be kidding," Big Sam yelled at him.

"Calm down, Sam," Hawkeye said.

"Go to hell, *Earl*."

"Whatever the problem is, we can talk about it in my room."

"You're my problem," Big Sam said, throwing Hawkeye's arm off his shoulder. "You're screwing me over, paying other guys more than me. I started with you, *Earl*. I did the first drop with you. Remember?"

"What's he talking about, Hawkeye?" Morgan asked.

"Nothing," Hawkeye said.

"Cut the shit, Hawkeye," Big Sam yelled. And he turned to Morgan. "Your family's dealing, man. How stupid can you be? Even she knows." And he pointed to me.

"Shut up," Hawkeye screamed, rushing Big Sam. "You're an idiot, man," and he pinned him against the wall.

"I'm an idiot? I'm an idiot? You drove around the city making a delivery with Casey at your side like you're on some kind of hot date, and I'm an idiot?"

Hawkeye backed away from Big Sam and turned to Morgan. "It wasn't like that."

o o o

Morgan drove me home and didn't utter a word the whole way. I just stared out the window, wishing I knew what to say. When we pulled up in front of my house, Morgan leaned over and kissed me, which was a surprise because he'd been so mad. He raised the volume on the radio and put his hand on my thigh just as Hawkeye had done, and I wondered if he'd seen. He ran a finger along the edge of my track shorts and then, gathering fabric, pushed them up. Pressing my head back against the car window, he kissed me harder than usual and placed my hand on his jean zipper. I went along, stroking back and forth once or twice, before I stopped and said, "I can't."

Holding my arm firmly, he said, "Of course you can."

But I couldn't and Morgan was annoyed. "What's your problem?"

"I don't have a problem," I said, straightening myself. "I just want to wait."

"Wait for what?" he said, irritably.

"I don't know," I said.

It wasn't that I thought losing my virginity was the biggest deal in the world. Or wrong. I just wasn't ready. That's all I knew.

Morgan moved away. "Well, when you figure it out, call me."

For the next three days, I couldn't stop crying. I stayed home from school on day one, and even though I could've used Tylenol on day two, I wouldn't go to Mrs. Graf's office. On day three, Tracey said I was being ridiculous. She'd been talking to Morgan, and she warned me that he'd break up with me if I didn't get with it. Plus, Morgan was tired of having a girlfriend who had to cheer at games every Friday and Saturday night.

I considered quitting the squad and wondered how it was possible, that something that had been so important to me no longer held significance if it meant losing Morgan. It was a mistake to think things couldn't get worse.

It was Alice who slipped. It was the night we played St. Martin's, and after we finished our halftime routine, she asked casually when Morgan and I had broken up. I told her that we hadn't exactly broken up, and she froze. "Oh, okay. Sorry," she said.

"Sorry about what?"

"Nothing."

"Alice, what made you think we broke up?"

And then she told me that her brother had seen Morgan and Tracey making out at a keg party the night before.

In the St. Martin's school bathroom, I cried and wiped mascara from under my eyes. After the game, I took a chance and drove to Fat Harry's. The bar was thick with smoke. I could barely breathe.

As I pushed through the crowd, The Police's "Message in a Bottle" permeated, and in a booth in the back, I saw Tracey and Morgan making out. I felt like I was going to be sick. When they stopped kissing, they looked up and saw me standing there.

Tracey jumped up. "Casey! What are you doing here?" Her cigarette burned between two fingers, the ash red hot. I looked to Morgan. He just shrugged.

o o o

Tracey called the next morning, but I wouldn't get on the phone. My mother asked what was going on, but I wouldn't tell her. Then Morgan called, and I wouldn't take his either. I disconnected the phone in my room and sat on the floor scooping mounds of onion dip onto Ruffles potato chips. I cried and cried and, dazed, stared at the telephone cord snaking across my shag carpet.

o o o

In the hallway at school the next day, I overheard some kids near the lockers talking about Tracey.

"She carries a blow-dryer in her purse."

"No way. That's weird."

"It's true. She blows her hair at school."

I joined their group. "That's not all she blows."

New Orleans, 1980

On the night Franklin Prep played Country Day, I grabbed my pom-poms and my purse and headed for the door. I'd been so out of it, not doing homework, not going to parties, even missing a game or two since the night I caught Tracey with Morgan making out, but I couldn't miss another game without risking being thrown off the squad, and I'd already lost enough.

After the game there was a Mardi Gras–themed open house. As a cheerleader, attendance was mandatory.

"Enjoy yourself tonight," my mother called as I walked out. She'd been concerned these last few weeks, as I hadn't been doing much of anything, and was glad to see me participating again.

It was a scorching night, even for New Orleans, the kind of Southern heat that makes your skin slippery and your hair frizz before you reach your car.

At the game, I cheered with all my heart, as if I could scream the hurt out of me. Hundreds of people shouted in the stands, and the lighting illuminated the field with a yellow glow. At halftime, the band played "Soul Man" and I shook my pom-poms hard, doing the routine I'd practiced countless times.

The game wasn't even close. Franklin Prep slaughtered Country Day, and after the victory, I drove myself, windows down, music turned up loud, to the open house on St. Charles Avenue. Still in my cheerleading uniform, I walked up the path lined with burning torches to the plantation-style mansion where the party was.

A wide staircase led to an enormous wraparound porch, and white columns supported a two-story balcony above. Inside, the house was already jam-packed. I made my way through the crowd, looking for people I knew.

In the dining room, guests crammed around the stately antique table, eating shrimp and baby quiche. There were platters of ribs, fried chicken, and bowls of gumbo. Mardi Gras masks and doubloons decorated the table. Purple, green, and gold feathers adorned a traditional chandelier, and strands of colorful beads dangled. I took in the high ceilings, ornate moldings, a well-polished wood floor—shiny and rich as Southern tradition. My house didn't have any of that, and while I wasn't usually one to notice such details, these things popped out, making me feel out of place and like despite my cheerleading uniform, I didn't really belong.

Franklin Prep football players, cheerleaders, band members, principals, teachers, and parents had two requirements: show up at open house parties and drink. In New Orleans, it was totally normal to party with school faculty. Some had Jägermeister. Some loitered around kegs. All chatted about the night's win.

"You look different."

I turned and saw Hawkeye.

"It's my hair," I said, a bit self-consciously. All the girls in the entire city of New Orleans it seemed had fine, straight hair. It was impossible to keep mine tame, but I didn't care anymore because I was starting to appreciate that mine was distinctive, wild, and thick.

"You look more grown-up."

"What are you doing here, Hawkeye? This isn't your kind of thing."

"Don't be so quick to judge. I come to open house parties." He lifted his sunglasses and checked out my legs. "Want a drink?"

"Sure," I said, and I let Hawkeye lead the way to the keg in the kitchen.

He clinked my red cup with his. "Bottoms up," he said.

He lifted a piece of king cake from a platter and took a bite, and the yellow sugar coated his lips like gold glitter. He offered me some. I hesitated for a moment, but then, tired of being such a goody-goody, I ate it and let his fingers touch my lips.

"I got the baby," I said, pulling the pink plastic toy from my mouth.

"Luck and prosperity coming your way. But now you have to buy the next king cake."

"Okay, sure."

From a table, I lifted a green eye mask and slipped the elastic band around my head. Remembering Tracey and Morgan, and the whole situation, I felt a pang in my heart.

Hawkeye handed me another drink. And then another. At some point, I lost count. Through the green mask, I studied Hawkeye's muscular arms, noticing that they were bigger than Morgan's. Drunk already, every part of me tingled, and what was meant to stay inside just blurted out. "I like your arms," I said. "They're big."

He pulled me close, and I wondered what would happen if Tracey walked in and saw Hawkeye holding me like that. To Tracey, Morgan was the safety school, the one she knew she could get into—Hawkeye was the reach. Smells of New Orleans infused the air: beer, magnolias, red beans and rice.

"I like this party," I said, holding out my red cup as if to cheers.

"You're slurring," Hawkeye said. "I think you're drunk."

I took off my green mask. "You must be a rocket scientist."

"Oh, being a wise guy, huh?" Hawkeye smiled and I smiled too. "I should take you home. Want me to take you home?"

"Noooo. I'm just starting to have fun. And anyway, I have a car."

"You can't drive," Hawkeye said.

"I'm a good driver."

"I'm sure you are. But you're also drunk."

"I'm not." And my words sounded so muffled I wondered if what I actually said was *I'm snot*.

"Follow me," Hawkeye said, grabbing hold of my hand. He led the way to the backyard, to a charming patio—ivy dripping everywhere, red and white begonias in terra-cotta pots. Even though the sun had been down for hours, it was still hot outside, New Orleans hot.

"Come here," Hawkeye said. "If you can walk from one end of the patio to the other, on this brick border, without falling, you can drive yourself home. Otherwise, you're coming with me."

"I like a challenge," I said. "And for your information, I'm part of the GAC. You know what that is? It's the Girls Athletic Committee, and I'm spectacular on the balance beam. This is no problem."

"Okay. So do it." And he stepped back to watch.

When I fumbled, he reached for me. Hawkeye smelled of pungent alcohol, and the world felt lusciously alive, wild with possibility. In the background, I heard drunken voices and laughter and "Let the Good Times Roll." Hawkeye walked me to his new car, a Mercedes 450SL. Unlike the jalopy, this car had no Christmas tree air freshener, no marijuana growing from the ashtray, and no bobblehead Jesus on the dash.

In the car, Hawkeye pushed in the lighter. A moment later, there was a pop and the lighter burned red hot. He lit a joint, holding it between two fingers, and passed it to me. I'd never smoked before, but it was already clear to me that this was a night of firsts.

"Hey, remember that day?" Hawkeye asked, "You know, that time we played Truth or Dare?"

I nodded.

"It wasn't supposed to turn out that way." He took off his sunglasses and looked at me. "Can I see?" he asked, pointing his chin at my stomach.

I lifted my cheerleading top, just a little, and he touched my scar with his finger. I let him stay there; nobody had ever touched it before.

"Sorry," he said. "I'm really sorry."

"It was dumb. Big Sam can be a jerk."

"For sure," Hawkeye said, downing his beer. He paused. "I fell for you that day."

"Me?"

"Yeah, you're pretty tough."

Hawkeye leaned in, his lips on mine, and we made out. I pictured Tracey and Morgan, then pushed their images away.

After what seemed like a long time, Hawkeye pulled back and lit a cigarette. The car filled with smoke, and it felt like I was floating on a cloud. It was odd, because we didn't talk then, but it was okay, because nothing needed to be said. The night had taken on a whole new feel, formless.

After a few minutes, Hawkeye stubbed his cigarette into the ashtray. "Come on," he said, opening his car door.

"Where are we going?" I asked, getting out of his car. Everything was spinning, and I had to concentrate hard in order not to fall.

He opened the trunk and I saw an alligator piñata.

He cradled the piñata with one arm and slammed his trunk shut with the other. "Where's your car?" he said. "I'll drive you home."

In my car, the alligator piñata rested at my feet.

"I'm going to drop you off," Hawkeye said. "Then I'll make this delivery. Tomorrow I'll bring you your car, and you can take me to get mine."

"Why do you do it, Hawkeye?"

"Do what?"

"Make deliveries."

He shrugged. "Easy money. Easy life. Things used to be too hard. Free delivery's the key, a game changer. Our customers get to stay home and interact with straight-laced high school kids instead of driving into seedy neighborhoods and dealing with shady characters."

"What about Big Sam? How'd he get involved?"

Hawkeye laughed. "My mother recruited him."

"How?"

"He hadn't studied for a final, so he went to the nurse's office. He wasn't sick but my mother let him stay. The next time he needed an excuse, she gave him Benadryl and wrote a note to his teacher explaining that he'd had an allergic reaction to something. He owed her. After that, they had a deal."

"And why piñatas?"

"It was code. *We have the best-quality piñatas. Do you want a piñata delivery?* They're a great cover."

Parked at the curb in front of my house, Hawkeye pressed a button, bringing his seat back. I leaned over and we kissed. I wanted this. And more.

Hawkeye put his hand between my legs, touching me how I knew he'd touched others, even Tracey. He had a reputation for messing with girls' heads, making them feel special, only to dump them in the most humiliating ways. I didn't care.

As I straddled his lap in the driver's seat, he lifted my cheerleader skirt and pulled my panties to the side. Before I knew it, he was inside me—my virginity gone.

A light flashed, and I jumped to the passenger's seat. A policeman knocked on Hawkeye's window and showed his badge. "We're looking for Earl Ritter," he said.

I turned to Hawkeye. "They're looking for you."

"They're always looking for me."

But Hawkeye was wrong, because they weren't policemen. They were FBI. They'd rung our bell at midnight, asking my father if he knew where I was or who I was with. My father told them I was at a football game, cheering. And that I had an open house party after. Having inside information, they told him they needed our house for a stakeout.

The car door swung open with force, and four armed agents dragged Hawkeye to the curb. I stared out the window into the dark night, trying to see what was going on. Within seconds, Hawkeye was on the sidewalk, facedown, hands cuffed behind his back. That's when I saw my father standing on the side, watching the whole episode go down.

Nothing between us was the same after that.

New Jersey, 1980

On Friday nights, Syrian families congregate around their dining room tables for Shabbat dinner, and my parents decide we are going to do the same. On our first Shabbat in New Jersey, my father holds open a prayer book and recites, in Hebrew, a blessing over a cup of red wine.

"Not bad," my mother says.

My father takes a sip of wine and hands the cup to my mother. "It's like riding a bike," he says. "It all came right back to me." My father turns a page in the siddur and recites a second blessing for the challah.

In the kitchen, on large platters, my mother dishes chicken and potatoes, a roast, string beans with allspice, *s'fiha*, white rice, and *kibbeh hamdah*. It is not unusual for Syrian women to cook an abundance of food, but it is unusual for my mother. Overnight, it seems, she realizes she's been playing by the wrong rules and is doing things the Syrian way now.

"Looks like Mom drank the Kool-Aid," Sam teases. "No cans? No TV dinners?"

"Cut it out, Sam," my mother says.

"Leftovers for a year," Sam goes on. "We could feed all of Africa."

"Sam," my father warns.

○   ○   ○

As my parents and Sam embrace our new life, I sit there recalling a Thanksgiving in New Orleans when my father invited his father, Grandpa Sam, and his girlfriend, Christina, for dinner. My mother didn't want to cook but agreed to since national holidays were all we had then as far as tradition went.

Nellie had offered to help. "I'll make a ham," she said.

Even though New Orleans was fourteen hundred miles from Brooklyn and the Syrian Jewish community, my parents exchanged guilty looks. It wasn't that they'd kept kosher till then; they hadn't. Right from the beginning, they agreed to put their Orthodox Jewish ways behind them, but a ham on the dining room table was a severe step, symbolizing a complete abandonment of culture and community.

"I don't want Nellie thinking I don't appreciate her. It's not worth the risk. It's not a big deal," my mother said. "I mean, I don't care, you don't care, and your father certainly doesn't care." She shrugged. "When in Rome."

"I'm not concerned about the ham, but no turkey?"

My mother waved a dismissive hand. "Turkey's always dry. Nobody eats it."

"I do," my father said.

On Thanksgiving Day, my mother set the table in the dining room and placed her contribution, a paper turkey she'd bought from K&B, in the middle. In the kitchen, she slapped Oscar Mayer turkey slices on a plate and set that on the table too.

When Grandpa Sam and Christina arrived, my father pointed to the glass coffee table. "Sharon, *maza*?" He didn't often speak Arabic.

"I didn't make any. We're going to eat soon."

My father's eyes darted to his father, and he pulled my mother to the side. With his father so close, he was utterly embarrassed by his wife's lack of hospitality. Syrian women were taught to serve, and being *shatra*, hospitable, was highly valued. Syrian women were supposed to say *fadal*—welcome to my home—regardless of convenience, and their freezers were always full of *maza*—*sambousak, kibbeh, laham b'ajeen*, and *eras b'ajweh*—in case an unexpected guest should drop by. And even though my mother's father was Syrian, her mother was an Ashkenazic Jew, her ancestors from Europe, not Aleppo, and these rules simply didn't apply.

"How many times have I told you to prepare appetizers when we have company?"

"The last time I made *laham b'ajeen*, you laughed at me."

"You made a Syrian appetizer that's supposed to be the size of a silver dollar into the size of a large pie from Pizza Hut."

My mother didn't have patience for tedious work and considered laboring over Syrian delicacies a waste of time. My father had turned what she believed was a clever idea, combining tradition and modernity, into a shortcoming, and she didn't appreciate being criticized. "It tasted the same," she said.

o o o

I push food around my plate, feeling depressed, thinking about how unfair it is that while Tracey gets to decide which college she wants to apply to, I get to pick what bathing suit I want to wear in the Marriage Box—a one piece or two. I sit up tall and clear my throat. "So, I was thinking, I'd like to go to New Orleans for Christmas."

"We don't celebrate Christmas," my father says, not looking at me.

I slump in my chair. Even though our house always sat bare, holiday time in New Orleans was spectacular. Lights flashed like smiles across rooftops, peppermint poles lined pathways, and Santa and his sleigh topped most every lawn.

"I want to go home," I say, trying again.

"You *are* home," my father says.

I stab a potato with my fork. "I want to go to New Orleans."

My father still doesn't look at me. He's looking down at his plate. "You know you can't go back."

"Oh, that reminds me," my mother says. "Your boss from Getaway, Mr. Betesh, called today. A rabbi got hold of him and gave him an earful about you working on the weekend. Apparently, Syrian girls don't work on Saturdays, and the rabbi made it clear that community members couldn't support an establishment that ignored the laws of Shabbat. Mr. Betesh doesn't want any trouble. He'd rather you work fewer days."

"But I need to work on Saturdays," I say. "I need the money."

"Don't shoot the messenger," my mother says, piercing a string bean. "The community's changing. This is all new to me too. It wasn't like this when I was young. A rabbi was there to give advice. That's all."

"Well, it's ridiculous. It's not their business when I work."

"Obviously, it is," my father says.

"They have rules about everything."

"Yes, they do. That's the way it is here."

"I don't have to follow their rules."

"That's enough, Casey," my father says, his lips tight.

I drop my knife, and it clanks against the side of my plate. "They can't control me."

"Casey, you've caused enough trouble. I've had it. Not another word," my father says.

"But I *need* the money. I'm saving up."

"Casey, I'm warning you."

"It's my life! I want to make my own decisions."

My father leaps from his chair and puts his hand over my mouth like a gag. "Not another word, you hear me? Not another word," he bellows, his face close to mine.

I'd seen my father lose his temper with strangers—the thief

who tried to rob his antique store, a drunk who jumped a red light and almost hit our car, but never with me. Across the table, my mother sits frozen in her chair, and Sam's eyes are wide and unblinking.

My father removes his hand from my mouth and mumbles, "I told you to keep quiet. You don't listen. Why can't you just listen?" He moves away slowly and sits down in his spot at the head of the table.

I keep my head down, eating heaping spoonfuls of potatoes, swallowing without chewing.

"I guess I went a bit crazy for a minute," my father says, not apologizing. "It's just you've been relentless."

"You're exactly like your Aunt Susie," my mother chimes in, her shoulders relaxing. "Susie doesn't know when to keep quiet either."

"Temporary insanity," my father says, as if pleading a case. Sam hits his spoon like a gavel on the table. "Guilty as charged."

When my parents aren't looking, Sam catches my eye. He circles his pointer finger at his temple and mouths, *Crazy.*

My father tries to make light of the whole incident, but I don't speak for the rest of the meal. Sometimes you can't take back what's happened. Not ever. I stuff my face with food until my stomach hurts so bad I think I might throw up.

o o o

"Those Syrians live in the dark ages," Grandma Rose says over the phone when she hears I'm not allowed to work on Shabbat.

Grandma is just what I need, so on Saturday, instead of handing out menus and collecting tips, I take the train to see her in New York City, where she lives. She sits next to me on the couch in her apartment and holds my hand. Through her translucent skin, blue veins pop like electric wires.

"I can't stand it here, Grandma."

"I know," she says.

If anyone can understand my plight, it's Grandma. She was Grandpa David's secretary, and nobody in Grandpa's family wanted him to marry her. Plus, she's Ashkenazi and feels like an outsider too.

"Saks," she says, raising a finger. "That's what you need."

o o o

The taxi fare from Grandma's apartment to Saks is $4.20, and Grandma reaches into her purple crocodile purse for a ten-dollar bill. "Keep the change," she tells the cab driver. He turns to us and smiles so wide I think his lips might rip. Grandma is known to be a great tipper, and nobody worships her more than her hair stylist, her manicurist, and her doorman.

We step out of the cab, and Grandma points to a black leather jacket in the window. "You're in New York City now, my love. Might as well look the part."

"I don't want to look like the other Syrian girls, Grandma."

"Understood."

Claire is Grandma's very own salesperson. Her auburn hair is loosely pinned in a bun, her cheeks white and smooth as bars of Ivory soap.

"There's nobody like your grandmother," Claire says. In black pumps and a dress with shoulder pads, she exudes chic elegance, owning a polished, put-together look like a real New Yorker. "Your grandmother's an amazing woman. What style, such grace, and she looks young enough to be your mother," Claire says, leading us to a dressing room. She unlocks the door and gestures to a sparkly beige dress already hanging on a silver rod.

"That's stunning," Grandma Rose says, sitting on an upholstered chair in the carpeted fitting room.

"I don't do glitter," I say.

"You don't do flashy," Grandma corrects, pinching the fabric between two fingers. "This is magnificent."

I turn over the price tag. "No way, Grandma. This is a fortune. I don't want it."

"Well, I want you to have it."

"I don't believe in spending money like this. I'd rather feed the homeless. In every state!"

"Cut it out, Casey. You need to have nice things in your closet. Just in case."

"Just in case what?"

Grandma Rose unzips the dress, taking it off the hanger. It's important that a woman always look her best, she says. "Think about it this way, Casey. Buying this dress is like a smile. When someone smiles, people smile back. It's contagious. And when a beautiful woman shines, the world radiates in return."

"Grandma," I say, "only you could change the selfish act of buying this dress into an altruistic one."

o o o

The rabbi gets his way, and I continue to work at Getaway, but not on Saturdays. Little by little, I piece together community expectations—some religious, some cultural, most archaic and long established. As I sweat over the hot dog grill or work the cash register making change at Getaway, the Syrian girls stare. They don't know what to make of me. To community members, the ones who grew up in Brooklyn, the rules are clear, and most follow contentedly, understanding that to stand out, or attempt to satisfy individual needs, threatens the community's existence. I try to mix what I've known my whole life with this brand-new way of living, but again and again, as I flip burgers, I'm asked, *Aren't you S.Y.?*

"S.Y.?"

"Syrian."

"Yes," I answer.

A girl with long black hair named Rochelle tells me she's going to be in my class at yeshivah in the fall. She wears a lamé sarong. "I don't get it," she says, standing on the other side of the cash register, a hand on her hip. "It's summer. Why are you working?"

"I need the money."

She chews pink gum. "Can't you just ask your parents?"

New Jersey, 1980

My first Syrian date is with a boy named Isaac. His mother cornered me at a bris and told me I'd be missing something if I didn't go out with her son.

Isaac calls a few days later. He asks why he never sees me around, why I don't hang out in the Marriage Box.

"I don't want to get married," I say. "Isn't that obvious?"

o o o

On our date, I wear the sparkly beige dress Grandma Rose bought me. In trying to hold on to some image I have of myself, I accessorize with brown feather earrings, two chunky silver rings, and a turquoise beaded cuff. I wear Maybelline very black mascara, high heels, and a brown leather ankle bracelet with a silver peace sign. The finished look is a compilation—part Flower Child, part Disco Queen.

While we wait to be seated at a table, I sit on a stool at the bar and Isaac stands next to me. "Funky Town" beats in the background. "What kind of name is Casey? I don't know any Syrian girls named Casey."

"I was supposed to be named Cynthia, after my father's mother," I say. "But my dad kind of broke that rule." I don't tell Isaac that my father breaks a lot of rules and that besides naming me what he wanted, he owns a gun and carries a purse.

"What's wrong with Cynthia?"

"Nothing. That's not the point. It's just that he met a girl named Casey and liked that name better."

"He doesn't care about Syrian customs?"

"He does. He just thought using the *C* was good enough. Plus, my mom was drugged during my delivery, knocked out for days. When the nurse came by with my birth certificate, she was out of it and let my father do what he wanted."

Isaac fidgets. It's obvious he isn't used to such transparency. Syrians tell stories about themselves that are promotional, not self-deprecating, because the reputations they acquire stick. Once you are labeled smart or pretty, that's what you are. If you are known as the girl with the crooked nose or thick thighs, that will never change. *And once a slut, always a slut.*

Isaac shifts his body weight and changes the subject. "This place is cool, no? *Shoof* the G's."

"What does that mean?" I ask, playing dumb, partially because his words are derogatory slang but mostly because I don't want to be with Isaac, and the sound of his Brooklyn accent is making things worse.

"*Shoof*? You don't know what *shoof* means? It means 'look' in Arabic. Look at the G's."

"What's a *G*?" I ask.

"You don't know what a *G* is?"

"No," I lie.

"You're *sketching*. Right? You're kidding?" He waves at a bartender, trying to get her attention. "A *G* is a girl. They're pretty, the bartenders. No?" He cocks his head. "I can't believe you didn't know that."

American Syrians have invented their own language—part Arabic, part slang, part Pig Latin. Speaking properly isn't a priority. In New Orleans, it wasn't important to me either, but amongst the Syrians, I do everything opposite.

"You could speak English," I say, sipping my drink. "We're in America, after all."

"No reason to." Isaac shrugs. "Everyone I know understands me."

"You might want to get out in the world a bit."

"Why should I? I like it right here, where everyone I know gets me. And agrees with me."

"Isn't that kind of tedious?"

"Kind of what?"

"Tedious," and when I see he doesn't understand, I clarify, "Boring."

The bartender places a bowl of nuts in front of us. I scoop some. Isaac palms my hand, hard, and yells, "Don't."

"Don't what?"

"Eat those. Not everyone washes. It's disgusting."

"I'm not a germy," I say, popping nut after nut into my mouth.

"I like your accent," he says to me.

"Thanks."

"It's why I asked you out. I overheard you talking at Getaway. You like it here?"

"It's been kind of tough. I miss my best friend."

"I mean, do you like the restaurant?"

"Oh, yeah. It's great."

"So, what's so special about New Orleans anyway?"

"It's a great city. I loved my school. I was a cheerleader."

Isaac leans in. "Maybe you'll do a cheer for me later."

"I don't think so."

"Oh, come on. Why not?" he says, sliding the bowl of nuts away from me.

As a rule, Syrian girls don't eat on dates. They eat at home in order not to appear gluttonous. And they don't drink—too avant-garde. But I do both. And all night, Isaac keeps looking at me funny, as if I am a circus act or something. I can't help but wonder what he'd think if he knew about my past.

After dessert, when I want to order another drink, Isaac says, "Maybe you've had enough."

"What? What makes you think I've had enough?"

"You're slurring."

"That's my Southern drawl."

By the end of the night, I've downed four screwdrivers, and feeling lonely, I invite Isaac inside when he drops me at home. In the kitchen, I offer him a snack.

"What've you got?" he asks.

I pull a package of kosher hot dogs from the freezer. I smack the package against the counter, and when a hot dog breaks free, I wrap it in a paper towel like a baby in a blanket. I place it in the microwave. A minute later, there's a ding, and I hand Isaac his hot dog.

"Are you kidding?"

"Does it look like I'm kidding?"

"Wow, aren't you *shatra*."

"I don't want to be *shatra*, thank you very much. *Shatra* is just another word for servant." I join him at the dinette table. He leaves his hot dog, uneaten, while I swirl mine in French's, making yellow designs around the edges of my plate.

"What? No. A woman who is *shatra* is amazing. She serves beautifully. Artfully."

"Oh, that's great. Brainwashing women into believing subservience is an art." I bite off the tip of my hot dog.

"If you don't like to serve, why are you a waitress?"

"Now, that's a good question."

"I have another question," Isaac says, leaning forward in his chair. "What's that about?" He points his chin to my peace sign ankle bracelet. "You some kind of hippie?"

"Maybe."

Memories surface from too much vodka. Hippies in the

French Quarter—their long hair, crocheted vests, bellbottom pants, and vibrant tattoos—dotting New Orleans like rainbow sprinkles. Strikingly keen is the sound of jazz, the smell of beer, the taste of uninhibited culture.

"When I was ten years old," I tell Isaac, wanting so badly to connect with another human being, "Cracker Jacks were my favorite snack because of the prize. I'd open the box, dig inside for the tattoo, spit on it, and apply it to my skin before eating any of the Cracker Jacks. When I wanted more tattoos, I started creating my own. In my room, I'd spend hours on end drawing swirling designs around words like LOVE, PEACE, HOPE, JOY." I leaned in, hooked eyes with Isaac, and touching my ankle bracelet, said, "I want to be an artist. I want to convey something. You know what I mean? An ideology. A worldview."

"Wow."

"Wow what?"

"You're deep."

I stand, stack our plates, and carry them to the sink. At the door, I kiss Isaac goodnight. Not because I like him but because Syrian girls aren't supposed to make out. Especially on a first date.

o   o   o

Upstairs, I wash my face. Looking in my New Jersey bathroom mirror, I remember coming home from one of my very first dates in New Orleans, way before Morgan and I started hanging out, and Tracey was there because her parents were away and she was staying at our house. She was rubbing Pond's cold cream on her cheeks in front of my bathroom mirror, and I scooted in next to her. As I splashed water on my face, she asked me about my night. Standing side by side, I told her I didn't like my date but that I'd kissed him anyway because I didn't want him to think I was a bitch. Dabbing her cheeks dry with a washcloth, Tracey said, "I like when guys think I'm a bitch."

○ ○ ○

Alone in my new life, in my new bathroom, I shut the light and head to my room, wishing for the millionth time I could be more like Tracey.

And that I could go home.

Brooklyn, 1980

On Labor Day we move like sheep along with all the other
Syrian families from the Jersey Shore to Brooklyn. Our black
Cadillac is packed tight with suitcases and shopping bags full of
our belongings, and we travel north on the Garden State Parkway. An hour later, my father crosses the Verrazano Bridge
while my mother calls out directions. Sam and I sit in the back,
looking away from each other and out our windows. Traffic on
the Belt Parkway is depressing, and I think it can't get worse
until I see Bay Parkway. It's crowded and dirty; it's the Brooklyn I recognize from TV. *Welcome Back, Kotter* or something.

The Midwood section, where we live, isn't much better. It's
aesthetically displeasing with houses lined up like dominoes, the
space between them filled with concrete, not grass. The streets
are congested, the honking—off-putting. Even the graffiti is drab.

We arrive at our two-story home by noon and spend the day
unpacking. My father hides his gun in a closet on the top shelf,
my mother stocks the kitchen, Sam watches television, and I
mark my calendar with a big X. One more day until school starts.

My parents want me and Sam to be part of community
life, so they've enrolled us at a second-rate Sephardic yeshivah,
even though we don't speak a word of Hebrew. My new school
is a narrow four-story building, and unlike Franklin Prep, there
is no gym, no field, and no auditorium. The next day when my
mother pulls up in front, I cry.

The rabbi is our principal. He wears a yarmulke and has a thick black beard. My mother extends her arm to shake his hand, but he pulls back.

"Oh, I'm so sorry," my mother says. "I forgot. No touching. You know, I like that rule. It makes sense."

"Follow me," the rabbi says, letting the awkward moment pass. He escorts my mother, Sam, and me to his office. The hallways are totally bare—no bulletin boards announcing pep rallies, no posters with famous quotes, and no blooming courtyard.

The rabbi's office has one small window, which faces a brick wall. He gestures for us to sit opposite his desk and points to the dress code on page thirty-six in the handbook. Sam has to wear a yarmulke and, under his button-down shirt, tzitzit, which resembles a Hanes tee shirt with knotted fringe attached to its four corners. Tzitzit are a constant reminder of one's obligation to God.

Girls are required to wear knee-length skirts and shirts that cover their elbows because being *tzniut*, modest, is not only valued but expected. I find this odd because at Getaway, all summer, girls my age, and their mothers, wore skimpy bikinis and high heels to the beach.

The rabbi explains how boys and girls are taught in separate classrooms so that we can't distract one another, but he has nothing to worry about, because I saw a couple of boys in the hallway on the way to his office, and they don't look anything like the boys at Franklin Prep. With yarmulkes on their heads, and tzitzit dangling from their shirts, they don't appeal to me. The rabbi hands me my schedule, and I read it.

Tefillah–Prayers (8:00–8:45)
Chumash–Bible (8:50–9:30)
Navi–Prophets (9:35–10:15)
Homeroom (10:16–10:34)
Ivrit–Hebrew Language (10:35–11:20)

Jewish History (11:25–12:00)
Mishlei–Proverbs (12:05–12:50)
Lunch (12:55–1:30)
American History (1:35–2:15)
Earth Science (2:20–3:00)
Mincha–Afternoon Prayers (3:01–3:19)
English (3:20–4:00)
Math (4:05–4:45)

"When do we have art?" I ask.

"You don't," he says. "Unfortunately, there isn't enough time in the day."

My heart sinks. "But the day is forever. We don't get out until four forty-five."

"There are time constraints," the rabbi says. "Music, gym, and art are not essentials."

I don't tell the rabbi how much I disagree. Junior year is important. I'm concerned because besides needing those extra-curriculars, I want to be prepared for the SATs. With all the time wasted on Hebrew subjects, I'll never get a good score. Not wanting to end up like a typical Syrian girl—uneducated and married at eighteen—I've already decided to get straight As and apply to some out-of-town schools. I feel trapped, and somewhat desperate, because college is my only way out.

When my mother leaves, the rabbi shows me to my first-period class. I stand in the doorway and watch as a group of girls polish their nails, their gold bangles clanking against their desks with each brush stroke. Chatting as if they are in a beauty parlor and not a classroom, they look like Middle Eastern goddesses, their summer tans deep as copper—a color my skin could never be.

I sit down at an empty desk in the back.

"Hi," Rochelle says.

"Hi," I say.

Since summer, she's traded in her gold lamé sarong for a black-fringed button-down. She waves her hands in front of me, air-drying pink nails. "You're the girl I met this summer, right?" She snaps gum. "The one from Louisiana."

"New Orleans," I say, as if she's wrong. I search for a pen in my purse.

Careful not to mess up her nails, Rochelle pulls over a chair. Our teacher calls for the class's attention, but Rochelle continues talking as if there's no reason in the world for her to stop. I stare straight ahead, determined to make a good impression.

"Girls, it's time to begin," Mrs. Hemstein says.

I open my notebook, deciding if I should apply to Tulane or BU—or both.

"She's nice," Rochelle says, pointing at Mrs. Hemstein. "She doesn't care if we talk." Rochelle blows a gigantic bubble, then sucks in.

"Getting a yeshivah education is a gift," Mrs. Hemstein says. She wears a wig because Jewish law requires observant married women to cover their hair.

Hair, I learned over the summer, is considered seductive and has sexual potency. Traditionally, Jewish women wore scarves to hide their hair, but somewhere along the way, women began to use wigs instead. Head coverings are supposed to make women less attractive to men, but I've seen women with wigs that are thick, long, highlighted, and much more eye-catching than their actual hair.

"You are very lucky, girls," Mrs. Hemstein reminds us. "Can I have your attention, please?" She writes with chalk on the blackboard in large letters. *Chumash*.

I cup my mouth with my hand and whisper to Rochelle, "What's *Chumash*?"

Rochelle's eyes widen. "The study of the Torah," she answers, as if I'd asked *What's ice cream?* which I think I'll do later in the day just to mess with her.

"You are very lucky to be Jewish," Mrs. Hemstein says, finally getting our class to settle down. "And let me say again, you are even luckier to attend yeshivah. But that comes with a price. You're the heart of the Jewish community, and each and every one of you is held responsible. What you do, and what you say, is a reflection on the entire Jewish world. *Chas Ve'shalom*, God forbid, you should behave in a way that brings shame to you, or your family, or Jews at large, for that is *Chilul Hashem*, disrespectful to God."

I sink lower in my chair. These girls probably never did anything worse than flirt with a boy or eat unkosher food. What I did with Hawkeye is so much worse. I take a deep breath.

"Don't take her so seriously," Rochelle says, seeing my face. "She's very *taeel*. She cries if we wear lipstick. Want to come with us for lunch later? We go to Lou's deli."

"Sure," I say, not wanting to eat alone.

"You're excused," Mrs. Hemstein announces, finally. "Hurry along so you're not late for your next class."

"Where's the bell?" I ask Rochelle.

"There isn't one."

Whoever thought a high school student would miss a bell? I unfold my course schedule and cross off *Chumash*. As the day drags on, one by one, I check off *Navi*, *Ivrit*, Jewish History, and *Mishlei* and, overeager, do the same to lunch before the period even starts.

o   o   o

The September sun hides behind tall bricks as we exit the building. Kings Highway resembles what a thriving market in Aleppo must have looked like. There are no Burger Kings or Piggly Wigglys. Instead, stores selling string cheese, *ka'ak*, *kibbeh*, and *laham b'ajeen* line the street. Olives, pickles, and nuts are scooped out of large vats and weighed. Allspice and cumin are freshly ground and displayed in sacks. The guttural sounds of Arabic—*bejenin, belash*—fly through the air and land on the sidewalk like spit. You can buy homemade Syrian dessert: *'ataiyef, kanafe*, and *ma'amoul*. In storefront windows, there are silver menorahs, wine cups, and candlesticks for Shabbat.

A black cat crosses our path, and Rochelle jumps back. I turn my head and spit three times, thinking of Tiger, Morgan's yellow cat, and Spooky, Hawkeye's black one, and how Hawkeye would grab the flesh of their necks and throw them from cushion to cushion. They'd hiss, claws splayed wide. The litter box, foul smelling, near the back door.

"What are you doing?" Rochelle asks.

"Spitting," I say. "Black cats are bad luck."

"They're so gross," a girl named Adele chimes in. "I hate cats."

"Me too," Rochelle says. "I like dogs but not cats." She turns to me. "Do you knock on wood too?"

"Sometimes," I say, not sure what she is getting at.

"It's a Christian thing." She waves her hand. "We don't do that."

The kosher deli is at the end of the block. My whole class, sixteen girls, sit around a long table, and for a moment I imagine fitting in. Over the summer, Sam's friends gathered to play football on a lawn, and when it started to rain, they ran inside, a tribe, leaving what must have been over forty sneakers piled outside the front door. Walking home from Getaway, I could see the mound from the street and felt jealous.

Rochelle informs me that she usually eats half a grapefruit for breakfast. And lettuce, no dressing, for dinner. She orders pickles with mustard for lunch.

"That's all you're having?" I ask her.

"I'm on the grapefruit diet. But they don't have grapefruits here."

"What's the grapefruit diet?"

"You only eat grapefruits."

"For how long?"

"As long as it takes. I have to lose five pounds."

"Why?"

"My boyfriend makes clothes in China, and he keeps bringing me samples, size zero. I'm really a two."

"Why don't you just tell him?"

"Because I already told him I was a zero."

"But, Rochelle, you're so skinny."

"That's not the point. A zero's better. Everyone knows it's better."

"Any smaller and you'll be invisible."

"Good," Rochelle says, shrugging a shoulder.

The waiter sets down Rochelle's lunch—pickles lined up on a plate like individual blades of grass. He places a pastrami sandwich in front of me, and the girls in my class look at me as if I am about to eat a rhinoceros.

"I bet you eat pasta, don't you?" Adele asks from the far end of the table. Everybody stops talking to hear my answer.

"Sure," I say.

Adele shakes her head as if this is the most outrageous thing she's ever heard. "Oh my God. Do you eat bread too?"

The Syrian girls are good at eliminating, knocking things off their lists—no dessert, no bread, no pasta, no sex. I'm not like that. Once I hear *no*, I want it more. I squirt mustard all over my pastrami sandwich and take a bite, discovering the first good thing about New York.

o   o   o

It is 3:20 and I'm already exhausted. At Franklin Prep, school would be over by now and I'd be at my locker packing up my books, getting ready to go home, but at yeshivah—we are just getting started. I whip out my schedule and put a check near English.

Mr. Salem, our English teacher, is twenty-six. He has curly hair that hangs in ringlets to his shoulders, and he plays the harmonica. You can tell from the second you walk into his classroom that something is different, all the desks arranged in a U. Mr. Salem quotes Bob Dylan, and his arms flay with excitement as he discusses characterization, theme, and plot.

While Syrians don't revere teachers, the Syrian girls love Mr. Salem. He drives a Mazda convertible, not a Honda, and undeniably handsome, manages to get his female students to read, participate in class, and do their homework.

Mr. Salem writes on the board. *The Scarlet Letter* by Nathaniel Hawthorne. I wasn't a great reader while at Franklin Prep, but now books supply a connection to feelings and thoughts no one around me seems to understand.

As much as Mr. Salem encourages our class to consider other ideas or to be open-minded, the girls are too scared they'll be ostracized, talked about, or labeled like Hester. When we discuss *The Scarlet Letter*, they judge, guardians of right and wrong, believing Syrian girls should not do anything sexual premarriage, while boys can do whatever they want but never with a Syrian girl. Blood on wedding night sheets a reward for chastity, the lack of it, a sin. There is no place for me in their world.

"What about love?" I ask.

"What about it?" Adele says.

"If two people are in love, you think the boy should be with someone else and not with the girl he loves?"

Adele puts her hands on her hips and faces me. "Girls who fool around are *hazita*. And sluts. Nobody will marry them."

o o o

By December the leaves on the trees are all gone, and Brooklyn is as ugly as ever. When I get home from school one freezing day, my mother is in her room with the door closed.

In the kitchen, I make Kraft macaroni and cheese. Just as I sprinkle the packet of cheesy powder over the noodles, the phone rings. I pick up the receiver that's mounted on the wall, and my mother picks up too. She doesn't realize I'm on the line. The telephone cord is long, and even though I can move around the kitchen, I don't dare. Covering the mouthpiece with my hand, I'm careful not to make a sound. Aunt Susie tells my mother that Tracey has a new boyfriend, a Franklin Prep football player, and that she got a 1250 on her PSATs.

What? I mouth. It's all I can do not to scream.

Aunt Susie says that Tracey is already talking about the homecoming dance and that she's excited about it.

I have to sit. I'm overwhelmed with fear and sadness, shocked by the fact that Tracey has moved on without me and that she's changed. I drop the receiver and it clanks to the floor. I pick it up fast.

"Is someone there?" my mother says. "I'm on the phone."

I don't move.

"Hang up, please," my mother says.

To avoid making any more noise, I press the button on the phone with my pointer finger, breaking the connection, before I place the receiver back on its cradle. Not bothering to get a bowl, I eat macaroni and cheese straight from the pot, thinking about Tracey and our giant fight. She said I was the one who hurt her and that I was the one who'd been disloyal. She blamed me for abandoning her, so consumed with cheerleading and with Morgan. When I accused her of stealing my boyfriend, she defended herself, insisting that Morgan and I were broken up. I claimed we weren't and said with friends like her, who needed enemies. Tracey jerked her head, her bangs flipping from her face, and she walked away. Scooping the last bite of macaroni and cheese, I remember standing there alone, near the lockers. Later when I saw her in the science lab, instead of sitting near the microscope next to me like she normally would, she sat at a different table, and during our lunch break, she left school and drove to get Humphrey's frozen yogurt without me.

o o o

That night, Rochelle calls and tells me that John Lennon was shot, murdered in cold blood outside The Dakota, his home near Central Park.

I walk down the hall to my parents' room. The bedsheets are pulled up to my mother's bare shoulders, and a negligee is crumpled on her night table. I step back.

"What is it?" my mother asks.

"Nothing."

"Casey, you can come in. We're just watching television."

On the screen, black-and-white footage of John and Yoko. "Imagine" plays in the background. A newscaster's voice: "John Lennon, a legend, an artist, activist—dead." I sit on the edge of my parents' bed. Once I belonged there in between them, their good little girl—the one my mother said woke up smiling, always smiling. The one my father taught to putt.

"I'd like to talk about my college plans," I say, facing them.

"What about college?" my father says.

"I'd like to go away. Maybe to Tulane or BU."

"I don't think so," my father says.

"What do you mean?"

"Casey, it's not going to happen."

"Why not?"

"You'll be married by the time you're eighteen."

"What? I will not."

My father pauses. "Wanna bet?"

"Bet what?"

"Bet you'll be married by the time you're eighteen."

"Who bets on something like that?"

"I do."

"You're gonna lose," I say.

He reaches into his nightstand drawer for a piece of paper and a pen.

I jot down the words to our bet.

We both sign at the bottom.

Brooklyn, 1981

Over the weekend, Rochelle's boyfriend, Rick, hired a pilot to write WILL YOU MARRY ME? via skywriting. She stops me in the hallway at school to tell me the news, and as she talks, I envision the words in the bright blue sky tailing the plane, letters fading and disappearing like clouds. She shows me her ring, a three-karat pear-shaped diamond, and she invites me to her *swanee*.

"What's a *swanee*?" I ask.

"It's a party. A Syrian tradition. My future in-laws give me presents." Her diamond sparkles on her manicured hand as she fishes a piece of gum from her purse. "You should come," she says, chewing.

Rochelle strolls into science class with her head held high as if she has every right to be there, but because of a newly instated policy, in actuality, she only has until the end of the week. Too many Syrian girls are getting engaged during junior year, and it's becoming a problem. They're a distraction, spending all their time studying engagement rings instead of their class notes; reading bridal magazines, not their textbooks; and writing guest lists and menus in lieu of term papers.

I am there when Rochelle cleans out her locker for the last time, and panicked that she won't have a high school diploma, I ask her how she feels about dropping out.

"School's not really for me," she says with total confidence. "And anyway, you don't need to know all this stuff after you graduate."

o   o   o

At home, my mother stands at the stove experimenting. In a pot of red beans, kosher hot dogs bob, taking the place of unkosher sausage. I scoop the beans over steaming white rice and tell my mother about Rochelle's *swanee*.

"Oh boy," she says. "You're in for quite a surprise."

"What do you mean?"

"In Aleppo, a *swanee* was a simple custom. Now it's an extravagant affair, a luncheon for over two hundred women."

"Don't some women work?"

"Not really." From a cabinet under the sink, my mother pulls out a bottle of Windex. She aims at the countertop and sprays, wiping away smudges and fingerprints with a paper towel. "Windex, Windex, Windex. All I do is Windex," she says, as if Windex is a verb.

"What was a *swanee* like in Aleppo?" I ask.

"The groom's family delivered presents, discreetly, to the bride's house. It was done kind of hush-hush, because people were afraid of the *ayin*."

"What's the *ayin*?"

"The evil eye. It was enough that a girl was getting married, but presents to boot was too much good luck." She sprays Windex once, twice, three times and cleans the countertop, the outside of the refrigerator, and the freezer. "It was safer to keep your good fortune to yourself."

"So, what changed?"

"The community got rich."

I snicker.

"Nothing's perfect," my mother says. She lifts a plastic bag from the garbage can and ties a knot. "With the good comes the bad."

"And this is what you want for me? You want me to get married and have a *swanee*?"

"Don't knock it, Casey."

"I want to go to college. I want to *be* something."

She turns to face me. "Being a wife and a mother *is* something." She carries the trash to the side door and puts the bulky bag down. "It took me too long to learn that," she says as she throws on a leopard-printed coat, a Grandma Rose hand-me-down, that she keeps on a hook near the door. She hauls the heavy bag outside.

It was 1973 when Billy Jean King played Bobby Riggs in a Battle of the Sexes tennis match. Bobby Riggs was obnoxious, claiming he could beat any woman, and he rubbed me the wrong way. I wanted Billy Jean to win so badly I could feel it in my bones, and my enthusiasm surprised Tracey. "She's not even pretty," Tracey had said. When the game finally aired, we watched in the den. My father sat in his leather chair, his legs up on the ottoman. Sam was next to him on the carpet, both of them rooting for Bobby Riggs. It wasn't often that my mother and I were on the same team, but that day, we sat side by side, bonded on the edge of our sofa, cheering and high-fiving every time Billy Jean got a point.

My mother comes in from outside and closes the door. "Brrrr," she says. "It's freezing out there." She aims her chin at the bowl of rice and beans, "How is that?"

"Disgusting."

"You'll get used to it," she says.

Leaving the red beans and rice behind, I take the stairs two at a time and slam my bedroom door shut. I hear my mother's muffled voice: "This is where we live now, Casey. You need to make the best of it."

Sitting cross-legged on my bed, it seems to me that the possibilities of what I can be, and who I can become, have shriveled like a Shrinky Dink toy. It feels like I'm living in a box, the Marriage Box, and my world has grown infinitely small. I stay in my room for a long time, feeling sorry for myself, tracing the S on my belly with a finger. If playing Truth or Dare with Hawkeye and Big Sam had been my only mistake, I'd still be a cheerleader at Franklin Prep, trying on tiaras and royal blue taffeta dresses, the next Homecoming Queen.

I haven't drawn since we left New Orleans, but I feel an urge to for the first time in months, so I take out my sketchpad and begin. Lying on my stomach, I write my name in bubble letters. I sketch a picture of a baby girl wearing a bonnet and a bikini, lounging in the Marriage Box. She's bawling, a Charlie Brown "good grief" cry, and the thought bubble says, *I want a pacifier and a marriage proposal and I want it now.* I think it's funny and sad, and alone in my room I cry.

After a few minutes, I wipe my tears and head down the hall to my mother's room. I find her sitting up against her headboard, reading Sydney Sheldon's *Bloodline.* She props the book against her lap and reaches for the glass of white wine on her nightstand.

"Where's Dad?" I ask, standing at the foot of her bed.

"It's Monday night. Where do you think he is?"

Since we moved, my parents' social life had built momentum and was jam-packed full of activity. Often, after work, my father would stay in the city and meet my mother and his group of sixteen friends, two tables of eight, at a restaurant. On the weekends, he took to leaving a duffel bag full of clothes in the trunk of his car. He'd shower at the club after tennis, head to a friend's house for gin rummy, and then go to the city for dinner. Saturday night after Saturday night, while I cried myself to sleep, my parents would stumble in around three in the morning, my mother's makeup smudged into two black eyes and my father's hair disheveled like a young boy who'd refused to brush. Sometimes my mother needed a break. She considered Monday, the night my father played cards, her day off.

"Your father likes to burn the candle at both ends," she says. "He's going to run himself ragged."

"Why'd you put me in the best school in New Orleans if you didn't care if I went to college?"

"Things change, Casey."

I throw my hands up in a huff and storm out of her room.

Brooklyn, 1981

I want what my parents have. I want friends. So as I drive to Rochelle's *swanee*, I mentally prepare, trying to see things from a fresh perspective, as if I'm Margaret Mead herself, collecting data on a group of people I desperately care to understand. Just as I pull up to Rochelle's house, I see it—a spray-painted gold fire hydrant, erect as a shrine.

You never know what's going to knock you off balance. And there's been so much lately I've had to get used to—my parents partying and behaving like teenagers, girls my age dropping out of high school and getting married, my father betting I won't go to college—that now my world feels totally inverted, my thoughts and beliefs upside down, as if I am seeing it all in a headstand.

But who, I need to know, *paints their fire hydrant gold?*

The valet takes my car.

The newly built corner house reaches the property line on all sides. Two cars—a Mercedes and a Porsche—are parked in the driveway. The garage door is open, and I see servers from the kosher catering company squeezing past the cars, carrying tins of food in through the basement entrance.

The house is all brick, and a man in a tuxedo greets guests in front of iron double doors. The foyer is three stories high with a gold dome at the top. A crystal chandelier hangs like a massive snowball, the floor is black granite, and a grand stair-case breaks into two, veering off in opposite directions. Red carpeting trails the winding steps, and the ambiance feels sur-real, as if I am stepping onto a set from *Gone with the Wind*. This is a far cry from the community's humble beginnings. A far cry from Grandpa David, a first-generation American, who, at seven, had to drop out of school to peddle on the boardwalk in order to eat.

Standing near the entrance, I scan the crowd, needing to find someone or something familiar, but what I see instead are hordes of women wearing colorful makeup, beauty parlor–teased hair, and diamonds. They all pose in heels, viewing and getting viewed.

I spot Rochelle. "Congratulations," I say, wishing I'd bothered to shave my legs and blow-dry my hair. In rebellion, I wore a beige and brown plaid skirt and navy clogs. Rochelle is dressed in a satin bustier the color of cotton candy, and her tea-length skirt is appliquéd with organza flowers. She matches the pink bouquet behind her, and I wonder if that was deliberate.

"Thanks for coming," Rochelle says.

She looks like a child playing dress-up. Her lips are per-fectly lined and shockingly rosy. Rochelle's mother stands by her side.

"Congratulations," I say.

She leans in to kiss me. "Thank you, sweetheart. *Abalac.*"

It's custom for her to wish me the same sought-after destiny as her daughter. It's supposed to be a blessing. I feel like ducking.

"Excuse me. Watch your back," a waiter says, carrying a tray of champagne.

I turn away from Rochelle and her mother.

"How are you, Casey?" my mother's friend, Irene, asks. Since our move, Irene has been invaluable to my mother. She showed her where to get her nails done and where to buy kosher meat; she told her which dry cleaner was the best and shared recipes for *s'fiha* and *yebra*, but at the moment, Irene can't help me. Her comment is a salutation, not a genuine question, so I don't confess that I'm having a hard time fitting in and that something at this party just isn't right.

In the living room, the *swanee* is set up for all to see. Women congregate around the display of gifts like sightseers gawking at the queen's jewels. I turn and head in the opposite direction.

On the dining room table, there are silver platters full of salad nicoise, smoked salmon, seared tuna, *sambousak*, *kelsones*, and string cheese. Crystal bowls hold *ka'ak*. On a separate marble table with gilded legs, there is dessert. Platters are lined with cubes of cantaloupe, honeydew, and pineapple on sticks. Trays are filled with baklava, *'ataiyef*, brownies, and chocolate chip cookies.

I fill my plate with *kelsones* and, standing, devour more than I should. I eat for two, three, four, an act of rebellion against all Syrian girls who won't eat, who wolf down diet pills, who throw up. I wrap four *sambousaks* into a paper napkin and slip them into my sweater pocket that runs across my stomach like a kangaroo's pouch.

Glancing out the window, my gaze lands on the gold fire hydrant. Rolling my eyes, I stroll to the kitchen and put my plate on the granite island near a sink. There is a second sink at the other end of the room. From what I can tell, there are two of everything in this house: two front doors, two sinks, two staircases, and two exotic cars.

A waiter enters and washes red grapes. The sound of running water, the beat of clinking glasses, the cadence of bustling waiters all come together in harmony, allowing me a moment of escape. But I can't stay in the kitchen forever, so I make my way to the den, where I find a group of girls from school talking in a corner. I walk over to them.

Adele nibbles on carrot sticks. Her turquoise eye shadow, shaped like mini umbrellas, hangs heavy on her lids, and I feel so sad for every Syrian girl my age wearing such serious eye makeup. "Did you see the fur Rochelle got on her *swanee?*" Adele says to the group.

"You've got to be kidding," a girl sipping champagne says. She has an air about her like a force field, and she throws her head back, finishing off her champagne. "That was once a live animal. Wearing it is disgraceful." She puts her glass down.

I like her immediately. "Agreed," I say.

"I'm Beatrice," she turns to me. "Call me Bee. B-e-e."

"It's supposed to be B-e-a," Adele says.

"Sure, if you want to do everything how you're supposed to." The sparkle in Bee's eye is as big as the sparkle in Rochelle's diamond.

"Don't listen to her," Adele says, waving me closer. "She's just jealous." Adele takes me by the hand and pulls me toward the living room. "You've got to see the *swanee.*"

"I'm *so* not jealous," Bee says. "But I am curious. I'll come with you."

The *swanee* shimmers and shines. A Daum crystal vase jam-packed with pink roses, a Lalique bowl filled with *lebas*, Baccarat wine glasses, a gold Rolex, diamond earrings from Ricarde's, sterling Tiffany candlesticks, a white silk nightgown, and a fur coat from Bergdorf's are all propped up and angled, displayed on white satin.

"You see these sheets," Adele says, pointing. "Frette. These are the finest. The decorative pillows and towels too."

"Uh-huh," I say, not knowing girls my age care about these things.

"That's just what Rochelle needs. The finest," Bee says. "We're talking about someone who wants a Hello Kitty–themed bridal shower."

"It's a dream," Adele says, looking around. "An absolute dream. You see that bag?" She points to a tear-shaped purse, gold and studded with crystals. "It's Judith Leiber. You could faint."

"My grandmother wears Judith Leiber," I say.

Adele goes on to explain that the whole point of a *swanee* is the purse. Inside is a ten-dollar bill, the amount the bride, a virgin, needs to go to the *mikveh*. It's customary for the groom's family to pay.

The *mikveh*, I learned, is where once a month a Jewish woman submerges in rainwater before having relations with her husband. It's a rule that when she gets her period, her husband isn't allowed to touch her because she's *niddah*, impure. When her period is done, she counts seven *clean* days before washing every nook and cranny of her body, swabbing her nostrils, belly button, and ears with a Q-tip. She flosses her teeth, removes her nail polish, washes her hair, and finally dunks in the ritual bath. Only then can she be with her husband.

"You have to take *mikveh* classes or a community rabbi won't marry you," Adele says.

"Can a rabbi do that?" I ask.

"He can," Adele says.

It all sounds so archaic. In New Orleans, girls our age were figuring out how to get birth control and, when things didn't go as planned, an abortion. This couldn't be more opposite.

"The *mikveh* is ridiculous," Bee says.

"It's not ridiculous," Adele snaps. "It keeps a marriage going."

"Yeah, how?"

"Holding back heightens desire and keeps the couple long-ing for each other, every time like a honeymoon."

"That's what they want you to believe," Bee says. "That's how they *get* you."

"They don't have to *get* you. It's the law."

"What if the bride isn't a virgin?" Bee asks. "Then what does she do?"

"Stop it, Bee. Of course she's a virgin."

I look down, fiddling with my skirt, not wanting to make eye contact with Adele. Picking at my bottom lip, I yank off a piece of skin and touch the raw spot with a finger. Blood. I step back from the circle of girls, nervous they can read my mind or somehow know my secrets. With a pink napkin, monogrammed with Rochelle and Rick, I pat my lip.

"What's your philosophy, Adele? Ignorance is bliss?" Bee gulps champagne.

"Something like that. Life's easier that way. Less stress."

"That's one way to look at it. Then you'll never know if you got screwed. So to speak." And Bee laughs at her own joke. I laugh too.

I miss Tracey right now so much and wish she could hear this. Our upbringing in New Orleans was so different, and I wonder what Adele would do if she knew about how once during a basketball game at half time, Tracey and I left the gymnasium and broke into the main school building by squeezing through a tiny separation in between doors bound by a chain. In the bathroom, we smoked cigarettes and scribbled Blondie lyrics on the bathroom wall. Tracey blew smoke rings inside smoke rings, and Mr. Catonio burst through the door, busting us, just as Tracey whisked out her brand-new diaphragm.

o o o

"I've had enough of this," Bee says, turning to me. "Let's get out of here."

This is the best invitation I've had in a long time, so I follow Bee into the kitchen. She swipes a bottle of kosher champagne from the counter and tucks it under her arm, cradling it like a baby. "Grab those," she says, pointing to fluted glasses. We exit through the back door, thieves.

Outside, the wind howls. Leaning against a tree, Bee pops the cork, and I remember the *sambousaks* in my pocket. Unfolding the napkin, I offer one to Bee, and sesame seeds rain to the ground. She pours champagne into our glasses, letting it bubble and fizz and spill over the sides.

○ ○ ○

For the next few weeks Bee and I are inseparable. We take the subway to Manhattan, shop on Canal Street, and buy colorful scarves, dangling earrings, and silver rings. We get ice cream from Carvel: vanilla with rainbow sprinkles and hot fudge sundaes.

One night, Bee and I go back to Rochelle's house, this time with toilet paper. First, we roll the gold fire hydrant in front, turning it white as a linen-wrapped mummy. Then we creep to the backyard. Under an eerie tree with bare branches, pointy as claws, Bee hands me an edge. "Hold this," she says. She throws the roll and it soars through the air. She catches it, rips, and does it again. Outsiders, we do this over and over. And in the darkness, the tree drips with white streamers.

Bee drapes toilet paper over her head like a veil. "Look, I'm a bride," she says. She takes hold of my arm. "*Abalac.*"

The sight of Bee strikes me. It's an image I go back to again and again. Bee—a bride, wearing a toilet paper veil, under a halogen light, in a dark backyard, in Brooklyn.

Brooklyn, 1981

Something is wrong with Bee. We've only been friends for a few months, but there are signs. There are always signs. I want to make her feel better, so I skip school with her, and when we come back to my house at noon, I lie, telling my mother we got out early.

Bee sits on my bedroom windowsill, half inside, half out, blowing cigarette smoke into the universe. "I'm bored," she says. "Totally bored."

Over the last few months, I haven't thought much about my father's gun, nor did I ever expect to touch it again, but in this moment, desperate for Bee's attention and admiration, I feel it calling, pulling me to revisit.

"Wait here," I say. "I'll be right back." From the hallway, I hear my mother closing cabinets and clanking pots downstairs in our kitchen. I sneak into her room, climb on her vanity chair, same as I'd done years before, and retrieve my father's gun. I'm pretty sure it's not loaded, but I guess it could be. I push the thought away, hide it under my shirt, and carry it back to my room, carefully placing it on my bed.

"Cool," Bee says.

"A girl's gotta protect herself. New York City is dangerous," I say, staring at the gun. "There are rapists in Central Park, and a lot of women carry Mace."

"True, true," Bee says.

"At Walgreen's yesterday, a kid flashed me. He was riding a bike, and he lifted the bottom of his track shorts. No underwear. Brooklyn's gross."

"The world's gross," Bee says, stubbing her cigarette out on the sill.

"Girls?" my mother says, knocking on the door. "Do I smell smoke?"

I jump up and cover the gun with my pillow. "No, Mom."

She jiggles the knob. "The door's locked. You sure?"

"Positive," I call back.

"Okay then. I'll see you later. I'm going out."

It takes me a few minutes to calm down, but then I turn to Bee. "Rochelle called. She wants us to come over. It's her turn to host."

"Thrills," Bee says.

Rochelle is months into her marriage and every Tuesday plays canasta. All the married Syrian girls do. They should still be in high school but instead dress in designer clothes and prepare extravagant lunches, playing cards in the middle of the day like little old ladies. It is shocking how fast Syrian girls go from girlhood to womanhood. Overnight.

"Let's go to Rochelle's," I say, and this surprises Bee. But I want more friends. As much as I like Bee, she is unreliable and often withdrawn.

"Maybe it'll be fun," I say, trying to sound upbeat.

Bee stretches her arms over her head and sighs. "I don't think so," she says. "Unless, of course"—she points at the gun—"we take that."

I want to change Bee's mood, and since the gun isn't loaded, it seems mostly harmless, just a bit of excitement. I hide it in a Lester's shopping bag under a Blondie sweatshirt.

o   o   o

Rochelle lives in a two-family house on Ocean Parkway. Bee and I are late, and when we arrive, Rochelle opens the door, beaming. "I'm so glad you came. Come in."

Rochelle is totally put together in stilettos and black Prada pants. With her nose-job nose and addicted-to-aerobics body, she is perfectly accessorized. I don't understand why Rochelle is so nice to me. But from my first day of school, she's included me in everything.

"Can I take your coat or your bag?" Rochelle asks.

Bee hands Rochelle her coat, and I eye my Blondie sweatshirt, making sure the gun is concealed. "No, thanks. I got it."

"Make a plate," Rochelle says to Bee and me, gesturing toward the dining room table. She's sprinkled fresh parsley over vegetable rice and placed sprigs of dill around grilled salmon. I circle the table, wondering how at seventeen she knows about garnish. But Syrian girls know a lot of things about being an adult. They run their homes like drill sergeants: towels folded in exactly the same way, freezers full so they'll be ready to serve, drawers neatly ordered, bathrooms Lysol clean, the walls, rugs, plates, and platters hospital white.

As I survey the table, Rochelle stands next to me and cups her hand over her mouth, whispering, "You see that pocketbook?" She points to a girl I've never seen. "It's Gucci. I want it, but it's a fortune."

"She's obsessed," Bee says. "*Pocketbook Anxiety.*"

"The right bag is essential," Rochelle says. "You know everything about a girl by her purse."

In some circles talking about money is considered impolite, but Syrians are different and they flaunt their wealth. Status is everything, and none of them would be caught dead with a no-name purse, or God forbid, last year's model. I know from Grandma Rose that it hasn't always been that way. She speaks negatively about the women of her generation who don't know one designer from another, who dress in housecoats and let themselves go.

Bee, Rochelle, and I sit on the couch. Three card tables with peach tablecloths are set up for canasta. A dozen girls play, concentrating and counting cards, eying the deck, tallying, and keeping track of what is thrown.

I get up to fill a plate with food, leaving Bee to guard our bright yellow Lester's bag. When I return, and the conversation turns to babies, I almost choke on my lentil salad.

"Anyone can get married. Not anyone can have a baby," Rochelle says, referring to Sarah, the first one in their card group to give birth. "Sarah's blessed. She'll have four kids before she's thirty."

"Is that the goal?" Bee asks.

"If you're lucky," Rochelle says.

Bee rolls her eyes and I hope nobody notices, because I want to belong at Rochelle's, and I worry Bee will ruin my chances. I'm confused and trying to straddle both worlds, not knowing where to firmly plant myself, behaving like a typical Syrian girl on one hand, and packing a gun to keep Bee amused and close by on the other.

"Anyway," Rochelle says, "Rick can't wait."

"Rick can't wait?" Bee asks. "He can't wait to change diapers?"

"*He* won't change diapers. The housekeeper will do it."

Just as Syrian girls are conditioned to want certain things, so are the boys. Their job is to get married, buy a house, and have at least four kids. They are taught to think that two halves make a whole, and like *The Emperor's New Clothes*, the community perpetuates the idea of *happily ever after* even though, from what I can see, Syrian boys, once married, grow bored or lonely and behave like spoiled little brats who picked a red lollipop and then changed their mind, wanting a purple one.

A girl in a rabbit-fur vest cuts broccoli with a knife. "Lunch is delicious, Rochelle," she says, changing the subject.

"Thanks," Rochelle says. "Shhhh, don't tell," she whispers in my ear. "I bought the desserts."

These girls won't eat anything fattening—a brownie or a chocolate chip cookie—but still they are expected to bake desserts homemade, always outdoing each other. Maybe that's why Rochelle likes having me around. I'm no threat.

Just then, Sarah walks in, and all the girls in the card club stand and clap as if she's just won best actress and deserves a standing ovation. Her body looks better than it did before pregnancy. Her hair is blown straight, she wears a Chanel tweed jacket, tight black pants, heels, and the same Gucci purse that Rochelle wants. Sarah smiles a movie star smile, and her eyes sparkle bright, matching the clarity in the diamond studs on her ears, a gift from her husband after delivery. Sarah accepts kisses and congratulations from everyone in the room. I follow protocol and kiss her too.

This is it; this is what my parents want for me. These girls are protected from the outside world; they are safe. For a second, I consider what it would be like to belong, the path set, the answers easy. I can choose to be part of their recipe swapping, a game they created, kind of like Secret Santa, where they each pick a name out of a bowl and then anonymously mail a recipe to one another. There is a sense of belonging, and taken with their closeness, I too want to drop out of school and have friends. I want a boy to love me. I want a standing ovation. Who wouldn't?

Sarah sits down next to me. I move the bag with the gun away from her feet. "How old is your baby?"

"*That* many weeks."

"How many weeks?"

"*That* many."

"What?"

Bee interjects. "Five weeks. Her baby is five weeks old. She won't say that because of the *ayin*. It's a superstition that the number five protects you from evil, and Sarah doesn't want you to think that she thinks she has to say 'five' in order to protect herself because you're jealous."

"You're kidding. Right? I mean, how do you avoid saying a number? That's so arbitrary. And impossible. It's like deciding not to use the letter *r*."

Bee shrugs.

"Wait. So if it's five o'clock"—I turn to Sarah—"and somebody asks you the time, what do you say?"

"It's *that* time."

"What if it's four forty-five?"

"It's a quarter to."

"A quarter to what?"

"*That* time."

"Are you kidding?" I look at Bee and she rolls her eyes. "What about five fifty-five?" I ask Sarah.

"Almost six."

"Oh, come on."

A girl wearing fingerless fur gloves approaches. Interrupting, she says, "Sarah, you're bones."

"Thank you," Sarah says, smiling.

"How did you do it?"

"For starters, I didn't nurse. Also, I drink coffee and eat celery. Chewing celery burns a lot of calories."

"Celery, that's a good one. I was eating tons of carrots, but then my skin turned orange and I had to stop."

"You look like a werewolf," Bee says, pointing at the girl's gloves.

"They're mink."

"Looks like hair to me. Waxing can get rid of that."

I laugh, and the girl with the fingerless mink gloves gives me a dirty look. Then she turns to Bee. "Oh, cut it out, Bee. You know they're sharp." She joins three girls at a table and gossips about a previous card game. She has the group's undivided attention, telling them how the hostess wore all her *swanee* jewelry, which was too much for the middle of the day, served on chipped platters, bought fish already fried, and used canned potatoes. "And not to be mean, but her apartment was a mess, books and toys everywhere."

Little by little as the day goes on, the illusion of warmth and friendship I imagined melts like the uneaten ice cream tower on the dining room table. I see the madness in these card games—the competition fierce, one's image on the line, and all creativity and individuality judged. There are strict guidelines to belonging, and everyone has to follow the rules. Deviation is tolerated only a tad, leaving tiny, orchestrated ways to express yourself. They are like schoolgirls mandated to wear a uniform but who get to choose a bow or their socks.

I turn to Bee. She looks upset. "What's wrong?" I ask her.

"Just bored, that's all." Bee yawns and picks raw red onions out of her lentil salad. She stacks the teeny purple cubes on the edge of her plate.

"Want to go? We can go if you want."

She continues to pile onions until the purple wall she's erected comes tumbling down. "No, I'll stay," she says. "I want dessert."

As the girls play, they talk about manicures and fan their cards, analyzing each other's nails—shape, color and shine—with intentness, as if they are huddled in a biology lab collecting important data and studying classification.

I try to be interested in this Syrian girl world, but all their attempts at perfection are infuriating, and it makes me want to ruin something. I consider flipping over the platter of grilled vegetables on the table. Eggplant flattened into the white carpet like roadkill.

Sometimes I don't notice things about myself until someone else tells me. I didn't know I looked good in red until Grandma Rose pointed it out. I didn't think I was smart until Mr. Salem encouraged me to apply to Barnard. I didn't consider myself pretty until Morgan whispered it in my ear. But suddenly I realize, all on my own: I don't fit in. I can't just forget or erase my past—Tracey, Morgan, Hawkeye, and Franklin Prep—because as complicated and messy as those things are, they are inside me. In an effort to save myself, and Bee too, from the monotony and triviality, I kind of snap. Needing to change the subject and talk about something else, anything else, I announce a bit too loudly, "Sandra Day O'Connor is going to be the first female Supreme Court Justice."

The Syrian girls hold their cards close to their chests and stare. Mute. I don't really have anything else to say. I didn't plan on interjecting, and I don't really care about politics or Sandra Day O'Connor. I just want to do the opposite of what they do.

"I'm glad a woman got the job," Bee says, excited for the first time all day. "But I don't like her, or her point of view. She's against abortion, and she's all for the Second Amendment." She eyes the Lester's bag on the floor.

"Abortion?" Rochelle says. "God forbid." These girls say "God forbid" as often as people use periods at the end of sentences.

"Republicans act like sex is wrong but carrying a gun is right," Bee says. "And that's just stupid." She smirks and nudges the yellow bag with her foot. "Some people," she says, shaking her head and laughing, "should not have a gun."

"Of course we should have the right to carry a gun," Sarah says. "We've been through so much. Inquisitions, pogroms, and holocausts. We need to be able to protect ourselves."

This is the first thought-provoking statement I've heard all day, and while I appreciate her point of view, it bothers me that the Syrian girls make everything exact. Black or white. No gray. It's obvious that guns get into the wrong hands. Sick people. Irresponsible people. Young people. And I am living proof.

I don't know how counterproductive it will be to challenge the S.Y. girls, how one individual can never change the thinking of such an old-fashioned community, but I want to show them that everything they believe isn't necessarily 100 percent solid. I look around at all these young girls, considering motherhood and designer clothes and gourmet recipes, and without thinking, just wanting to contest or get a reaction, I stand, the gun in my hands. I hold it high above my head, aiming at the ceiling.

The girls scream. "What are you doing? Are you crazy?" And they duck and crawl and scurry under card tables, white carpet fuzz all over their black Prada pants.

I lower the gun and rest it at my side, scanning the room and registering their frightened faces. "It's fake," I say. "It's not real. What, I'm not crazy."

And of course, they believe me.

Brooklyn, 1981

The stunt I pulled at Rochelle's card game makes the Syrian girls wary of me. I'm not excluded exactly, because there is an unspoken rule in the community, which is actually working on my behalf, and that is that once you are *in*, you'll never really be out. No matter what—scandals, lies, addictions, jail sentences, infidelities—you belong.

But word about the card game got around, and the girls at school started treating me differently than they did before the gun incident. I knew they thought I was odd from the beginning, but now, it seems, my strangeness has taken on a whole new dimension, and in the hallways at school, they keep their distance, and instead of inviting me for lunch at the deli, they leave me out, saying afterward, "Where were you? You should've come."

"They're a bunch of losers if they can't take a joke," Bee says, defending me and flicking her cigarette into a Kings Highway gutter. But Bee can't understand why I feel bad because she didn't want to be friends with them anyway.

"Hey, can I tell you a secret?"

"Sure," I say, ecstatic that Bee wants to confide in me.

"I didn't tell you because I promised I wouldn't say anything, but I'm busting." She leans in close. "I'm sleeping with Mr. Salem." She stares directly into my eyes as if daring me to react.

I act cool even though I'm flipping out inside. And I must seem composed because she goes on, telling me that she's been having an affair with Mr. Salem for months and that sometimes he gives her a hard time. It isn't that he doesn't like her; he fell for her immediately. But he is her teacher. And she is his student. So, he tries really hard to stay away. It's during those times, when he tries to resist her, that Bee is distraught and impossible to reach.

When Bee is available and happy, she's a good friend, and she sticks up for me with the girls at school. But they don't care what she has to say.

From a bathroom stall, I overhear girls gossiping about Bee at the sink. They talk about her, judging her for flirting with Mr. Salem, and they all agree she's a slut, which is a surefire way to lose standing with the Syrian girls.

○   ○   ○

I miss Tracey so much. Now and then, I consider reaching out to her. But I don't.

I buy a goldfish. I carry him home in a plastic bag and dump him into a bowl with blue gravel. I purchase a green net for scooping him up and transferring him into the sink when his bowl needs cleaning. Sometimes when he's in his net midair, he flops around, struggling, breathless, stuck, and I have to use a finger to push him through. His wet orange skin feels alive; he is a heart-throbbing, vibrant creature. A two-inch blob of hope.

I name him Fish. "Hello, Fish." I wave.

I watch him swim. I imitate his mouth puckering. Bored, I carry him down the hall to my parents' room.

"Where are you going?" I ask my parents, sitting on their bed and setting Fish down on my father's nightstand.

"Dinner," my mother says. "Elios."

"You go out every night."

"Not every night."

"Okay, most nights."

"Casey," my mother says, "must you always find something to complain about?"

Fish darts across his bowl with purpose, as if even he has a destination. My father leans down and kisses the top of my head, "Goodnight, sweetheart." From across the room my mother blows a kiss.

They leave.

Fish swims.

Bee calls. "What are you doing?" she asks.

"Nothing," I say. "What are you doing?"

"Nothing. I'm going crazy. Brad's busy."

I'm still not used to her calling Mr. Salem Brad. At school, needing to keep their relationship a secret, she calls him Mr. Salem, but in private she says whatever she wants. They've been meeting in shady all-night diners, and Mr. Salem told her he's never been happier, that he loves how their relationship is so exciting, and he can't get over how they make out for hours like teenagers.

"You *are* a teenager," I remind Bee.

"Ugh!" Bee screams into the phone. "He's so frustrating."

"Come over," I say, lounging on my parents' bed. Fish stops moving. I tap his bowl. He swims freestyle through the water.

"No. I'm going to eat a bag of Doritos and smoke a pack of cigarettes."

"Sounds like fun," I say, and I hang up.

My heart aches. I watch Fish, my only companion, and remember hanging out with Morgan at Café du Monde, pigging out at midnight. We drank coffee with chicory, café au lait, and blew on piping-hot beignets, gobbling mouth-watering deep-fried dough. Powdered sugar caked our lips. Morgan used his pinky to scoop up a tip-full of sugar and brought it to his nose, cocaine. He laughed at himself, unknowing, thinking he was really funny. Cool.

o   o   o

On Saturday, Bee and I go to Manhattan to have lunch with Grandma Rose. She likes when I bring Bee along, the three of us anti–anything Syrian. Grandma Rose thinks Bee is refreshing, and Bee thinks Grandma Rose is a trip.

At Smith and Wolensky, Grandma Rose orders a martini and flits from story to story, entertaining us. "Did I ever tell you I wanted to be a dancer? Actually," she says, "I was a dancer until I met your grandfather, and then I gave it all up." I picture Grandma on stage, dressed in white, under a gleaming light. In my mind Grandpa David appears out of nowhere and yanks her from the stage.

The waiter hands us menus and Grandma sighs. Once her second martini hits the table, Grandma tends to reveal too much about her marriage, and the retellings don't always go well. "Your grandfather and I are from two different planets. He likes *meshe*. I like steak. He speaks Arabic. I speak Yiddish. He likes to stay home. I like to go out. Shall I go on?"

Bee nods.

Grandma leans in, pretending to whisper, "He's cheap. I'm not."

Bee laughs. She is an only child and her parents are divorced—a Syrian cautionary tale—so to her, my family is normal. Bee loves Grandma's stories. So do I.

"I'm not kidding," Grandma says. She looks at me. "On the same day I bought myself an extravagant diamond choker, your grandfather cut coupons and went to the grocery store to get oranges on sale. He must've bought a hundred."

We finish our main courses, and Bee excuses herself from the table. She doesn't come back for a long time, and Grandma sends me to check on her. Through the bathroom stall, I hear her throwing up. "You okay?" I ask.

"Fine," she says, her voice muffled. "Must be something I ate."

o   o   o

Bee elopes with Mr. Salem. *Brad.* The rumor is she's pregnant and that Mr. Salem is the father. Whatever. She just takes off. Doesn't say goodbye. Sometimes I wonder how things might've been different if I'd been a better friend, because as much as I liked hanging out with Bee—buying albums at Music Factory on Kings Highway, dancing with her in my room to Earth, Wind & Fire, and eating Chinese food on Nostrand Avenue—I always compared her to Tracey, a tally constantly going on in my head. And in my heart—Tracey is skin, Bee a sweater.

o   o   o

Alone in my room, I study Fish. He isn't moving. His eyes bulge. I tap his bowl. Murky water swooshes. "Fish," I say, "can you hear me? Are you okay?" Fish floats upside down to the surface. I use the green net to scoop him out. He lies still, as if playing dead. I hold him like that until he starts flopping around.

Fish dies the same day Rochelle's father does. Adele calls to tell me. Jewish law requires a body to be buried as soon as possible, so by ten the next morning the synagogue is jam-packed with over two hundred people. I've never been to a funeral, and it's nothing like what I've seen on television. There are no flowers. There is no organ player, no fancy hats. In life, Syrians work to one-up each other, always needing to have the best of everything, but in death they all go out the same way, naked in a pinewood box.

Rochelle wears no makeup and her white blouse is torn, a symbol of her sadness. Women sit on one side of the synagogue, men on the other. Without Bee, I'm on my own and sit in the back, by myself.

The rabbi eulogizes Rochelle's father, talking about how he was a leader of our community, how he lived a full life, and how he is going to a better place. *Olam Haba.* He addresses Rochelle's family, reminding them that the afterlife is the true life, that this time on earth is just a passageway on our journey to our real resting place in heaven.

I cry so hard I can barely hear what the rabbi is saying. I'm thinking about my own father and how for the last few weeks, I've been trying to get back at him for making us move to New York. I wouldn't leave the house and watched TV day and night, never taking off my dirty sweatpants. I wouldn't wash or brush my hair and ate repulsively, nonstop: beef jerky, Doritos, Velveeta. My father came into my room one night. He sat on my bed. "Try, Casey."

But I wouldn't.

I stopped cleaning Fish's bowl. I let algae accumulate and take over. It got so bad I could hardly find Fish through the gunk. Earlier that morning, I patted my dead orange fish dry and rolled him in a paper towel. On all fours, I reached for my boot box, which I kept under my bed, and not ready to let go, I placed Fish inside.

After the funeral, I drive to Rochelle's house to pay respects. Her eyes are red and puffy. As is customary, she sits with her mother, her two brothers, her sister, and three aunts on the floor. The rabbi reminds Rochelle's family that they shouldn't listen to music for a year—not at home or in a car. *Weren't they sad enough?*

Fifty folding chairs line the room, ready for visitors. The mirrors in the house are covered with sheets. There is food on the dining room table: bowls of nuts, dried fruit, *sambousak*, *ka'ak*. A handwritten sign reminds visitors to say a *beracha*, a blessing, before eating in order to lift the soul of the deceased.

I don't even bother to take my coat off, as I want to leave as soon as I can, and I stand near the table, waiting for the right moment to approach Rochelle.

"I heard about you," a gruff voice says.

"Me?" I turn around.

"Casey, right?"

"Uh, right. Who are you?"

"Michael. Rick's friend." He smiles. "Did you really pull out a gun at Rochelle's card game?"

"It wasn't loaded."

"I think that's not the point."

"Look, I don't need a lecture."

"I'm not lecturing you. I think it's funny."

"You do?" I face him. "So, how bad was it? How far did the news travel?"

"Not too far. Your secret is relatively safe."

"Why don't I believe you?" I pick up a *sambousak* and turn to walk away, then turn back. "But hey, thanks for trying to make me feel better."

Michael has short curly hair and dark skin and is handsome in a way I'm not used to, unfamiliar, as if he's just arrived from far away. He tells me he is twenty-three, a businessman, and a lover of Jim Morrison and lives in his own apartment in New York City. I still sneak cigarettes and wear argyle knee socks. It feels like there is a whole generation between us.

"I need to spend time with Rochelle. It was nice to meet you."

"The pleasure's all mine," Michael says. His Adam's apple moves like a ping-pong ball under his skin, and I can't help but stare.

All the girls from the card game sit around Rochelle, comforting her. They don't leave her side, and I can't get near. Once again, I feel out of place. I am back to where I was before I met Bee.

Alone.

Brooklyn, 1982

My parents and their friends are approaching forty, and they are rich. As second-generation Americans, they still hold some old-world values when it comes to gender roles and religion, but wanting to be cool, and eager to participate in modern New York City life, they push against some cultural limitations. They call themselves jet-setters, behaving in ways that others in our community never did before.

I keep catching my mother checking herself out in the rearview mirror of our car. She turns her head from side to side and pulls back the skin on her cheeks.

"Mothers are supposed to have wrinkles," I say.

"That's easy for you to say."

It's New Year's Eve, and my parents are having a party in our Brooklyn house. The zebra area rug in the living room is brought down to the basement so the hard wood can be the dance floor. Instead of putting the furniture into storage for the night, my father checks the weather, and when he sees snow isn't forecasted, he has movers lug it all to our backyard.

"I just want to go on record," my mother says, red Velcro rollers in her hair. "Leaving our furniture out here overnight isn't smart. It's risky. And I don't like it. It could rain. It could snow. A number of things could go wrong." My father directs movers to set the couch under a tree.

Our house is perfect for a party; it's decorated with mirrored walls, metallic blinds, and a built-in bar, stocked with enough alcohol to get every guest at the party dead-drunk four times over. The food is kept light, pick-ups only. "Let's call a spade a spade," my mother said to my father while planning the party. "Heavy food ruins a good buzz."

She's decided to serve nuts, olives, and crudités at the bar. Platters of Syrian appetizers: fried *kibbeh*, *laham b'ajeen*, and meat *sambousak* are on the dining room table, and hot-pink feathers are scattered like fallen wings in between them.

In the entrance foyer, silver glitter top hats and gold tinsel crowns that say Happy New Year are lined up on glass shelves.

The DJ wheels in two speakers, big as tombs, and on my way upstairs, I trip on his orange extension cord. "Almost killed myself," I say, grabbing hold of the banister.

"Sorry," he says, looking at me as if I have no reason to be so snippy.

A few hours later, I sit on my parents' upholstered bed and watch as they try on outfits. They parade back and forth like runway models, taking themselves way too seriously. Again and again, they disappear into their walk-in closet, where my father keeps his gun. Since putting it back after Rochelle's card game, I try not to think about it, as that gun has only ever led to trouble.

Finally choosing what to wear, my mother cuts tags off black leather pants and slips a silver sequined halter over her head. She looks glamorous, dazzling as a character on *Dallas*, and my father's cologne and her perfume fill the room. I can hear Tracey's voice, clear as if she's standing right next to me. "What the hell? You're supposed to be living it up and having a blast. Not them. They've had their turn."

"I should be in New Orleans right now," I say, watching my mother brush her hair at her vanity table.

"Oh, no. Don't start that again, Casey. There's a party down the block. You should go."

"I don't want to."

"Why not?"

"Parties are just another version of the Marriage Box, a place to go if you want to meet someone and get married."

"So, you'd rather stay in your room and sulk?"

"Kind of."

"Don't cut off your nose to spite your face, Casey. Go to the party."

"I'm getting old," my father calls from the bathroom. "The gray hairs are coming in faster than I can pluck them."

"You're not supposed to pluck," my mother yells over her shoulder. "They grow back faster if you do." She softens her mouth into an O and applies lipstick, red as a stop sign.

"That's an old wives' tale," my father says, at her side.

My mother stands. "Suit yourself. What do I care?" She pushes her vanity drawer shut with her hip. "Come on, let's go downstairs. Our guests will be here soon."

o o o

Around midnight, I get hungry and creep downstairs. Music blasts. It's dark in our living room, misty from a fog machine. Through the haze, I see one of my mother's friends dancing on our bar, her spiked heels grinding into the wood. Sober, my mother would never allow that. A female bartender wears a holster rimmed with shot glasses. She pours tequila, one after another, in rapid succession, handing them out. Husbands and wives dance, but not with each other. I make a left into the kitchen.

There are tins of fried *kibbeh* on the dinette table, but I'm not in the mood for Syrian food. I take out a package of hot dogs from the freezer, break one free, and wrap it in a paper towel. While it cooks in the microwave, I grab a bag of Ruffles potato chips and, learning from Bee, swipe a bottle of champagne.

Back in my room, I eat. Hungrily, I chew and swallow, gobbling the hot dog and then the bag of chips, trying to satisfy an emptiness that feels brutal. I fill the tub in my connecting bathroom. Music from downstairs ricochets off the walls. Alone in the bath, I pop open the bottle of champagne and take big gulps, one after another, waiting for it to work and make me feel better. I place the bottle down on the bathmat and dunk, wetting my hair. Water rushes over my face, temporarily drowning out the music. *This is it. There is no place darker or lonelier in the world.*

Clobbered by the thought, I step from the tub and spread the towel, green as a sod of grass, in front of the full-length mirror glued to my door. I get on my knees, naked. Wet curls sprawl over my shoulders, and I stare as Kool and the Gang's "Celebration" invades, flooding my room, pouring in from all sides.

I place my hands over the S on my stomach, and my mind wanders to Tracey and how in New Orleans, whenever Grandma Rose and Grandpa David were in town visiting from New York, we'd spend the night with them at the Fontainebleau Hotel. We'd play Monopoly and Tracey was always the banker and SPY, a game we invented to show our bravery and camaraderie, daring each other to do things that, at eight, felt highly mischievous. In reality, we never did anything more serious than stand near the water fountain in the lobby with drops of water on our cheeks, drawing strangers into our web of lies, pretending to cry because our pennies had fallen in; we'd pocket chocolate mint candies wrapped in green foil from a dish in the hotel restaurant and then secretly eat them in a stairwell made of iron and cement, incarcerated.

I get up and slide the boot box from under my bed. Unraveling the paper towel, I see Fish in between my purple boots, and he is whitish, his eyes cloudy. I take a deep breath and a swig of champagne. "Bye, Fish," I say, flushing him down the toilet.

The doorknob jiggles and I jump, covering myself with the green towel. "Who is it?" I yell. It's probably one of my parents' friends looking for a bathroom, but whoever it is, they can't hear me over the music. I throw on a Pretenders tee shirt and track shorts and open the door. Nobody is there.

In bed, light-headed and totally drunk, I stare at the collage of photographs on my wall. Tracey and me at sleepaway camp, age nine; a shot of us at a holiday dinner all dressed up; and a candid, casual one in front of Franklin Prep, our hair in ponytails.

Curling into a ball, I cry and everything around me spins.

Brooklyn, 1982

Michael calls. "**What do you** say we get together?"

I stand at the side of my mother's bed; the phone is nestled in between my shoulder and chin. "I don't go out much," I say.

"Well, you should. I'll pick you up Thursday. Around seven."

o o o

Michael rings the bell twice before I can get to the door, and immediately, I have a sense about him.

"I like your boots," he says, pointing.

"Thanks. My grandmother got them for me. Never thought I'd wear purple boots."

"Well, they're cool." He smiles and waves his hand, gesturing for me to walk out the door first.

o o o

Michael drives a Porsche, and I'm intrigued even though I don't want to be. He brags about a recent trip to Cortina, his old girlfriend who happens to be a fashion model, and his thriving new business. At a red light, he stops, looks both ways, and proceeds through the intersection. Since that one night with Hawkeye, I've become someone who panics at the sight of police cars. I appreciate his boldness.

"So, Annie Oakley, want to tell me why you have a gun?"

"I don't want to talk about it," I say. "And please don't call me that."

Michael smiles and stares straight ahead.

He speeds through the Brooklyn Battery Tunnel, up the West Side Highway, and through Central Park. The trees in front of Tavern on the Green are strewed with hundreds of teeny lights, and it all looks so elegant. I'm not used to going to such fancy places on dates, and I feel immediately grown-up. Stepping out of the car, the cold New York air hits me with a slap, and I close my jacket around me.

"Hey," Michael says. He has dimples. "Don't button up so fast. You're always wearing a coat. Let me see what you look like under there."

Shocked as if I've been savagely awakened from a deep sleep, and disempowered somehow, I hesitate. But then, not knowing what to do, I open up. With no shame, Michael stares, and his eyes scan my body. Both humiliated and roused, I close my coat and strut my purple boots into the restaurant.

Michael speaks to the maître d' with poise, cupping the man's hand with a ten-dollar bill, and we are escorted to the best table near the window.

Michael orders champagne. "To us," he says, clinking his glass against mine, and I wish I could report every detail of this date to Tracey.

I picture us laughing on the phone, miles between us, and I tell her about sipping champagne from fluted glasses instead of chugging beer from a bottle. I divulge that instead of a single yellow lightbulb in the ceiling, there are enormous chandeliers whose ornate arms sprawl like golden branches on majestic, upside-down winter trees. I describe every detail—petite portions of endive salad with grapes and walnut oil dressing, comparing it to our usual Red Lobster *All You Can Eat* salad bar, sole amandine to barbeque chicken wings, and porcini ravioli to chili cheese dogs, which, late at night, is what Morgan and I liked best. Baroque paintings in gilded frames decorate pleated upholstered walls, which is a far cry from the collection of paper-mache fish and dartboards tacked to the dark wood paneling at Fat Harry's, and even though I hate to admit it, it's suddenly a little exciting to be experiencing this whole new world.

"McCartney was a pop artist," Michael says, continuing the conversation we'd started in the car. "Lennon was the soul of the Beatles. The revolutionary."

"That's what people think, but Paul McCartney was the inspiration behind Sgt. Pepper. He was an incredible song-writer too. He wrote 'Yesterday' and 'Hey Jude.'"

Michael dips bread in olive oil. "McCartney was the front man. A pretty face."

"You just give Lennon more credit because he was politi-cally active and married to Yoko Ono. But Paul and John were a team. They needed each other."

"Feisty, aren't you?" Michael says. "That's okay. I like a challenge."

"You like to play the devil's advocate."

"I like to play the devil." He lifts the candle from the center of the table and holds it close to my face as if to get a better look at me.

Michael tells me how he's just opened an electronics store in the city and is determined to be the best. He works long hours providing his customers with top-quality merchandise at reasonable prices. His company motto is *We can't be beat.*

When the waiter pops the cork on the second bottle of champagne, Michael tells me that his mother was recently ill, and her doctor gave her three months to live.

"Fuck him," he says. "You know what I mean? He's not God."

I'm not sure if his denial of the doctor's diagnosis is the ultimate in intelligence, a spiritual smarts unfamiliar to me, or the most ignorant perspective imaginable.

I lean in.

He tells me that as his mother deteriorated, his anger grew and grew until one night he ripped the living room curtains from the rod.

Distraught, Michael visited the rabbi, who told him to pray and keep kosher and Shabbat, which until then Michael and his family hadn't done.

"He wanted me to put some skin in the deal," Michael explains nonchalantly, as if accepting these life-changing tasks is as easy as changing his socks. Soon after, his mother miraculously recovered. "That was a year ago and she's perfect," he says, as if he is personally responsible.

"So, you grew up reformed like me."

"Oh, no. We're Orthodox," he says, as if being reformed is reprehensible, a different religion entirely.

"But you said you weren't observant. That's what reformed Judaism is."

"We always belonged to an Orthodox congregation, an Orthodox community."

I'm not used to religious discussions on dates. And it's clear we've had different experiences growing up Jewish in America. Michael believes his Judaism is a gift and the core of his identity. But ever since second grade when, at Franklin Prep, our class made Christmas wreaths, I see religion as a divider. Tracey and I were separated from all the other kids, and we sat alone in the back of the room. While everybody else decorated wire hangers shaped in a circle, our hangers were twisted into triangles and placed on top of each other to make Jewish stars. The distance between the tables was huge, and we felt like castaways on a remote island.

For dessert, the waiter suggests gelato. "You get three scoops."

"What flavors do you have?" Michael asks.

"Pistachio and chocolate," the waiter says, refilling our champagne glasses.

"That's it? Two choices? But you get three scoops. That doesn't make any sense."

The waiter looks at Michael as if to say, *I just work here, mister. I don't make the decisions.*

While I sort of wish Michael wouldn't bother the waiter, and I worry he is being rude, I like that he speaks his mind. He is right. There should be more choices.

"Did you go to yeshivah?" I ask.

"I did until I was six, and then the rabbi whacked me with a ruler on the back of my hand because I wasn't paying attention during prayers. I told him to *fuck off*, left the building, and walked home alone."

"Really?"

"Yep."

"A six-year-old heretic. Good for you. I could never do that."

"You're a lot nicer than I am."

That's when I tell him how hard my transition into community life has been.

"You probably shouldn't have brought a gun to Rochelle's card game."

And drunk, we both laugh.

He holds my hand and says he likes the sound of my voice. Like a song, he remarks. He asks me why my family moved back to New York after all those years in New Orleans, and I say something about my parents missing community life, and then I quickly change the subject.

"I want to go to college," I say. "I want to learn about the world."

"You don't learn about the world in a classroom," Michael says, leaning in. "You have to see it."

Michael didn't go to college, and he's completely okay with the fact that he has street smarts, not book smarts.

I question why you can't have both.

"It's rare," he says, with absolute clarity. He plucks a rose from the center of the table and hands it to me. "You have a beautiful smile," he says, staring into my eyes. "To the most special girl I've ever met." And again, he clinks his champagne glass against mine.

We are imagining things, projecting and believing. We are drunk, and this is the first time I feel happy since we moved to New York. I smile, rescued, carefree, and alive, and I am young again, maybe six, and my father is driving home from the country club, my mother in the passenger's seat, and after a day of ice cream and tennis and the high diving board, the windows down, I sit in the back of our black Cadillac in my wet bathing suit, the hot wind blowing and whipping my hair around my face, and as we cross the Mississippi River Bridge, I sing to my favorite song, "Jeremiah was a bullfrog . . . Joy to the fishes and the deep blue sea. Joy to you and me."

o o o

Michael begins sending flowers every Friday. My mother lifts the card from the bouquet of red roses week six and reads out loud, "All my love, Michael."

She pins the card back to the satin bow. "Casey," she says, attempting to tell me what she knows about marriage, "life isn't a bowl of cherries."

She wants me to get married; all Syrian mothers do. It's a desire that seems to be genetically coded. But as Michael and I get serious, something inside her stirs.

It's irrelevant, anyway. I'm not listening. I pick a single rose from the bouquet. With eyes closed, I bring it to my nose and inhale.

Brooklyn, 1982

Michael yanks me from my misery. Over the next few months, we dance at The Red Parrot and Xenon. We ice skate at Rockefeller Center, ski on Hunter Mountain, and picnic in Central Park. He brings me presents on a whim: a red rose from a street vendor, a cashmere scarf from Bergdorf, expensive perfume from Italy.

We stay out late, breaking curfew, and when my father hears us at four in the morning, he comes to the head of the stairs, calling my name. Michael doesn't sneak out the back door how other boys might. He stands there facing my father, assuring him he'll keep me safe.

"Now that's a real man," my father says, drinking coffee the next morning.

o o o

Sometimes, I miss Michael and need reassurance, so I ride my bike to Ocean Parkway knowing he's on his way home from work. I synchronize our encounter, timing things just right, and when I see him, I'm euphoric as a bird-watcher who's spotted some exotic, rare breed.

His car comes to a stop on Eighteenth Avenue and Ocean Parkway. I ride to the corner, pulling up next to him. Pretending this is pure coincidence, I smile, a cheerleader smile, looking surprised but delighted by this exquisite serendipity.

"Hi," I say when he puts his window down.

"Hi to you," he says, smiling back with equal enthusiasm. "What are you doing here?"

"Just riding my bike." And I wonder if he knows I'm lying.

He checks me out, from my high ponytail to my Adidas sneakers, and I can tell he sees what I want him to—that I'm athletic, sheer vitality.

"Great seeing you." He smirks.

The light turns green.

Michael tilts his head, his dimple deep. "Gotta go," he says.

"Okay," I wave, maintaining my cool. But I ride home as if my bike has wings.

o   o   o

That night my bike is stolen from my Brooklyn garage, and I'm devastated.

"*Kapara*," Michael says when I tell him. "Better the bike than something worse. Better to lose your ring than your finger."

I think that's easy for him to say since he hasn't lost anything at all, but then Michael says *kapara* when he loses money in the stock market, when his store is robbed, and when someone crashes into his parked Porsche. He doesn't get attached to things the way I do; he believes he has what is rightfully his. No more, no less.

I come to understand the concept of *kapara* more fully on Yom Kippur. We've been dating for around eight months, and in the Syrian community that is equal to a lifetime. Michael's mother orders a chicken for me, as she does for all her children. This isn't a chicken to eat; it's a chicken the butcher will slaughter. A sacrifice. This tradition happens all over Brooklyn, and I presume other parts of the world, although I doubt there are many Jews killing chickens in New Orleans.

"So, the chicken gets my sins?" I ask Michael.

"Yep. It takes the bullet."

"I don't want a chicken to die on my account." But then I picture Hawkeye, the piñatas, and the FBI, vivid and clear as a movie, and I think that one chicken isn't going to be enough; I'll need the whole coop. Plus, Michael explains they're donated to poor families, so I give in.

I don't let it bother me that Michael's family belongs to an ultra-Orthodox synagogue, even when I see for the first time the *mechitzah*, a wall separating men and women. Not only am I not allowed to sit with Michael; I'm demoted to the back. I can't see or hear the rabbi.

"I don't like sitting separate from you," I say to Michael after the service.

"You want to change thousands of years of tradition?"

I don't answer. With God on his side, it's clear I won't win.

o   o   o

After Yom Kippur, I announce to Michael that I'm becoming a vegetarian.

"What? Why?"

"It's wrong to kill animals," I say.

"Why do you think God put them on earth? He put them here for us."

"I don't believe that."

My reason for turning vegetarian is twofold. I care about the animals, I do, but I'm also beginning to feel uncomfortable about eating food that isn't kosher, and I don't know how to make this religious leap, become kosher, without my entire identity—everything I've been about, plus all the New Orleans in me—getting swept away. Tracey will think I'm being brainwashed. Which maybe I am. Who knows?

Becoming a vegetarian is a brilliant solution. Save the animals and save face at the same time. But Michael can't stand the idea. He drives us to Second Avenue Deli and orders a chicken salad sandwich. "You have to eat it," he says, holding it out to me. "It's delicious. And"—he winks—"if we're going to be together, we should be on the same page." Michael is clear about his values. He keeps kosher and the laws of Shabbat, and that will never change. But wanting Michael's approval, I eat a chicken salad sandwich.

o o o

Michael tells me that from the moment he laid eyes on me, he knew I was the one, his *naseeb*, his God-given intended.

"How'd you know?" I ask.

"I just did."

"But you hardly knew me."

"I knew what I needed to know."

o o o

But Michael's wrong. He didn't know me. Or my secrets. He didn't know I lost my virginity in a one-night stand, or that the reason I never take my shirt off when we fool around is because of a scar on my stomach, a scar that will mark my body for the rest of my life.

What he does know is how important Tracey is to me and that we had a falling out. I've been opening up lately, telling him how much I miss her, but he doesn't care about the details.

"Family's family," he says. "You both need to forget and move on." He mails her a round-trip plane ticket to New York.

Tracey calls immediately. "Hi," she says, as if not one day has passed since the last time we talked. "Who is this Michael guy? He bought me a plane ticket. Kind of extreme, don't you think?"

"Not if you know Michael."

"Are all the Syrians like that?"

"No."

o o o

A few days later Tracey arrives at JFK. Michael and I pick her up from the airport. Michael waits in the car while I linger at baggage claim. When I see Tracey, my arms and heart open wide. We hug for the longest time while suitcases circle the luggage carousel.

"I'm so happy to see you," I say.

"Me too," Tracey says. She fishes a stick of Big Red from her purse and unwraps it.

"I can't wait for you to meet Michael." I shift my weight from one leg to the other and twirl hair around a finger. I take a deep breath. "He doesn't know, Tracey."

"He doesn't know what?" she asks, folding the stick of red gum into her mouth.

"About Morgan or Hawkeye. About the mess I was in."

"Why not?"

"Things are different here. I've had a chance to start over."

"It was a mistake, Casey. A teenage mistake, that's all."

"Yes, and it's behind me now."

Tracey takes another piece of gum from her purse. She unwraps the foil, bends the stick in half, and then folds it in half again before plopping it into her mouth. Our friendship is like that now, smaller—a fraction of what it used to be.

"Hawkeye used us. He used both of us."

"Michael's old-fashioned," I say. "And kind of religious, which is weird, I know, and totally unexpected. But I like him. He does these really odd but charming things like sending you a plane ticket. He bought me a bike after mine was stolen, hired a limo on my birthday, and I know he has something amazing planned for after graduation because at yeshivah there's no prom, no party, no mixed dancing. And he wants it to be special for me. He's really generous."

"He's really rich."

"I've moved on, Tracey. Things change."

"You've changed."

"Good," I say, not caring she didn't mean that as a compliment.

"Religion. Money. Next you'll tell me you aren't going to college."

Tracey and I have our differences. Growing up, I said Shema every night before bed, while she would never pray. To her, God is a fantasy as real as Prince Charming. And money just equals greed. She blows a red bubble.

"Tracey," I say, facing her, "promise me you won't say anything to Michael."

When we were younger I confided in her, told her I had a crush on Morgan, made her swear not to tell, made her cross her heart and hope to die, but she told him anyway.

"Are you going to marry this guy? My mother says you're going to marry him."

"That's ridiculous. I love him. I do. But I don't want to get married."

Together we pull her duffel from the spinning carousel.

"Tracey, he gets me," I say, wanting her to approve of my relationship with Michael.

"What world are you living in, Casey? He doesn't even know you."

o   o   o

Outside, Michael pulls up to the curb.

"A Porsche?" Tracey says, looking at me when she sees Michael's car.

She sits with me in the passenger seat, and Michael heads toward Manhattan. "So, where to, girls?"

We go to Yellowfingers, and Michael orders a bottle of white wine. Tracey runs through the list of boys she's dated since the last time I saw her, and the list is long. I know Michael is judging her, but I also know she doesn't care.

Tracey's interest is piqued when Michael orders without looking at the menu. He just asks for what we want, and whether it's on the menu or not, we get it: spaghetti with tomato and basil, penne with truffle oil and mushrooms, grilled snapper with capers. And a Margherita pizza for the table.

Tracey interrogates Michael about the rules of kashrut. "Wait, so how does this work? This restaurant isn't kosher," she says.

"Technically, no," Michael says. "It's not."

"Well, it either is or it isn't."

"We do our best," Michael says, sipping wine. "We don't eat meat here. Or shellfish. Observing a little is better than not observing at all."

"You just made that up. That's not how it goes."

"The community has its own rules, Tracey," I say. "Syrians do some things the Orthodox way, but they also eat in unkosher restaurants."

"You can't pick and choose."

"Why not?" Michael leans in, both elbows on the table.

Thankfully, the waiter appears, interrupting. He serves our food and offers us fresh pepper. : Michael wants pepper on his slice of pizza. When the waiter stops grinding, Michael says, "Keep going. Until your arm hurts."

"Michael," I whisper.

"What?"

"Be nice."

"I am nice," he says, unaware of how his abruptness is perceived by the world.

I want Tracey to like Michael. I watch him, trying to see what she sees. He uses a fork and a spoon to twirl pasta instead of letting strands of spaghetti dangle from his lips. He eats slowly, never talking with his mouth full, and holds his plate up generously, offering, "Want some?"

But Tracey barely pays attention. She's too busy smiling at our handsome waiter, a John Travolta lookalike, who keeps her wine glass full. The waiter tells Tracey he likes her accent and asks her where she's from. Turns out, he loves New Orleans and thinks New York City is really awesome too, despite the current transit strike.

Michael rolls his eyes and pontificates about workers and unions and how they have too much power. The vein near his temple bulges.

"You don't use public transportation, do you?" Tracey asks him. "Oh, no, that's right." She smacks her head with her hand as if just realizing. "You drive a Porsche." She locks eyes with Michael and dabs the corner of her mouth with a napkin.

"Who wants dessert?" I ask, changing the subject.

"Not me," Michael says. "But get whatever you want."

I read the menu, and before I decide, the waiter, trying to get in good with Tracey, serves us limoncello. "On the house," he says, pouring.

"Cool glass," Michael says, holding it high. "Look at this."

I'm used to Michael pointing things out I'd never notice, like elegant crystal and fine china, but Tracey, I can tell, thinks it's weird that Michael admires the glass and that he holds it up for what feels like an eternity. "Love this shape," he says. "Sexy as hell."

That's how Michael is. One minute he's ready for a fight, the next, enamored by beauty. "He's a rough, tough cream puff," his mother once said, and I think that's right.

The three of us clink glasses and down limoncello.

o   o   o

Back at home, alone in my room, Tracey tells me that Big Sam went away for a while, to some kind of boarding school, but he's back in New Orleans and doing fine now.

Mrs. Graf is still behind bars, and Tracey doesn't know where Hawkeye and Morgan are. "At some point after you left, I went by their house," Tracey says. "The grass was dead. The roof was crumbling. I peeked inside a window and the house was empty, totally abandoned. Anyway, who cares," she says. "I'm so over that whole time in my life."

We snack on Doritos, and I tell Tracey about the Marriage Box and how I avoided it at all costs. What seemed unbearable when I was alone is now hilarious. We laugh at the Syrian girls and their extensive beauty regimes: waxes, manicures, facials, and hair appointments. We make fun of rich Syrian boys and their antiquated ways of flirting, which always includes a put-down.

"Once when I was waitressing and taking a balding twenty-five-year-old guy's order, he told me I was a pretty girl but that it wouldn't kill me to knock off a pound or two. He actually patted my stomach."

"That's insane," Tracey laughs. Even Bruce Springsteen wrote about them. And she falls back on my bed, singing, "And the boys dance with their shirts open like Latin lovers along the shore, chasin' all them silly New York girls."

"You gotta love Bruce." I smile and tell Tracey how much I missed her and how depressed I've been. I tell her about the card game at Rochelle's and the gun. "I couldn't take it anymore," I say. "I felt so stifled. I was really losing my mind before I met Michael. He's different. He lives in the city and has traveled all over the world. He's not a typical Syrian."

"Well, you're also different, Casey. You're not like the other Syrian girls, desperate to get married. You're eighteen years old and you know Michael's a boyfriend. A boyfriend. Not a potential husband. That's why people date, to try on different relationships."

And then as if I need to defend Michael, or myself, or our bond, I blurt, "People aren't jeans, Tracey."

o o o

My father says falling in love and getting married is like falling down a staircase. You take a step, slip, and before you know it, you're at the bottom. I think that's the most ridiculous thing I've ever heard.

Three nights into Tracey's visit, she makes plans to have dinner with Grandma Rose. I haven't seen Michael since Tracey's first day in town, so we have a date.

Michael wears a pink leather tie, and it's a joke all night long. Everywhere we go, people comment—the parking lot attendant, our waitress, a bouncer at the club—and the more he's teased, the more brazen he gets. Michael behaves as if he's in a never-ending game of Truth or Dare, always picking dare. *I'm going to wear a pink tie. Dare you to question my manhood. I'm going to speed. Dare you to stop me.*

After our delicious meal at Nani's and dancing at The Red Parrot, we drive back to Brooklyn, top down. We sing along with the Rolling Stones to "Under My Thumb," playfully pressing our thumbs into each other's thighs.

The East River, black at night, flickers with city lights. Michael shifts gears and speeds on the FDR. Within moments, sirens flash, and a cop pulls us over. Terrified of policemen, still traumatized from my night with Hawkeye, I try to remain calm. Michael snaps at the cop, asking him if he's had nails for dinner.

The cop doesn't hesitate. He jerks Michael from the driver's seat, throws him against the side of the car, and cuffs him. He grabs Michael's pink tie and yanks it above his head like a noose.

"What's this, buddy? A pink tie? You like pink?"

I jump out of the car and stand by Michael's side. "Michael, what are you doing?"

"I'm not doing anything," Michael says. "It's this guy; he's on some kind of power trip."

"Stop," I beg Michael, scared he'll get into even more trouble.

"There's only one way to stop this," the cop yells, staring at me.

"How?" I holler over the whizzing cars.

"One way, you hear me?" the cop shouts, his hand smashing Michael's cheek against the car window.

"How?" I plead.

"Marry me," Michael screams over his shoulder. In his hands, which are still cuffed, he holds a diamond ring.

It takes me a minute to put all the pieces together. Michael has friends in the police department. And this proposal is why he sent for Tracey, imagining I'd want my best friend with me during this happy time.

"Well?" Michael says.

My mind races as the highway shakes beneath my feet. I want more time to decide, but I know Michael will not understand that. And I don't want to lose him.

I hug him tight around his neck, and laughing and crying at the same time, jumping up and down, I scream, "Yes, I'll marry you!"

With Michael things are clear: you are either with him or against him.

Brooklyn, 1982

Tracey spends the summer preparing for college, buying bedding and some posters for her dorm room wall. She receives a letter in the mail from her roommate, Chloe, and Tracey decides Chloe is the best. She's from California and has a collection of tapes so vast they could listen to music nonstop for days. Tracey picks classes, registering for freshman English, Psychology 101, Intro to Spanish, and Philosophy: Matters of the Mind. It bothers me that I'm missing out on that, but I focus on how much I love Michael, and my honeymoon, and I push my uncomfortable feelings away.

○ ○ ○

My wedding night comes in no time, and screens printed with cherry blossoms line the synagogue walls, setting the tone for our Asian-inspired affair. Bamboo runners and black pebbles decorate tables, and at sushi stations, enameled chopsticks crisscross like Samurai swords in wide goblets. On black trays, waiters serve iced sake and arak in shot glasses— all thanks to Wilder Cooper, the most prominent wedding planner in New York City. Wilder is known for designing extravaganzas meant to whisk guests away, transporting them to another time and place, creating atmosphere like a different world, and as the guests from New Orleans pile into the shul, they stare wide-eyed at gigantic rice-paper lanterns.

Wilder took care of most of the decor, but my father was instrumental in three ways. "One," he told Wilder, "I want a bar near the dance floor long as the Mississippi. Two, all alcohol must be top shelf. Three, I want a disco ball in the center of the dance floor big and bright as the sun."

When Wilder said that Japanese decorations, and paper lanterns in particular, wouldn't look authentic next to a disco ball, my father said he didn't care. Wilder turned to my mother for support.

"The disco ball stays," my mother said. "I'm not trucking with him over nonsense. No siree. Win the battle, but lose the war."

Wilder looked at me.

I just shrugged.

o o o

It doesn't matter. Top of her field, Wilder knows how to please her clients, and she creates an eclectic, multicultural atmosphere, even going so far as to allow, in a corner, some traditional Syrian appetizers: meat *sambousak*, *laham b'ajeen*, fried *kibbeh*.

Wanting Tracey to be my maid of honor, I planned my wedding around her school schedule. She's off for Thanksgiving break and is spending the weekend in New York City with Aunt Susie, Uncle Bobby, and Cathy. While Tracey doesn't usually have the best things to say about community life, she loves Syrian food. She poses for pictures with me and, in between shots, eats *kibbeh* after *kibbeh*.

My mother walks toward me in her sparkling gold gown, and I get sentimental thinking about this moment in my life, about moving on and moving out. It wasn't all that long ago that I was small and standing next to her in New Orleans, so enamored, as she curled her eyelashes. She'd pluck and shape her brows into arcs, stylish as state-of-the-art bridges, with painstaking care, while for some reason, she was never as meticulous about her lipstick and often applied it in a rush, looking like a kid who'd eaten red ices.

But tonight, on my wedding night, she's thirty-six and flawless, her makeup and hair professionally done.

"You ready?" she asks, putting her arm around me.

Aunt Susie interrupts, "For God's sake, where's the shrimp cocktail?" After living in New Orleans for more than thirty years, she wasn't used to celebrations without a raw bar. "What kind of party is this?" she asks, kissing my mother.

"A strictly kosher affair, Susie," my mother says, hugging her. "No shrimp, that's for sure, but the bar in the social hall is long as a football field. You'll be fine."

A waitress holding a bamboo tray filled with shots of sake walks by. She's wearing a black kimono; her hair is swept up in a bun pinned with floral ornaments like a geisha. I scoop a shot glass off her tray and present it to Aunt Susie.

Smiling, Aunt Susie looks me up and down. "You look gorgeous. I've never seen a more spectacular bride." She takes the shot glass from me. "Thank you, darling," she says. "I've always said you were like one of my own. Like another daughter. Although if you were mine," she says, shaking her head, "I wouldn't let you marry at eighteen. But I will say this—that Michael is a charmer."

It's pure luck that Big Sam has to work and can't make it to my wedding. Maybe he's grown up since the last time I saw him, but I'm glad not to have to take that chance, as he might think it would be funny to tease me about our past, not understanding the damage he could cause.

Aunt Susie is a potential problem too; she has no filter. She could say anything, at any time, and I need to keep Michael away from her. I scan the room, looking for him, and instead see Colette, his old girlfriend, kissing Michael's father hello.

It wasn't my decision to decorate the social hall with square tables—the centerpieces, low arrangements of white orchids and votive candles—or to have cherry blossom branches at the entrance. And it wasn't my idea to butterfly black napkins on white plates or lay paper fans on each chair. It *was* my idea, however, to keep ex-girlfriends and ex-boyfriends off the guest list.

I pull Tracey to the side and point. "That's her. That's Colette."

"How do you know?"

"I saw her once at Getaway. I didn't know who she was then. I was about to start work, and she was near the Marriage Box, wearing a high-rise bikini, heels, and you're not going to believe this, a cowboy hat."

"That's ridiculous."

"I know. Pretty tough not to notice." Feeling anxious, I fidget with the collar on my gown.

"Why is she here? Did she crash?"

"Probably." I lean in close to Tracey. "She's capable of anything. Michael told me that she came to his house last week, uninvited, dressed up in a sexy waitress costume, and delivered a hand-drawn menu she'd made to Colette's Café."

"No way," Tracey says, laughing.

"Yep, it's true. She used a calligraphy pen and wrote in fancy letters: *Entrées: Tongue, Breast, Rump Roast.*"

"Stop it, Casey, that's too much."

"Then she asked him if he was ready to order. I guess she was trying to win him back or something before it was too late."

"These Syrian girls are crazy. What they wouldn't do for a husband."

"It's not funny, Tracey."

"Okay. We can handle this. Calm down and give me a minute to think. I can be obvious and trip her? Or spill a drink on her?" She pauses and then lifts a finger. "But soy sauce would be better."

"Soy sauce *would* be better," I say, totally amused.

Michael is in the center of the foyer, mingling with our guests. Handsome in his Bergdorf tuxedo, he corners a waitress holding a tray of sake and hands shots to a circle of friends. I walk over, loop my arm through his, and whisper in his ear, "What's she doing here?" I aim my chin at Colette.

"Oh," Michael says, unflustered. "I meant to tell you. My mother wanted me to apologize. She mentioned this morning that my grandmother called Colette and told her that her invitation came back in the mail."

"But she wasn't invited. There was no invitation."

"She lied."

Colette grew up in the Syrian community and attended yeshivah. Her family is observant and wealthy. Michael's grandmother doesn't like that I was raised out of town, without religion and community, and from the start, she disapproved.

"So, what was your grandmother thinking? That you'd see Colette on our wedding night and you'd realize you loved her and not me?"

"I guess."

Jealousy's a wicked drug, a stimulant of the central nervous system, an appetite suppressant, an anesthetic numbing my toes and fingertips. I watch Colette eat celery and sip champagne. I stare as she flirts with Eric, one of Michael's best friends, and keep an eye on her as she drums up conversation, flitting from group to group like a bee flying from flower to flower.

Because of my lost virginity and my scar, I haven't slept with Michael. Since the Syrian community values and expects abstinence, my withholding doesn't seem odd. In fact, it appears virtuous. Watching Colette, I feel threatened. Her body isn't scarred, and sex oozes from her like golden honey—her virginity, unlike mine, up for grabs. I make sure to know where she is at all times.

"Earth to Casey. You with me here?" Michael asks.

"I'm with you."

Wilder, a Lucite clipboard in hand, wears an Asian-inspired short black dress and murderous heels, and diamonds hang from her earlobes like mini-chandeliers. Her black bangs are ironed flat. "Everything's moving like clockwork," she says. "The rabbi's waiting for you in his study."

"Don't let her out of your sight," I tell Tracey, pointing at Colette.

o   o   o

The rabbi sits across from Michael and me, behind a large desk. "This is your commitment," he says to Michael. He holds the ketubah. "Do you accept?"

"I accept," Michael says.

The rabbi leans forward in his brown leather chair, adjusts the yarmulke on his head, and strokes his long black beard. He tells us the story of Jacob and how he fell in love with Rachel. He tells us how Jacob agreed to work for seven years for Laban in return for her hand in marriage. On their wedding night, the bride was veiled, and Jacob didn't realize that Leah, Rachel's older sister, had been substituted.

"That's why the groom lifts the veil. You need to make sure you're marrying the right girl," the rabbi concludes.

"When is she actually mine?" Michael asks the rabbi.

"When you step on the glass."

"Okay then," Michaels says, standing. "Let's get this show on the road."

o   o   o

Under the chuppah, the rabbi speaks with precision about how a person is not complete until they are joined in matrimony, and he explains that the groom steps on a glass because it reminds us of the fragility of a marriage. "You cannot repair a shattered glass," he says.

Michael crushes the wine cup under his foot, and our guests stand and chant, "*Marbrook.*"

After the ceremony, Michael and I dance to Arabic music, holding a black napkin between us like a scarf. Rochelle taps my shoulder. "Lift your hands in the air. Twist at the wrist like you're changing light bulbs," she says, trying to teach me how to dance to Arabic music.

The guests from New Orleans are in awe. Not used to any of this, they stand on the side, watching.

After just a few songs, the DJ switches to disco music. My mother boogies to "It's Raining Men" like she's never heard a better song, and my father is relieved his job of raising and marrying a daughter is done. "You're not coming back," he says during our father-daughter dance. He grins as if he's kidding.

"You won," I say.

"Won what?"

"Our bet."

"I did, didn't I?" he says, smiling and spinning me around.

The wedding cake is five layers high and all white. As usual, Michael takes charge and cuts it while the DJ plays "All You Need Is Love." He scoops large forkfuls of cake into the mouths of whoever stands nearby. Even my mother, who hasn't eaten dessert in over fifteen years, takes a bite. I'm so secure in my new role as Michael's wife I forget all about Colette.

Exhausted, I take a break, talking to Tracey near the bar. We order screwdrivers.

"I can't wait for my honeymoon," I tell her. "I got the cutest bathing suits."

"Bikinis?"

"No." And I look at her as if to say, *Oh come on, you know the answer to that.*

"Michael's going to see your stomach, Casey." She takes her drink from the bartender and faces me. "I can't believe you haven't slept with him yet. Only in this antiquated, old-fashioned community could you get away with that. What are you going to say when you don't bleed?"

"Cheerleading mishap. Consequences of a perfect split." I lift my glass toward her.

"Here's to starting off your marriage on the right foot," Tracey says, clinking her glass against mine.

The room goes black. No lights. No music. And the disco ball stops spinning. There is a moment of stillness before our guests panic. Fumbling, they knock down bamboo chairs and slip on paper fans. Michael is at my side. "Don't move," he says, anchoring me to the bar. He grabs candles from tables, creating decent light. He finds his grandmother and mine, and he sits them down in a safe spot. "Everything's fine," he shouts. "Everything's going to be fine. Come to the bar."

In the darkness, I hear my mother calling for Wilder. "Where is she? I'm going to kill her."

"Relax," Michael says. "It's okay."

"Okay? How is this okay?" My mother can hardly catch her breath. "We don't even know what's happening." She sits, lifts a paper fan from a chair, and fans her face.

Wilder makes her way to my mother, a flashlight in her hands.

"I'm fit to be tied, Wilder. What's going on?" my mother asks.

"There's nothing to worry about. It's only a blackout. Flashlights and more candles are on the way."

"Only a blackout? Are you kidding? This is a disaster."

Trying to calm my mother down and keep things under control, I say, "Mom, it's not a disaster. It'll be all right." But what I'm really thinking is *This is a bad sign.*

"Where's your father? Why's he never around when I need him?"

"I'm right here, Sharon. Right behind you."

Michael uses his hands, cupping his mouth like a megaphone, and announces, "People, let's party. Drinks for everyone. Who needs a disc jockey? We'll make our own music."

While our guests huddle around the bar, their eyes adjusting, Michael sings "Sympathy for the Devil," and bartenders pour drinks as fast as they can. Michael swipes a bottle of Stolichnaya off the bar and drinks from it. He holds the bottle in one hand and pulls me toward him with his other, twirling me around how he did one night, on a date at Club A.

Through the candlelight, I see Colette, looking sultry, leaning against the bar and watching. She fans herself, not taking her eyes off of us, and puts the paper fan down on the bar, placing it on top of a candle. Someone screams, "Fire!"

Tracey appears out of nowhere, a superhero. She reaches for a glass of water from a nearby table and squelches the flame. I don't know if Tracey wet Colette on purpose or not, but it doesn't matter. I'm just glad she got to throw a drink on her after all. As quickly as the thought passes through my mind, Michael swoops a napkin off a table and, without hesitation, comes to Colette's rescue, wiping the front of her dress.

"I'm all wet," Colette says, gazing into Michael's eyes.

"I can see that."

I stand frozen, my body numb, as the lights come on and the disco ball starts spinning. The DJ calls everyone to dance, and I suppose thinking he's funny, he plays "Disco Inferno."

Wilder informs my mother and me that an electrician has changed a faulty panel, and while he isn't expecting any more trouble, he's staying on for the rest of the night.

I walk away from Wilder so I can get a closer look at Michael and Colette when they start to dance. Her black sequin dress glitters in the disco lights, and they stare into each other's eyes, smiling. Colette bumps Michael's hip. Michael bumps her back.

A few weeks before our wedding, at The Red Parrot, Michael got drunk. On the dance floor, he pointed out the length of a girl's dress, more like a shirt. The girl's nails shined glossy red, and her golden hair swayed down her back to her butt. With one finger, Michael plucked at her hem, at the dark space in between her thighs.

"Be cool," Michael said over the music, seeing my concern. "All in good fun."

I pushed the uneasy feeling away, but his action beat deep, straight to my soul.

o   o   o

Michael finds me at the edge of the dance floor. I move away from his touch.

"What?" He shrugs. "You're mad at me?"

I don't answer.

"You're mad at me on our wedding night?" He reaches for my face, but I pull back. "Come on, Casey. Don't make this a big deal. She's my friend."

I've relinquished all my power—I can't go home, threaten to never see him again, or give him the silent treatment. My mother's words boom in my head. *Life isn't a bowl of cherries.*

I keep one eye on Colette and pull Michael close, kissing him hard and long on the mouth.

New York City, 1983

We move into an apartment on the Upper East Side right after our honeymoon. The base of our glass coffee table is black lacquer and built on a slant, making it look as if it's about to tip over.

"I'm not sure," I say, tilting my head, staring at the table when it first arrives.

"It's cool," Michael says. "I like it."

"Well, if you like it, I like it."

That's how things were at first.

○ ○ ○

Away from the Syrian community in Brooklyn, and even farther away from my past in New Orleans, I'm happy in New York City. I can count on the fact that my parents and Sam won't be knocking on my door or barging in anytime soon, and I can spend as much time as I want blasting music, dancing around in a crop top and short-shorts, watching TV and eating chips on the couch.

Every morning, I press my forehead against the sun-warmed windowpane, gazing at the East River, and on sunny days when a boat goes by, the water ripples and the current glitters gold.

Five days a week Michael goes to work, and I learn to cook. The first time I make *hashu* the rice is hard as if I've poured it straight from the box. When I tell Tracey what a disaster my cooking is, she says, "That's because you should be putting your energy into bigger and better things."

I open my nightstand drawer, glance at my NYU bulletin, and slam the drawer shut. "I gotta go," I say, hanging up fast.

Even though Michael says he doesn't mind if I go to NYU, I don't believe him because he also says, "I don't want to hear you can't make dinner because you have *homework.*"

Michael works long hours selling TVs, clocks, cameras, boom boxes, video games, and stereo systems. When his alarm goes off at seven, I hold him tight under the covers, interlocking my legs with his. "Don't go."

Every morning he says, "I have to."

Sipping coffee on the couch, I watch Michael as he prays, reading from a book and wearing tefillin. It's as if I'm a detective trying to solve some great mystery. I can't get used to the fact that Michael takes religion so seriously, and every time I see him worshipping this way, it's as if an imposter has barged in and taken the place of my husband.

In reality, I'm the fraud, hiding in plain sight. I've gotten good at keeping secrets. The hard part is behind me. On our wedding night, nestled in Michael's arms, I explained that due to an impressive cheerleading split, there'd be no blood, and since then I've learned to undress in front of him—hiding my body, and my scar—in ways that aren't stiff or unattractive. Michael has taken it as fact, or the way things are, that I prefer having sex with a tee shirt on. He isn't happy about it, but he accepts it as he understands I like my eggs well done, not runny; summer more than winter; and Fleetwood Mac over Ray Charles.

o   o   o

In time, I get better at cooking. I fill my days buying ingredients, preparing meals, and cleaning up after. Our kitchen is a typical New York City kitchen, which is to say, small. Small enough so that if I stand on one end and take a giant leap, I land at the other. It requires a certain kind of ingenuity to work in such a tight space, and I feel proud of how I can create so much from so little.

There is a satisfying and meditative quality to chopping onions and cubing potatoes. In that tranquility sometimes I zone out, remembering warm moments, like the time my mother and I sat in our kitchen in New Orleans, making *kibbeh hamdah*. She didn't call it that then. She called it meatballs, and I was enchanted with how there was a baby meatball tucked inside a big one. Storms in New Orleans could be unsettling, frightening even, but that day when it poured, it wasn't scary at all. As rain hit our ranch house windows, a smooth, even beat prevailed, and my mother relaxed into the rhythm. Rolling raw meat, my mother said, "You make the inside, I'll make the outside," and she cupped my hands, helping me with size and shape.

But other times, my thoughts go dark, and my memories are the opposite of soothing. I tense up, remembering how I betrayed Morgan, and how he betrayed me. And Hawkeye, how he touched my leg, and how my body—hot—responded.

o o o

One night, a few months into our marriage, I panfry breaded chicken for dinner. Michael strolls in from work with *Time* magazine under his arm, rolled up like a police club. He throws it on the kitchen counter. "Now this is worth reading," he says as if we are in the middle of a debate. "Not that made-up crap." He is referring to the collection of books in my room: *The Great Gatsby, Pride and Prejudice, The Grapes* *of Wrath, The Sun Also Rises.* I pledged to read the classics in an attempt to squash the shame I felt for not being in college.

"Fiction, Michael. It's called fiction." Oil sizzles in the pan. One by one, I flip chicken pieces. "How was your day?"

"Torture. I'm going to get washed up." He kisses my cheek and heads for the bathroom. "You plan on leaving this mess here?"

From the day we moved in, I took my clothes off in the exact same way, dropping my coat near the front door, then pulling my sweater over my head and leaving it on the floor near the couch, with boots, socks, jeans dotting the carpet on the way to our bedroom—leaving a trail as if I'd need those markers to find my way out.

"Why can't you just pick one spot in a corner somewhere?" Michael says, lifting lace panties. They dangle from his finger like a flag.

I lean on the frame of the kitchen door. "I like it this way. Makes me feel like I can do whatever I want. Like this is my apartment, my life."

"Well, you can't," he says, stepping over my bra. "There are rules. Remember?"

"I remember, Your Royal Highness. No sandwiches for dinner, and always make the bed."

o o o

I set the table and wait for Michael on our sixteenth-floor balcony. The air is sharp as the city itself, and I stare out into the endless New York sky—the lights, the vastness—pure possibility. Michael comes up behind me.

"Must you stand so close to the edge?" he asks, stepping back and taking me with him.

"What's wrong? You scared?"

"Me? Scared?" He hugs me tight from behind. "Never."

"It *is* a long way down," I say, turning to face him. I run my fingers through his hair and feel something new. "What's that?"

"A scar. I've had it forever." He pulls back.

"I can't believe I never noticed that before. How'd you get it?" This comes out fast, without me thinking, and I panic because I don't want him asking me the same about my scar.

"Neighbor threw a beer bottle at my head. He was *mezhnun*."

"What's *mezhnun*?" I ask, circling the smooth spot on his head with my finger.

"Crazy. He was crazy."

"Did you get stitches?"

"Yep."

"And then what happened?"

"Nothing. Can we eat?"

Michael hasn't always been so tough. His older sister told me that when he was four his favorite game was crawling around on the yellow linoleum tile in their kitchen purring like a kitten and sipping milk from a bowl. He'd curl himself into a ball, planting his body on her lap so she could stroke the top of his head. But over time, Michael hardened, and when his father downed a couple of scotches and beat him with a belt, Michael wouldn't cry. He simply learned to wear two pairs of pants to ease the blows.

I place Michael's plate in front of him at the table. "Why was your day so torturous?"

"Nothing gets done unless I do it myself. And nobody wants to work anymore. I lost it with two employees today." He stabs a bite of chicken with his fork and holds it up to me. "Delicious," he says, chewing. "Anyway, they were supposed to be unpacking a huge shipment, merchandise I needed on the floor, and instead I found them smoking in the back. I yelled at them in front of everyone. Fired them on the spot." He waves his arms in front of his chest, a referee making a final call. "We're short on help, but I had to set a standard, you know? Or else everybody sees what's going on and they think they can slack off too. And before you know it, you're running an out-of-business sale. *Everything Must Go.*"

"Did you have to fire them?"

"Yes, I had to fire them. Weren't you listening?"

"Of course I was listening." I fidget in my chair. "It just seems extreme. They must've been mad."

"Mad? You think I care if they were mad? I'm running a business, Casey. Not a popularity contest."

There was a time Michael cared what people thought about him. He told me that all through junior high he slept with a pair of cut pantyhose on his head, attempting to flatten his kinky hair, but by the time he got to high school, he got rid of the pantyhose routine and grew an Afro. He wore ripped blue jeans and brown leather sandals, and whenever I pictured him as a teenager, I envisioned his hairy toes sticking out of the straps like ten furry caterpillars just waiting to butterfly. Stoned, more often than not, he had encounters with the law and developed his *I don't give a shit* attitude.

I stack our plates and head to the kitchen. Michael goes to the couch and flips on the TV. After the news, we fool around and I cling to him, my head in the nook of his solid arm. He sings a cappella "While My Guitar Gently Weeps," and I feel as if I've been doused with opiates. He puts his hand on my belly, and I carefully move it away. Even though Michael has just told me about his scar, I'm not ready to tell him about mine. That story will lead to others, and wanting to avoid his questions, I shoot up fast.

o   o   o

I wash my face and change into a sleeping tee shirt. In bed, I lie next to him, staring across the room at my wooden bookcase. "Hey," I say, turning toward Michael. "Would you love me if I got fat?"

I've been reading a lot lately but also watching Donahue and am becoming more and more interested in people, relationships, and psychology.

"No," Michael says, unapologetically.

"What do you mean no?"

"No." He pauses. "I mean, maybe I'd love you in some way, but I wouldn't be attracted to you."

"So much for unconditional love." I move away and lean against the headboard.

"There's no such thing."

"What? How can you say that?"

"It's true. You don't get love for free."

"When did you become so cynical?"

"I've always been cynical." He pulls me close and swings his leg over mine, heavy as dead weight. I stare, fascinated yet again by the contrast of our skin: his dark as chocolate ice cream, mine vanilla.

"Well, I don't know about you, but I believe in true love, and if you don't—well, then, maybe you shouldn't have gotten married."

"Oh, you're right. Only people who are in love are married."

"Michael, what are you saying?"

"Calm down, sweetie," he says, propping his head on his elbow. "I love *you*, so don't worry."

"Awww." I roll toward him and take a breath. "Why do you love me?"

"Stop it, Casey. You know why."

"No, I don't. Tell me."

"No one makes salad dressing like you."

"That's not a good answer."

"Yes, it is." He smiles. "You make great soup too."

"I'm not liking these answers."

"Well, you should. I love how you take care of me. And you have a big heart."

I think of Nellie telling me I have a black one. She whispered it in my ear the day she left. A prophecy. I believed her.

Any fleeting desire I might have about confessing my past to Michael flies right out our sixteenth-floor window. I like how he sees me—all good—and want to keep it that way.

"Also, you're not like other Syrian girls," he says.

"And that's a good thing?"

"I married you, didn't I?" He kisses my cheek and fluffs his pillow, getting comfortable.

As we lie on our backs, a few seconds go by, and neither of us says a word.

"You sleeping?" I ask.

"No."

"Seems like you're sleeping."

"I'm not but I wish I were."

And he closes his eyes, tiny doors shutting.

o o o

Every morning when Michael leaves for work, I stay in bed drinking coffee and reading cookbooks: red snapper on a bed of sautéed spinach, salmon with warm lentil salad, thinly sliced steak with mushrooms. Alone in my morning bed, I explore all kinds of options. Later, in my kitchen, I'll substitute one ingredient for another, mixing and combining like any artist.

After Donahue, I get up and make the bed. I dress in a leotard and leg warmers and slide our coffee table over, making room for my mat. I slip my Jane Fonda aerobics video into our VHS machine and think about sliding *Deep Throat* into Aunt Susie's machine. Even though it feels like a lifetime ago, it's only been six years. Pushing the memory away, I lie in front of the TV and do leg lifts. After, I shower and change and head to the grocery store.

It's noon in New York City, and as I reach for a cart, I consider what my classmates from Franklin Prep might be doing—they'd be in a college classroom, studying in their dorm, or possibly sleeping late. They wouldn't be months into a marriage, gathering ingredients for pesto.

While I like my new life, I feel confused. Tracey sees home-making as subservience, and I'm not sure what I think. All I know is that cooking gives me direction and I'm good at it. Plus, it makes Michael happy.

Roaming down the spice aisle looking for some variety, I toss allspice and cumin into my cart. In the produce section, I pick up fresh thyme, basil, and rosemary. I have to hike all the way to the back for necessities: milk, juice, eggs. At the checkout line, I grab a pack of Life Savers and eat them one after another: red, yellow, green.

"Delivery?" the cashier asks.

"No, thanks. I've got it," I say, helping her bag.

On my way out, I slip a quarter in the gumball machine, hoping for red. I get white. As I walk home, I think about adding walnuts to my pesto. The grocery bags get heavier and heavier with each block. They cut into my wrists like handcuffs.

New York City, 1983

"Let's go out tonight," **Michael** says, calling from work. "You spend too much time in that tiny kitchen of yours. I want to take you out."

"I like my kitchen," I say, unpacking groceries and smelling fresh basil.

"Eric and Colette want to go out. Let's go."

A month after our wedding, Michael's oldest friend, Eric, asked if he could take Colette out on a date. Three months later, they were married.

"I was going to make pesto tonight," I say.

"Make it tomorrow. It'll be fun."

I wasn't into hanging out with Colette, but Michael said I didn't understand how things worked in the community. He said I should loosen up because Colette didn't want anything from him now that she was married. "The community's small," Michael said. "This kind of thing happens all the time. Trust me. It's no big deal."

I don't want Colette around for obvious reasons, but in addition, she isn't my type. She thinks it's funny that her older sister pays her son's bus driver to change his route so her son is the last drop-off after school. For $10 her sister buys herself an extra thirty minutes of free time every day, while her son circles their neighborhood, passing their house two times before the driver actually stops.

o   o   o

We meet at a new restaurant on the Upper East Side. Rochelle and Rick join us. Both Colette and Rochelle have fresh manicures, some kind of glamorous red, and they've had their dark hair blown and styled. Colette's is parted down the middle; it's plush with a sheen like velvet.

I'm the only one at the table who didn't grow up between Avenue S and Avenue T in Brooklyn, where they all met at Oscar's candy store after school. On high holidays and Shabbat, they prayed at the same shul. They went to the same parties, ate the same foods, and held the same beliefs. Whenever I'm around them, I feel like a schoolgirl left out at recess.

"Michael," Colette says, reaching for her vodka, "remember how you used to walk around our neighborhood in shorts and black socks?"

"You didn't wear shoes?" I ask, loving this detail.

Michael shrugs. "I don't recall."

"Well, I do," Colette says. "And what were those little figures you played with?"

"G.I. Joes." Michael smiles. "Now, *that* I remember. Rick and I used to make them go to war." He swigs scotch. "And there was that Italian kid. What was his name? Tommy. He was the badass of our neighborhood."

The waiter hands us menus, and I study mine, glad to have something of my own to focus on. I read it, getting cooking ideas. Michael and Colette decide to share salmon, and as they confer about how they want the salmon cooked, their heads tip toward each other, and their bodies form a triangle.

"Would you like to hear the specials?" the waiter asks, placing a basket of bread on the table.

"Let me save you some time," Michael says. "We have a few dietary restrictions." Michael shoots off a list in rapid fire: no meat, no chicken, no veal, no lamb, no pig, no shellfish.

The waiter looks stunned, and I imagine he isn't used to people speaking so curtly. He takes a moment before responding. "Then there are no specials," he says.

Keeping kosher still feels new to me, and restrictive. Reading a menu has become more a process of elimination than it is an exercise in choice. My eyes scan the appetizers. *No, no, no.* Finally, I see something I can have. "I'll have the vegetable soup," I say. And just as I'm about to order my main course, Michael chimes in, "There's no stock in that, right? No chicken or veal?"

"Uh, no. Not that I know of," the waiter says, averting his eyes.

"This is not a guessing game," Michael says, eyeing the waiter. "We're strict vegetarians, except we eat fish."

"We're kosher," Eric interrupts. He turns to Michael. "You're confusing the guy. Why can't you just say we're kosher?"

"Because no one knows what that means," Michael says. "And I want to be crystal clear."

"Eating in a trendy New York City restaurant is in no way kosher. You know what's been on these plates—steamed lobsters, prime rib, grilled chicken."

"We do our best, Eric."

"You're the boss." Eric shrugs.

The waiter looks eager to get away. "I'll check with the chef."

When he returns, Rochelle orders, and as she substitutes one side dish for another, specifies the use of olive oil as opposed to butter, and asks for the whole thing well done, Rick rolls his eyes. "Everything's a production," he says. "Can't you ever order straight off the menu?" He swirls the ice in his single malt scotch with a finger and raises his glass. "Here's to the Eight to Eleven Rule." Rick clinks his glass with Eric's and Michael's.

"What's the Eight to Eleven Rule?" I ask.

"You have to be able to tolerate your spouse from eight p.m. to eleven p.m.," Rick says. If you can do that, you've got it made."

I want to say something about how offensive I find this, but I don't. Instead, I kick Michael under the table.

All through appetizers, I keep my eye on Colette, studying her every move, because recently, I asked Michael if he thought she was pretty, and he said, "Pretty's not the right word. Striking. I think she's striking."

It was my own fault. I shouldn't have asked. "You think she's prettier than I am, don't you?"

"No," Michael said. "You're just different. She's like Ginger. You're like Mary Ann."

He didn't mean to insult me, but I felt slighted nonetheless.

Colette plops a grape tomato into Michael's mouth as if she is an Egyptian princess dangling a bunch of grapes above the king's head.

Rick twirls pasta around his fork. "This is incredible," he says. "Best food in the city." And then he sneezes.

"See, it's true," Rochelle says.

"Oh, sneezing makes whatever you say true? Okay then," Rick says, "see that tall blonde over there? She's not even pretty. Hachoo."

Michael and Eric laugh.

"I'd never touch her," Rick continues. "Hachoo."

Syrian men think this kind of talk is cool, even manly. When we first started dating, Michael told me about community boys and how he was raised, revealing that his older brother, Joe, brought him to a prostitute right before his Bar Mitzvah.

"But that's so young," I said when he told me.

"Yeah, well, that's the way it was."

"That's child abuse."

"Relax, Casey. It wasn't child abuse."

o o o

Rick, Eric, and Michael are still looking at the tall blonde and laughing. I hate their macho talk and attitude, but I don't know how to explain what I'm feeling. Their chauvinistic lingo is standard for many American men, not just Syrians, and if there is a line of acceptability, I don't know where it is. It's all hazy, and it seems like I'm the only one at the table who is conflicted, so I don't say anything.

Rochelle taps my shoulder. She says softly, "Bergdorf is forty off. Don't miss it."

Sales and designer clothes don't interest me, but I listen as if I care.

"I found an Alaia dress for twelve hundred dollars," she says. "It was originally two thousand." Rochelle leans in and whispers, "I put four hundred on my American Express, four hundred on my Mastercard, and paid four hundred cash. That way Rick can't track it."

"He doesn't know?"

"No. Of course not. He'd kill me."

Even though I'd never spend $1,200 on a dress, lying and secret keeping Rochelle and I have in common.

o   o   o

At home, I drop my coat on the floor near the door. "Those Syrian girls are crazy," I say, peeling off my sweater and letting it fall to the carpet.

"Oh, come on. They're harmless and you know it."

"It rubs me the wrong way."

"What does?"

"How they talk. Their values." I open the freezer, reach for Breyer's butter pecan, and grab two spoons. I plop on the couch next to Michael.

"Well, there's your problem," Michael says, taking a bite of ice cream. "You have to appreciate people for what they have to offer. You can't take them so seriously. You take everything so seriously."

I scoop ice cream onto my spoon. "I told you when we first started dating I could be heavy. You can't say I didn't warn you."

"Fair enough," Michael says.

"But really. Who talks that way?"

"What way?"

"Did you hear what Colette said when I told her I wanted to live in the city and you wanted to move to Brooklyn?"

"No. What'd she say?"

"She said she knew how to get Eric to do whatever she wanted. And like it's some big secret and not a woman's most ancient, not to mention manipulative, tactic, she said, *Make him happy*."

"Oh, yeah. I heard that." Michael laughs, and I'm reminded of how much I like it when he does.

"And *you*," I say, dragging out the words, "tilting back on your chair, arms behind your head, as if willing to accept such services."

"You bet. Why not?"

"Because that's not what marriage is about," I say.

"Being happy?"

"Very funny."

"There you go getting all serious again," Michael says, eating a bite of ice cream. He shuts his eyes tight, and his forehead scrunches.

"What's the matter?"

"Brain freeze."

"And if that's not bad enough," I go on, "Colette said she was going to teach me all of her tricks. She actually used the word *tricks*."

"Big deal."

"That's prostitution, Michael. Not marriage." With my spoon, I dig out extra pecans, adjusting the proportions to get the perfect bite.

"They're happy. Who cares?"

I place the tub of ice cream on the coffee table and straddle Michael's lap. He leans back, taken off guard.

I look him dead in the eyes. "I care."

New York City, 1983

As couples do, Michael and I develop a routine. Every Friday night, we spend Shabbat in Brooklyn. One week at my family's house, one week at his. Not able to drive on the Sabbath, we stay over, sleeping in the beds we slept in as children, the bed I cried in, night after night, when we first moved to New York. I want to stay in Manhattan, alone with Michael now and then, but Michael's father won't hear of it. "What kind of thing is that? You have to be in Brooklyn on Shabbat."

When Michael and I first started dating, I took down the collage of photographs on my bedroom wall. Michael knew a lot about Franklin Prep and how I wanted to be a cheerleader, but he knew nothing about Mrs. Graf, Morgan, and especially Hawkeye.

Every weekend, at my parents' house, Michael complains that the food is like hospital food, no love, and the house is like a sauna. Seventy-six degrees. Late at night, our mouths dry, he stands near the thermostat in the hallway and shoots his chin toward my mother's closed bedroom door. "She's trying to cook us," he says.

At his house, his father calls me *Rochi*, an Arabic word for sweetheart. And his mother, a glamorous woman with a French manicure, wears a turquoise ring the size of a quail egg. She cooks Syrian food better than our ancestors in Aleppo and makes delicious *hata*, which is basically crispy chicken and spaghetti. We ooh and ahh over her *kibbehs* with mushrooms, chicken with eggplant, and *keftes*. The trick, she tells me, is lots of oil and allspice.

I prefer the weekends at Michael's. His house always smells like deep-fried *kibbeh* and love, the warmth coming from two stuffed ovens set at 350 degrees. There is something about my mother-in-law that I find alluring, and I can't stop staring. On Friday nights, she wears a black silk kimono and gold slippers, and when she slides her feet out of the slippers and lounges on the living room couch, I admire her toenail polish, rich as rubies. Without his mother's approval, Michael would've never married me, so I know she likes me well enough, but I also know her own children are number one. I'm second string—on the team but forever on the bench.

Eating Friday night dinner with Michael's family is always the highlight of the weekend. Everybody talks over each other. While some would think the noise and confusion chaotic, I think it's heaven. There is an inescapable energy around the table, pitfalls too, and you never know who is going to be the target. Michael's older brother, Joe, dishes out scorn with a zing, just as Big Sam used to do. I make sure to stay on his good side, buttering him up whenever possible. Michael says I have nothing to worry about, that Joe would never mess with me since that would mean messing with him. Ever since he was fifteen and stabbed Joe in the back with a fork, Joe has been careful around him.

On one of my first Friday nights at Michael's house, his mother prepares something she's never made before—chicken with apricots and dates. Michael's father says the prayer over the wine and the challah, and his mother and I serve the new chicken dish plus some of her staples: brick roast, *rubuh' b'bizeh*, and *fasoulia*. To a typical Syrian family, her dining room table is a display of love, to a wannabe vegetarian—a doomed petting zoo.

"I hate sweet food," Michael says as his mother places the new chicken dish on the table. "We all hate sweet food."

I nudge him.

"What?" Michael says. "It's true. Who puts fruit in food?"

"Airlines do," Joe says, picking apricots from the chicken with his fork.

Michael's father takes a bite. "It's delicious," he says, and with comedic timing adds, "but don't ever make it again." Everyone laughs, even Michael's mother. We talk, and eat, and drink red wine, and as much as I need New York City and treasure being away from the community and its many restraints, I have to admit—I love this too. All my loneliness is behind me, and my secrets are safe, locked deep inside. And lately, while I'm cooking or doing a Jane Fonda workout, Hawkeye's face materializes but doesn't linger anymore; it distorts and disappears like a cloud.

In Michael's childhood bed we stay awake talking, our legs entwined. Michael tells me that when he was young, his father used to come home from parties, drunk.

"He'd shake me awake as if there was a fire in the house," Michael says. "He'd jump on my bed, his breath smelling of scotch, and rattle on and on, *Do you love me? How much do you love me? Who do you love more, your mother or me?*"

"I love you both the same," Michael would answer.

"No. No. You can't say that. Okay, how about this. If you, your mother, and me were on a boat in the middle of the ocean, and your mother and I were drowning, but you could only save one of us, who would you save?"

"Mom doesn't know how to swim."

"So, you'd save her?" he'd ask, springing to an elbow.

"I'd jump off the boat and put you two in it."

"That's not a choice. You have to pick. Your mother or me?"

Michael wouldn't comply. Eventually, his father would stop harassing him and pass out.

o o o

"Let's get a snack," I say, wanting to stay awake and talk some more.

"Are you kidding? I'm still stuffed from dinner."

"I'm not." I jump out of bed. "Come on."

We creep downstairs like naughty children sneaking around after bedtime, and the staircase creaks beneath us. In the soundless kitchen, I open the refrigerator.

"I can't see a thing. The light's broken in here," I say to Michael.

"It's not broken. It's taped down."

"Why?"

"So the light doesn't go on."

I know that on Shabbat, Orthodox Jews don't use electricity, including turning lights on or off, but I hadn't considered the refrigerator.

"Ahhh," I say, "learn something new every day."

"We should do the same thing in our apartment," Michael says.

"Sure," I say, with sarcasm. "If your dad ever lets us stay in the city on a Friday night."

In the pantry, I look for something sweet to eat. There is nothing. But the freezer, which also has tape over the light button, is stocked, as any good Syrian woman's freezer should be, and I find chocolate-covered almonds.

"Are they parve?" Michael asks.

If the package is marked *parve*, it means the snack is dairy free, and after a meat dinner, we can have some. If milk or butter is used, we can't.

"Rules, rules, and more rules," I say, reading the ingredients. "Parve," I cheer, and Michael and I each take a handful. Michael throws a nut in the air and opens his mouth wide. He throws his head back, attempting to catch the almond, but it bounces off his lip and lands on the linoleum floor, near the basement door. He picks it up, gives it a kiss, and eats it.

"Gross. Don't eat off the floor."

"Six-second rule," Michael says, chewing. He points to where the nut landed. "My Bar Mitzvah party was down there. It's not a finished basement. But it's all my father could afford. Hardly anyone came."

My heart sinks.

Back in bed, we hug and fall asleep nose-to-nose, his breath on my skin like light wind.

When Shabbat ends the following evening, while Michael loads our luggage into the car, I stand at the top of the basement steps and flick a switch. A single bulb lights up. The basement is wet and cold, and I imagine Michael, the Bar Mitzvah boy, wearing a burgundy velvet blazer, dancing alone to the Jukebox music.

I love him more than ever.

New York City, 1984

A week before Passover, Michael says we have to start cleaning for the holiday.

"You mean get rid of the bread?"

"All chametz. All leavened products," Michael says. "All wheat, barley, oats, spelt, and rye."

"That's everything we have," I say, looking into our kitchen cabinet, taking inventory.

Michael gathers boxes of spaghetti, a sack of flour, and a tub of oatmeal, and he dumps them into our garbage. He does the same to a bag of pita bread and a box of Raisin Bran.

"Holidays are supposed to be fun," I say.

The community has started taking religion more seriously, and according to the head rabbi, Chanukah is not about a bush or gift giving. Those are Christian traditions introduced in an attempt to keep Jews practicing because Chanukah doesn't hold a candle to Christmas, and everybody knows it. Rabbis now warn that these reforms will not produce divine inspiration. It's like rewarding children with cash for doing well on their report cards instead of cultivating their natural curiosity.

When I was young in New Orleans, I loved Chanukah and the fact that a Chanukah Fairy left a present on my bed eight nights in a row. As a reminder of the oil miraculously lasting during the time of the Holy Temple, we burned tall, thin candles and watched wax drip—golden yellow, cherry red, midnight blue.

But presently, in New York, this is all wrong. There are rules about when to light (when stars appear in the night sky), where to light (near a window), and what to light (not candles, pure olive oil, pale yellow).

Even with all these dos and don'ts, Passover is an entirely different story. Passover takes rule abiding to a whole new level.

It's all so predictable. Cyclical. Expected. And I'm getting bored. As soon as one holiday is over, another begins. Rosh Hashanah, Yom Kippur, Sukkot, and, finally, Simchat Torah, the one I can never remember. The one that feels tacked on like a triathlon adding a fourth event.

o　o　o

Over the next few days, Michael reminds me that we can't use our regular year-round pots, plates, or cooking utensils. Everything in our kitchen has to be brand new, or koshered, or used exclusively for Passover. Koshering entails immersing every single item (all flatware, spatulas, can openers, ladles) into a pot of boiling water with a stone in it.

All the food in our entire apartment (salt, sugar, tomato sauce, mayonnaise) has to be new, unopened, and marked *kosher* for Passover.

I clean the refrigerator, freezer, microwave, sink, and stove, and the day before the holiday, I wear yellow Playtex gloves and scrub the oven. Soap bubbles foam. When I turn to face Michael, oven grime drips down my arms. "This holiday is supposed to be about the Jews getting out of Egypt, escaping slavery," I say.

"Your point?" he says, standing over me.

"Slavery can't be worse than this."

EZ Off fumes swirl in the air. I open a window. "It's messed up, don't you think? We're supposed to relive our bondage year after year, but would an ex-con go back to jail to remind himself how lucky he was to be free?"

"It's halacha, Casey. We're doing the rice next."

Ashkenazic Jews don't eat rice on Passover, but Sephardic Jews do. The only stipulation is we have to *check* for specks of wheat. That means going through each bag three times—grain by grain. We spread what must be thousands of grains across our black marble dining room table.

"I'm crazy for loving you," I say.

"You'd be crazy not to." Michael smiles. He brushes a pile of *clean* rice to the side. "You know most men don't get involved in this."

"You're so ahead of your time."

Michael plucks a kernel of wheat from his pile. "Aha! See?" He holds it high between two fingers, a needle in a haystack.

o o o

The night before the holiday, we search our apartment for chametz, a Passover ritual. Michael breaks pita bread into ten pieces and wraps each piece in tin foil in order not to leave crumbs behind. I hide the tin foil balls around our apartment. Michael lights a candle, and in the dark, he searches for the bits of bread, looking in the oven, under the dishwasher, and in between couch cushions.

I follow him around our apartment. "This is like a *not* fun Easter egg hunt. Come on, Michael, you have to admit it. Colorful Easter eggs are better. Why's everything we do so drab?"

o o o

A Seder in New York is nothing like a Seder in New Orleans. As I help my mother-in-law set the table, I remember a Passover at Aunt Susie's house before all the trouble with Big Sam.

Grandma Rose and Grandpa David had flown in from New York for it. Aunt Susie was known to host the best parties, fussing over every detail from gorgeous female bartenders, to live jazz, to catered shrimp cocktail and chicken à la king. According to her, the key to a successful party was to set the mood, beginning with custom-made invitations. On the outside, a hand-drawn Moses was depicted begging Pharaoh, "Let My People Go . . ." And on the inside under a drawing of people drinking and dancing, it read, ". . . to Susie and Bobby's Seder." Aunt Susie's brick patio was dotted with terra-cotta pots full of red begonias. There was the velvety taste of potatoes au gratin and the crunch of her fried chicken. After, upstairs in Big Sam's room, the sound of David Bowie, "Changes."

I miss Tracey and the rhythm of New Orleans. Taking a deep breath, I bring myself back to reality and continue placing a single hard-boiled egg on each plate.

Our New York Seder consists of a two-hour reading of the Haggadah, which is a prayer book detailing the story of the Exodus. Michael's entire family sits around the dining room table, taking turns reading sections, alternating between Hebrew and English, reenacting our escape from slavery. The table is set with the customary Seder plate in the middle. Bottles of wine stud the white cloth. At ten o'clock, when Michael reads *Why is this night different than all other nights*, I want to say because usually we get to eat.

Since we aren't allowed to drive a car on the holiday, for two days we live with Michael's family. Michael talks endlessly about how much he misses Brooklyn and how he wants to move back, which freaks me out because, to me, Brooklyn is out of the question. It's a monochromatic canvas: brown brick houses, brown bare trees, brown dirty air. Manhattan is where the color is.

Michael keeps saying how important it is for Syrians to stick together, but by the time the holiday ends, feeling trapped, I can't wait to get to the city. The Brooklyn Battery Tunnel might as well be the Red Sea, and when we emerge on the other side in the New York night, I turn on the radio and sing out loud to Michael Jackson's "Thriller," dancing in my seat.

o o o

For thirty-three days after Passover, during a period known as the Omer, no Syrian will host a party, get a haircut, or shave. But after the Omer ends, an invitation is hand-delivered to our apartment. It is a leather-bound book—a pop-up. Elephants, giraffes, dinosaurs, bears, wolves, and snakes spring up across the sparkly page. In the center, there is a whale, and right below the whale is a picture of the bride and groom to be, hand in hand. Michael's first cousin Ruthie is having her engagement party at the Museum of Natural History. Wilder's in charge.

"Now, that's a happening," my mother says when I tell her about it.

Even though my wedding was considered top-notch, it didn't compare to the excessive affairs that came after. At first, I didn't feel comfortable with such opulence. Growing up in New Orleans, Aunt Susie's parties were as extravagant as it got. Gatherings during Mardi Gras and Jazz Fest might have nothing more than a keg. And at hurricane parties, for those who chose to ride out a storm instead of evacuating, nothing more was required than some high-speed wind, a power outage, and a couple batches of hurricanes—a mix of rum, vodka, amaretto, and triple sec—served in a tall glass shaped like a naked lady.

But things have changed, and I no longer watch *All in the Family* and *Good Times*. I now prefer *Dynasty* and *Dallas*. Attending black-tie affairs at Radio City Music Hall and Rockefeller Center seems kind of cool.

○ ○ ○

We take a cab to the Museum of Natural History. Michael wears a tuxedo, and I wear a black strapless gown. In the main entrance, there is a pianist, and waiters pass champagne on silver trays.

"Oh, man. That's really funny," I say, pointing to the information desk, which has been transformed into a bar.

After cocktails, we're directed into a corridor lined with violinists leading to the Hall of Ocean Life, the party room. Suspended from the ceiling, centered over the dance floor, is a hundred-foot blue whale. Wilder custom ordered water-blue banquettes, adorned with gold starfish-shaped throw pillows. Along the back wall, a DJ plays on a platform textured and colorful as a coral reef.

"This is incredible," I say, looking up at the whale.

Colette pushes her way through the crowd. "Where have you guys been?"

Over the last few months, we have spent a lot more time with Colette and Eric, and as much as I resisted, I've gotten used to her. We aren't best friends or anything, but I'm not threatened by her anymore. She has her man; she doesn't need mine. Plus, with Rochelle being pregnant and throwing up all the time, we've been hanging out just the four of us.

Eric heads to the bar. "Let's get drinks."

"You look great," I say to Colette. "I love your dress."

"Thanks," she says, twirling and showing it off. "It's new."

Michael hands me a drink and I take a sip. "What'd you do today?" I ask Colette.

"What do you think I did? Hair, makeup, nails. You?"

"Hung out with Michael. Read."

Colette rolls her eyes. "Seriously?"

I know Colette thinks I'm strange, but she likes me too. She has zero patience and wouldn't hang out with me if she didn't.

"*Shoof*," Colette says, leaning in and whispering in my ear. She points to a tall girl wearing a silver lamé gown. "She looks like the Empire State Building."

Colette has super cool style, and if there is such a thing as fashion IQ, she's a genius. She has a lot of rules. Sometimes, Rochelle wears a fitted top with a tight bottom, and according to Colette, that is a big no-no. "One or the other," she says. "Tight top, loose bottom, or oversized top, tight bottom. Skin-tight top and body-hugging bottom is just plain tacky."

Colette sips her cocktail. "And believe me," she says, still staring at the girl dressed in silver, "it's better than what she wore to the wedding at Shaare Zion. Yellow feathers. She looked like Big Bird."

"Yikes. That's kind of harsh," I say, swallowing my drink.

"You agree with me, Casey. And you know it. You just don't want to say it. But saying it doesn't change anything. Whether I say it or not, she still looks like one of the tallest buildings in New York City."

Michael explained to me early on that Colette speaks as if her opinions are facts. He also told me that when she was in school, if she got a sixty-five on a test, her father would hug her and say, "*Aboose Hayat*," my blessed heart. Someone else might have been troubled by the idea that their father didn't believe they could do better, but she wasn't. She took it to mean she was perfect just as she was.

"Enjoy people for what they have to offer," Michael coaches time and again, wanting me to get along with his friends. And I'm learning to do that, so when Colette says a college diploma isn't worth more than the paper it was printed on, I don't argue. And when she says nonchalantly, in regard to life, marriage, and friendship, *No expectations, no disappoint-ments*, I take a deep breath and don't say a thing.

Four vodkas later, Colette and I need to go to the bath-room. Drunk, everything is hazy and getting lost, we pass stuffed wolves, coyotes, and bears. Animal eyes peer at us behind glass.

In the bathroom, Colette stares at herself in the mirror. She runs her hand over her stomach. "Shouldn't have eaten so much broccoli today. I'm bloated."

"Your stomach is flat as a board, Colette."

The bathroom attendant points to an empty stall, and I head toward it. Back at the mirror, I wash my hands and, looking up, meet Colette's reflection. "I didn't know you had green eyes."

"Contacts," she says. "Just got them."

Her dark skin and new tiger-green eyes make her look entirely exotic, a Ban de Soleil model. Plastic combs, hairspray, and Tic Tacs are arranged on a small side table. Colette puts on lipstick and sprays her teased hair. Turning from side to side, she says, "It's fun to be pretty, don't you think?" She smiles and bats her eyelashes.

Aware of the bathroom attendant, I'm embarrassed.

"You know, Casey, now that I'm getting to know you better"—she faces me—"I have to say, I hear you talking to Michael sometimes, and I'm just being honest—you're too smart for your own good."

"What does that mean?"

"You think too much."

"Seriously?"

"College, college, college. You believe that will solve everything." She pops a single Tic Tac in her mouth.

"I haven't mentioned school in a long time."

"You still act like you want to go."

"I've been feeling a little bored lately."

"You never hang out with us," Colette says, not looking at me. She reads the calorie label on the Tic Tac dispenser. "We go for lunch almost every day."

"Colette," I start to explain but then stop. What was I going to tell her? That I want to learn about the world, spread my wings, do my own thing? She wouldn't understand.

"What?" Colette says, sucking on a Tic Tac. "What were you going to say?"

"Nothing. Forget it."

"There's a path, Casey. Just follow it."

New York City, 1985

Michael and I sit on the couch watching MTV. I press a button on the channel changer, muting Robert Palmer's voice midsentence. Four women, all with their hair slicked back, red lipstick and nails, wear skintight Alaia dresses. Their long, model-like legs continue moving in unison. One of them discloses a glistening tongue. Palmer, dead-center, mouths, *Might as well face it. You're addicted to love.*

"You sure about this?" Michael asks.

"Positive." It took some prying, weeks of begging, but Michael is finally ready to reveal his fantasy.

"Okay, you asked for it." He turns to face me. "You. Vacuuming. Naked. In high heels. Very high heels."

"What? You have a vacuum in your fantasy?"

"I do."

"And it's me? I'm the one vacuuming?"

"It's you."

"I don't get it."

"It's my fantasy, Casey. You don't have to get it."

But I want to get it, so I go to my bedroom, close the door, and call Tracey. She's a second-semester junior and has already dated almost every guy in the state of Colorado. Tracey doesn't understand marriage but she understands men.

"He's right," Tracey says after I tell her Michael's fantasy. "You've got to keep things fresh."

"So, you think that's normal?"

"I didn't say that. But let's face it—sex with the same person, day in and day out, can go from hot to boring faster than Michael's Porsche can go from zero to sixty."

"I hate when you talk like that. It makes me nervous."

"Okay, so don't vacuum naked; at least wear sexy lingerie."

"Michael likes lingerie."

"Of course he likes lingerie. All men like lingerie."

"Some prefer tee shirts," I say, less like a statement, more like a question, or wish.

I hold the phone with my chin against my shoulder, open my nightstand drawer, and take out my NYU bulletin. I fish out a bottle of nail polish, bluish-black, and resting my foot on the brochure, labor over my toes.

"That's what men who are married to women who wear tee shirts say. It's not true. All men prefer lingerie."

"Where do you get your philosophies? Truisms according to Tracey: All men like lingerie. All men cheat."

"I know what I know," Tracey says. "I'll never get married."

My mother thinks that Aunt Susie has allowed Tracey too much freedom and that having too many choices is not always a good thing.

"I mean, really," Tracey says. "Why would I get married? Show me one happy couple."

"I'm happy."

Tracey is silent.

"So, you think I should wear lingerie?"

"I do."

"Those slutty outfits make me feel like Chris Owens."

"Chris Owens? The Bourbon Street stripper?"

"Yeah, from our childhood. I think we got messed up."

"You *think* we got messed up?"

We both laugh.

"Have I got a story for you," Tracey says. "Did you hear that Mr. Druffin, the guy who lives across the street from my parents, died? Well, my mother told me he wanted to be cremated. He wanted his ashes spread along the levee, so his wife agreed to have a ceremony and sprinkle him around like freak'n fertilizer. Picture this: The wind kicked up, his ashes soared, and his lover, in the middle of the crowd, became hysterical, inconsolable, tears streaming down her face. And you know what she did? She lifted her shirt, showing her boobs, and screamed, 'Here's one for the road, baby.'"

"That's too much," I shriek, accidentally stroking the flesh of my foot with the nail polish brush. I dab at the spot with a tissue, and the color smears; it looks like a bruise. "That's unbelievable," I say. And as if we are in the middle of a game, a game of I Can Top That, I say, "Remember my father's fortieth birthday party? Remember the cake my mother got him? It was in the shape of a naked lady with boobs the size of oranges."

"I remember. That's so disgusting. Anyway, I have to go. A bunch of kids from my Spanish class are getting together for margaritas. We're going to Juan's. Adios." And she hangs up.

o o o

I go back to the living room and find Michael on the couch watching *NBC Nightly News*. The topic: guns in America. A two-year-old fatally shot his mom.

I wince, picturing my father's gun and how I wanted to show it to Tracey and found my parents' X-rated video instead, and how then we played Truth or Dare with Big Sam and Hawkeye to get it back—all of which led to my scar. I see myself holding the gun high over my head at Rochelle's card game. The news segment makes me understand the seriousness of my actions, and I feel uneasy, so when Michael reaches for me during a commercial, I'm happy to be held. Before I know it, we're having sex. Not eyes open, sweet, slow, honeymoon sex. Not raw, wild, late-night, drunken sex. This is different— his eyes are closed, and me, I'm hardly moving in order not to mess up my nail polish. It's getting harder and harder to justify keeping my tee shirt on.

When we are done, I say, "You know what I was thinking . . . ?"

"Shhh," Michael says, staring at the TV. "I want to hear this."

I sit up and jerk my pants back on, never imagining we'd be *that* couple. I want to be like one of those couples who talk late into the night, nonstop, as if they'd never be able to get it all in, as if when time ran out, their biggest regret would be they hadn't shared some obscure emotion, or tiny idea, because in those cases of perfect love, every insight and every moment together matters.

Michael aims the channel changer at the TV and raises the volume. I get up and go to the kitchen, looking for a snack. On the counter, there is a roll of silver electric tape. Michael's parents are out of town for the weekend, and we are finally going to spend Shabbat alone together in the city. I've already planned the menu, and Michael bought the tape for the light in the refrigerator so it wouldn't go on during Shabbat. As if he's joking around, or going through a phase, I still can't believe Michael thinks these religious acts are important, and each and every time he follows a random, new religious law, I get this nagging feeling deep inside that I don't really know him at all.

Hungry, I turn on the stove and shake Jiffy Pop across a blazing flame. The sound of aluminum scraping against the metal burner grates on my nerves, so I stop moving it around, and within seconds, I smell kernels burning. The fire alarm rings and I jump, startled. "Scared the daylights out of me," I scream. The alarm blares, and I don't know how to stop it.

When Michael doesn't say anything, I peek into the living room and find him fast asleep, his head nuzzled on a couch pillow. I stand over him, staring in disbelief. "Are you serious?" I gently nudge him. "Helloooo," I yell over the ringing. He mutters, his words inaudible, and rolls over, adjusting his position, still asleep.

It's a joke between us—his ability to sleep through any-thing—loud television, blasting music, sirens. "A gift from God," he's said.

The alarm rings and rings until the smoke clears.

o   o   o

The following morning, as I leaf through the NYU bulletin on my nightstand, Grandma Rose calls asking if I want to go for lunch. I say yes, but before I get into the shower, I read the course descriptions for Introduction to Psychology, Mythology, and Anthropology. I've taken to doing this. It feels strangely satisfying, immersive, as if I'm actually taking the classes.

At noon, I meet Grandma for lunch at Smith and Wolensky. Grandma is already sitting at a table.

"This worked out perfectly, darling," she says as I bend to kiss her. "Excuse me," she calls to a waiter. "I'd like to order a drink please."

"Sure," the waiter says. "What can I get you?"

"I'd like Stolichnaya vodka. Straight up. In a martini glass."

"Rocks?"

"I said straight up."

"Twist?"

Grandma's red lips pucker. "No."

I stiffen, never knowing what Grandma might say or do.

"Olives?" the waiter asks.

"Nothing else. Just vodka." Grandma places her fist on the

table as if it is a period at the end of her sentence. "People hear what they want to hear," she says when the waiter walks away.

Grandma is a vision of elegance. She wears thin heels, a black leather pencil skirt, and a gold snake bracelet; the eyes are emeralds. "How've you been, darling? I've missed you." After a few sips of vodka, Grandma puts her menu down and asks, "Did I ever tell you about Whitey?"

I nod, and while she nurses her cocktail, she tells me, again, how he was her first love. He was an Ashkenazic Jew and the man she abandoned in order to marry my Syrian grandfather.

"If only these purses could talk," my mother once said. We were in Grandma's closet, seeing what was new—a Thierry Mugler skirt, Calvin Klein leather pants, Charles Jordan pumps. "There's more alligator in here than in the Everglades," my mother said, showing me a purple Dolce and Gabbana clutch.

Throughout their childhood, Aunt Susie and my mother knew Grandma was keeping secrets or, at least, not telling the whole truth, but lately, Grandma has been blurting out bits and pieces of old stories, realities of her heart, that had once been folded away in the pockets of her Yves St. Laurent blazers and hidden beneath extravagant hats from Bonwitt Teller.

Grandma puts her martini glass down on the table. "They say it's just as easy to marry a rich man as a poor man. Maybe not. Let me tell you something." She seems unable to keep it all contained any longer.

"One day, your grandfather came home with a new car. His brother lived next door. We all wanted to go for a ride. Your grandfather told me to get in the back, and he put his brother in the front next to him. 'I'm not a second-class citizen,' I said, but I sat in the back and burned. And you know what I was thinking as we drove around the neighborhood waving to people we knew? I thought Whitey would never put me in the back. Never." She picks up her martini glass and holds it close to her lips. "It would've been a different life. A completely different life."

Grandma takes a deep breath and a sip of her drink. "Look what I just got on Madison Avenue." She reaches for her shopping bag, unwraps tissue paper, and shows me a black needlepoint pillow. Stitched in shocking pink letters are the words *Good girls go to heaven, bad girls go everywhere.* Grandma is proud of the ways in which she's rebelled against community life, and she holds her pillow up as if she's a first-place winner and this is her prize.

o   o   o

After lunch, I hail a cab. *A completely different life,* Grandma said, and I can't stop thinking about that. I too made a choice and could have been doing shots at a frat party—my biggest worry an upcoming psychology exam. Instead, I'm married and reading *The Road Less Traveled.*

Alone at home, I find paper and a pencil, and for the first time in a long time, I begin to sketch. I'm hesitant and uncertain; it's been too long. But as my hand moves around the page, I grow more confident, and the quality of my lines gets bolder. I remember the Butterfly in Audubon Park, and drawing with Morgan, and how I loved being around him. I wonder where he is and if he's doing okay.

The light off the East River shines through my dining room window and across the page. My drawing starts out random, haphazard even, but morphs into a comic strip. In the first frame, there is a stick figure of me. I'm reaching for allspice on a grocery store shelf. The frame next to it is Tracey, reaching for a book on a college library shelf. There is me lugging groceries into my apartment, and by its side, Tracey is carrying textbooks into her dorm room. The bottom frames show us both side by side, thought bubbles coming from our heads. Mine reads, *What should I make for dinner?* And Tracey's says, *In which European city should I study?* The drawings are childlike but pertinent, profound in a way that surprises me. Amused, I put the paper where Michael will never find it—wedged in between *Gone with the Wind* and *The Sun Also Rises* on my bookshelf.

New York City, 1985

I start sleeping later and later. By the time I get up most mornings, Michael has already showered, dressed, and prayed. I usually find him sitting at the dining room table reading *The New York Times*. Michael doesn't ease into the day as I do. He starts out ready to pounce. Or at least, debate.

"The Holocaust could happen again," he says, lowering the newspaper. He folds it, places it on the table next to his plate, and bites into a poppy seed bagel.

"Good morning," I say.

"Morning," he says.

I reach for the pot of coffee in the kitchen.

"Really," Michael continues. "It could happen again."

"Not in this country." I join him at the table and drink coffee.

"Casey, Casey, you're so naïve," he says.

"This is the United States of America, Michael."

He looks at me with wide-open, anxious eyes. "That's what the Jews in Germany thought. So they assimilated and lived like everyone else. They didn't protect themselves. They were in complete denial and didn't see what was right in front of their faces."

"You can't believe the Jews were at fault, Michael."

"Well, let's just say we need to learn from their mistakes." He lifts the newspaper. "They needed to be Jews first, Germans second. And they forgot that."

Michael believes that if he lives a certain way, follows certain rules, he can control things like holocausts and his mother's recovery. And I don't want to argue, so I change the subject. "Want to go to the movies tonight?"

"Sure," Michael says.

"Great."

"Why don't you call and see if Colette and Eric want to go."

I like our friends well enough, but I'm not in the mood. "I'd rather not."

"Okay," he says. But I can tell he's disappointed.

"What do you want to see?" he asks.

"*Terms of Endearment*?"

"You're kidding, right?"

"No. Why? What do you want to see?"

"*Scarface*."

And he leaves for work.

o   o   o

I strip off my Madonna tee shirt and boxer shorts, dropping them on the floor in the bathroom. I hold my stomach, inspecting my scar, which I don't stop to notice often anymore. Ignoring it is easier. Paying attention to it brings up too much discomfort. Not just the memory of the physical agony, the searing wire hanger on my flesh, but all the events that followed. Eight years have gone by since the day we played Truth or Dare, and yet in some ways, it feels fresh, as if no time has passed at all.

I shower and head to the grocery store for capers and lemons, ingredients I need for a chicken piccata dinner. On Second Avenue, I see a homeless man, sitting slumped against a brick wall. I've seen him around our neighborhood before. He's wearing a black knit cap and a green sweatshirt. He holds a cardboard sign that says, I HAVE A DREAM.

I walk past him, Michael's words in my head. *He could buy alcohol with the money you give him, and you wouldn't be doing him, or anyone, a favor.*

I saunter through the automatic doors at the grocery and put four lemons and a jar of capers in my cart. There is a floral section, and I admire carnations and roses and lilies and greens in large buckets. White orchids in terra-cotta pots crowd a shelf. I turn to a man working nearby. He's cutting the stems of roses with a sharp knife, and he wears a white lab coat with embroidery on his chest, Bruce.

"Is this orchid okay?" I ask him, choosing a plant whose petals are wilting.

"Yeah, should be okay," he says.

I step in closer, wanting Bruce to take a better look. "You sure?"

"Needs water," Bruce says. "Not much, just a little. But you can pick a different one if you want."

Orthodox Jews don't celebrate Halloween, but in New Orleans, the Halloween I was six, my father took me to buy a pumpkin. I selected a plump, perfectly round one from a heap.

"What about this one?" my father said, pointing to a misshapen pumpkin, discarded on the side.

"That one's ugly," I said, holding the beautiful one close to my chest.

My father stood over the ugly one. "Nobody's going to choose it. It's going to be abandoned here."

Having empathy for the pumpkin, we bought it and gave that orphaned, ugly pumpkin a home. It sat on our kitchen table all through Thanksgiving, Chanukah, and Christmas.

"I'll take this one," I say to Bruce. And I carry the struggling orchid to the register.

o   o   o

Outside, the homeless man catches my attention again. Michael's warnings echo. He told me how he once gave an unemployed man on the street his business card, inviting him to report for work the next day. When the man didn't show up, Michael determined that the homeless, all of them, can help themselves but choose not to.

I disagree. I have a sense about the man in front of me, his eyes warm brown. Pushing away Michael's cautions that this man could be a fraud or dangerous, I follow my gut and put a dollar in his coffee cup.

"Thank you, darling. That makes a difference," he says, looking up at me. The whites of his eyes gleam bright against his black skin.

"You're welcome," I answer, allowing myself to wonder for a moment, but only for one painful moment, where he sleeps and showers.

o   o   o

At home, I water my orchid plant and place it near the dining room window in the sun. Billy Joel plays on the stereo, and in the kitchen, I squeeze fresh lemons, preparing for dinner.

I can't concentrate. I keep thinking of the homeless man, alone, against the wall. Changing my plans, I mash tuna fish with a fork and plunk in a tablespoon of mayonnaise, a dash of dill, and fresh lemon. On toasted rye, I add lettuce and tomato and cut the sandwich into triangles, just how Nellie used to.

o   o   o

Back on Second Avenue, I hand the homeless man his sandwich. He smiles, his mouth a dark cave. "Thank you," he says.

"You're welcome. What's your name?" I ask him.

"Carl," he says, unwrapping tin foil. "Boy oh boy. You can cook," he says, chewing.

"Well, that's not exactly cooking."

"It tastes like cooking to me." He closes his eyes and swallows. "What's your name?"

"Casey."

"Casey, what are you doing here? How come you're not in school?"

"I graduated."

"Ahhh, so you're a college student."

"No, I'm not."

"You work?"

"No."

"Well, if you don't mind me asking, what do you do?"

In the Syrian community it is perfectly normal to be married at my age, expected even, but outside in the real world, people react as if I have four heads. I hesitate before answering. "I'm married."

"You're what? You're just a kid."

"I am not. I've been married a while already."

"Well, you look like a kid to me. How old are you?"

"Twenty."

"Twenty." He shakes his head. "Ewww. Somebody robbed the cradle."

I don't say anything.

"I didn't mean to insult you." Carl chuckles. "I'd do anything to be your age again." He holds a slice of tomato above his head and just stares at it, red and full as an evening sun. He lets it dangle and glisten in the air before eating it.

"Carl, how'd this happen? How'd you get here?"

"I lost my job and couldn't get another," Carl says. "Things got out of control quickly. Couldn't pay my bills. Lost everything."

My heart breaks.

"Hey, don't you go feeling sorry for me," he says. "You know what Abraham Lincoln says. He says, *Folks are just as happy as they make up their minds to be.*"

Carl takes the last bite of his sandwich and crushes the empty tin foil into a ball. "It happens. It can happen. People who are highly intelligent can be homeless."

o   o   o

I suppose in an attempt to please me, Michael calls around noon to say he wants to take me out for dinner, go on a date, just the two of us. He books Picalo Mondo. Eight o'clock reservation. Waiting for him to show up at the restaurant, I slosh wine around in my glass.

At a quarter to nine he rushes in and kisses my cheek. "Sorry I'm a little late."

"A little late? You're forty-five minutes late."

He looks at his wrist. "Well, you get a fifteen-minute window," he says, tapping the face of his watch with a finger. "Counting from eight fifteen, I'm technically thirty minutes late." He relays this logic with sincerity, as if this is fact and not arguable, as if he is not really late at all. "Anyway, here. I bought you something." He hands me a white box wrapped with a gold bow. Inside is a neon pink Versace miniskirt.

"Thanks," I say, even though I don't wear flashy, expensive clothes. Michael is well aware of my preferences, but I've been noticing lately that little by little, he's trying to change me—what I want, what I believe, what I wear.

Back at home, sex is equally fraught. He lifts my tee shirt up. I pull it down. We are always struggling for position.

o   o   o

The following morning, all I can think about is what I'm going to make Carl for lunch. After Michael leaves for work, I go buy ingredients. I stock up on Tupperware, plastic cutlery, paper napkins, and brown paper bags. Not wanting Michael to question me about Carl and what I'm doing, I hide the inventory under our bed.

I sauté garlic, Portobello mushrooms, and baby spinach in extra virgin olive oil and boil linguini. I pack up the pasta and find Carl one block south of the grocery store. "You changed spots."

"I go where the sun goes," Carl says, squinting and looking up at me. The grooves in his forehead are deep and squiggly, a maze full of lots of dead ends.

I hand him the bag and he opens it. "This world," he says, peeking inside, "the people in this world never cease to amaze me."

I wonder how he can remain so upbeat. People walk by like he isn't even there, as if he's invisible. "Carl, can I sit next to you?"

"Of course you can, darling."

I sit down in a stream of sunshine, right next to Carl, not even considering that someone might recognize me. The ray of sunlight is like a superhero's ray gun, making me invisible too.

o o o

Over the next few days, I make Carl chicken with potatoes, stir-fried vegetables with brown rice, and spaghetti Bolognese. And every afternoon, I sit with him while he eats.

"Don't you have better things to do?" Carl asks, twirling spaghetti around a plastic fork.

"Not really," I say. The wind blows and I zip up my jacket. "It's getting cold, Carl. Will you go to a shelter?"

"Never. Those places aren't safe," he says, peeling the orange I packed for him. "I prefer the streets."

The fruit's rind snakes across the sidewalk, and Carl gets

real serious. "These politicians, they talk about the American dream. What does that even mean?" Carl sighs as he leans back against the brick. "They call us street people. They say we're here by choice. Isn't that ridiculous? I want to work. I'm smart. And I know this guy on the streets who's a poet. I mean, a real poet."

He puts his face close to mine, closer than he's ever been before, his white mustache and beard a halo of hope around his mouth, and I am taken aback, but I don't budge. Carl's eyes get watery. "I don't need all that much. I don't need a living room; I don't need a big old house in the suburbs. I need twenty by twenty, that's all. A kitchenette, a commode, a shower. A bit of land in the back where I can grow some crops, feed myself. Make my own sandwich."

o   o   o

The bathroom in our apartment is tiny, and Michael and I can't both be in it at the same time. Invariably, while I wash my face or brush my teeth, Michael comes in anyway and reaches over me, opening the medicine cabinet or getting something from a drawer.

"Can't you wait until I'm done?"

Shirtless, he grabs a bottle of Scope, marked *Casey*, from the counter. He takes a swig.

"Hey, this is yours," I say, showing him the bottle that says *Michael*.

"You're ridiculous," he says. "You kiss me, don't you? What's the difference?"

"It's called hygiene."

"Your germs are my germs," he says, giving me a quick kiss before he walks away.

Standing before the mirror, I take a deep breath and pull the cap off my roll-on deodorant. A black curly hair lies across the top. "Michael," I call to him in the bedroom, "you used my deodorant."

"So?" he calls back.

"It's for women."

"I'm trying to get in touch with my feminine side." He laughs.

Lifting my toothbrush, I see it's wet. I march into our bedroom, waving it at him. "This has gone too far."

"It was dark. I couldn't see."

"Come on, Michael."

"We're one," he says, ignoring any line between us, preferring us melded—synchronized as an Olympic ice-skating duo.

"Yeah, okay, we're like one," I say, softening. I wash my toothbrush with soap and head to the kitchen. I open the refrigerator and splash milk in my coffee, stir with a spoon, and watch the milk disappear.

Michael leafs through mail on the counter. "What's this?" he asks, holding a manila envelope addressed to me.

"That's mine," I say, reaching for it.

He pulls it back.

I step toward him. "How many times do I have to ask you not to open my mail?"

He lifts the envelope high above his head, a game of Monkey in the Middle. "What's the big secret?"

"It's not about secrets." I jump for the envelope. "It's about privacy."

He turns his back to me, rips the envelope open, and pulls out an NYU application. "I have a right to know what my wife's been up to," he says, staring at it.

"I just wanted to see what it looked like. I didn't apply."

"That's not the point. You did it without consulting me. This is our decision."

"*Our* decision? I don't think so," I say, sticking up for myself. "It's *my* decision."

"Oh, excuse me. I didn't realize you were so independent. You want to be on your own? Be my guest."

Michael grabs his coat and leaves our apartment, slamming the door behind him. He doesn't call all day, and when I call him at work, he has all the salespeople at his store say he's busy. At four in the afternoon, I'm furious, at seven, frantic, but by the time he strolls in, drunk, at midnight, I'm mostly grateful.

o o o

In the morning, we don't talk about what happened. Michael gets out of bed, eyes the application in the garbage can, and I imagine because he's satisfied, heads to the kitchen without saying a word.

I sit at the dining room table and sip coffee. Michael points to my orchid plant on the windowsill. "That thing's dead."

I put my mug down and carry the orchid to the kitchen sink. "Bruce said it'll be okay if I take care of it."

"Who's Bruce?"

"A guy at the grocery store."

Michael shakes his head. "Bruce is wrong."

I water it anyway.

o o o

When Michael goes to work, I lift my NYU application from the garbage can. I iron it flat with my hand and sandwich it between *The World According to Garp* and *The Thorn Birds* on my bookshelf.

New York City, 1985

I'm lying on the couch reading *Lolita*, waiting for Michael to come home from work, when the phone rings.

I reach for it. "Hello," I say, putting the book down.

There's no answer.

"Hello," I say again, leafing through *Lolita*, trying to find my place. It's hard getting back into the story. I'm still not a great reader, but I'm determined to read the classics so that when Tracey refers to Jo from *Little Women* or Humbert Humbert from *Lolita*, I know what she's talking about. I've started reading with a pencil in my hand, circling words I'm not familiar with, then looking them up in the dictionary.

"And you're learning all this vocabulary. Why?" Tracey asks. "No one around you cares."

But I keep at it.

The phone rings a second time, and when I answer, there is silence. Just as I hang up, Michael knocks. A pair of my jeans, a sweater, and some socks are on the floor, and I kick them out of the way and across the carpet before opening the door.

"You're late," I say, and turn and walk away.

"I know," Michael says, tossing *Time* magazine onto the coffee table.

"Why didn't you call?"

"Sorry," he says.

"But you keep doing this."

"I know."

"You really have to call when you're going to be late."

"I heard you, Casey. I'll call."

In the kitchen, I heat up our dinner—meatballs and spaghetti. The phone rings a third time, and Michael picks up in the living room. He sounds nervous, speaking in one-word answers. "Yes. Okay. Uh-huh." It sounds like code. He holds the phone close to his ear, and while his appearance is unrecognizable, a version of Michael I've never seen, the scene—my mother suspicious of my father—is eerily familiar.

My mind floods with thoughts of long ago, coming home from Aunt Susie's house after a holiday dinner. I sat in the back seat of our car while my parents fought about the bartender at the party—a woman with eyelashes black and graceful as the legs of a spider—who'd served me a Coke. My father had commented on her low-cut blouse and my mother overheard. When she confronted him, my father said he didn't appreciate being interrogated and, furious, hit the steering wheel, smacking it with the flat of his hands, before he slammed the car door shut and walked away.

"I'm not stupid," my mother called after him.

With my forehead glued to the car window, tears streamed down my face as I watched my father get smaller and smaller. "I didn't do anything wrong," he yelled back, disappearing into the night. That darkness has haunted me, resided in my heart.

I join Michael at our black marble dining room table. He drapes a white paper napkin over his lap.

"Who was that on the phone?" I ask, trying to act cool.

"Nobody," Michael says, cutting a meatball in half.

I take a deep breath. "*Nobody* called?"

"Wrong number." He twirls spaghetti around his fork just like Carl did earlier that morning.

I pour us each a glass of wine, as if we are simply two adults having dinner, even though at twenty, I'm still below the drinking age. "Why were you talking to someone who dialed the wrong number?"

"Why so many questions?"

The marble is cold and hard beneath my elbows. "Curiosity."

"Can't we just eat?"

"Michael"—I reach for my glass of wine—"who was on the phone?"

He slams his hand on the table, and I jump. "Stop grilling me, Casey. I told you I don't know."

"I don't believe you," I say.

He stands up to leave, triggering something old and tired and ancient in me—an abandonment, disillusionment cocktail— and I grab hold of his arm. "Where are you going?"

"Casey, if you don't stop this," he threatens.

"What? What are you going to do?"

"I'm going to throw this." His hands are on his plate.

I know better than to dare him. "Throw it," I say.

And he does. The white ceramic cracks, and spaghetti dangles from the edges of our table.

My heartbeat quickens.

o o o

When Michael falls asleep, I check his pockets, not sure what I'm looking for. Clues, I guess: matches, receipts, gum. I open and close closets and drawers. There is nothing. As I snoop to uncover what I can about my husband, he sleeps soundly.

From what I can put together, there are two kinds of couples: cold and hot. Cold couples withdraw. They stew. They don't raise their voices. Hot couples fight. They yell and throw things. Every time I try to talk to Michael about our relationship, our differences, or anything of importance, the vein in his forehead bulges. "Oh, I see," he rages, "you wanna go a few rounds?" And like boxers in a ring, we are at it again.

o   o   o

After the spaghetti incident, feeling bad for overreacting, Michael buys me flowers every night for a week. He cuts each stem, one by one, and puts the flowers in water, adding plant food before I can decide which vase to use. Yellow tulips by my bedside. Red roses on the coffee table. White lilies at the entrance door.

"You can't buy me with flowers," I say, *night seven.*

"I'm not trying to," he says, unwrapping a new bunch and placing more red roses and pink lilies on the kitchen counter.

"Looks like you're trying to."

"I said I was sorry, didn't I?" Facing me, he cups my shoulders. "Let's go away. Italy. You and me. Pasta. Amore. Fun."

"Italy? You want to fly to Italy?"

"Sure, why not?"

"Tell me who you were talking to on the phone."

"Really? You want to go back there again? I told you it was a wrong number." And then, bottom lining me, he says, "You want to go to Italy or not?"

I don't know what a married person is supposed to do when something in their relationship isn't right. You can't just break up. I want so badly for everything to be good again. Couples not only have temperature; they have shape, and because I love Michael, or think I do, I need to figure out ours.

"It'll be great," he says, handing me a red rose.

I picture us, before we married, sitting in a booth in the back of some fancy Italian restaurant. We couldn't keep our hands off each other. We kissed, our lips playful, our eyes wide open and gleaming with desire. I wasn't one to kiss in public, but the attraction was beyond my control, and we couldn't stop, attached like waves in the ocean, joined like one vast beautiful body.

Allowing myself to get seduced, I imagine being in Italy twirling homemade pasta around my fork, viewing Michelangelo's *David*, hearing the tantalizing sound of a foreign language.

"Are you serious?" I ask, wanting what he is offering—romance, love, adventure.

"Dead serious."

I step in, and immediately he inches back.

"I just have to check what's happening at work," he says.

It's subtle, but I'm getting good at recognizing the space between us. "So, we might not go?"

"I said I have to check."

"Oh," I say, flatly.

"You act like I don't *want* to go. You know Casey, it's not about *desire*. It's about reality. I," he says, "have a job. Bills to pay. Responsibilities."

And just like that, our tender moment turns sour. Lectured and belittled, I'm always stepping on these land mines. But then as if nothing troublesome has transpired between us, Michael lifts a pink lily from the kitchen counter. "Amazing, don't you think? Like a jewel."

Through most of dinner that night, we sit quiet. But halfway through, Michael breaks the silence. "Okay, I can't hold it in anymore. I have to say it."

"Say what?" I take a bite of lentils with rice, *mujedrah*.

"No, nothing. Forget it."

"Tell me," I say, craving connection.

Michael points to my orchid plant on the windowsill. "I'm sorry to inform you, but unlike all our fresh flowers, *that* is dead."

"It's mine. Don't worry about it."

"So, you're just going to leave it there, dying?"

"It's not dying."

"You're right, it's dead. Might as well say Kaddish for that thing."

"Well, I like it." I stand and carry my empty plate to the sink.

o o o

I wait for Michael to fall asleep, and then I call Tracey using the living room phone. "We fight so much," I say. It takes me a minute to gather my courage before I tell her about the mysterious phone calls.

"Syrian men feel entitled," Tracey says. "They don't see anything wrong with cheating."

"Do you think Michael's cheating on me?"

"Don't take it personally, Casey. It's part of the culture."

"Not my culture," I say, feeling yet again like I am living in a foreign land, a place I don't belong.

"Michael loves you, he does, but Syrian men are a different breed."

o o o

After we hang up, I get ready for bed. I'm not careful—I know no matter how much noise I make, or how high I lift the comforter before climbing into bed next to Michael, he won't wake up. Lying in bed, resentments accumulate and build like dust. Stuck, I don't know how to get unstuck. The thought of losing Michael, or leaving him, makes my stomach churn, and it feels like without his love, I'll die—I don't have many friends, I've given up on going to college, I've given up on myself.

Moving closer to Michael, I feel the warmth of his body. I close my eyes and fall asleep.

o o o

In the morning, I get up and fill a Maxwell House coffee can with water and arrange the flowers Michael gave me inside. I parade down Second Avenue, the water sloshing, and hand it to Carl. "Here," I say, "these are for you."

"Thanks," he says, placing them on the sidewalk next to him.

"I'm going to follow Michael," I tell Carl.

He strokes his beard, which has grown considerably over the last few weeks. "You should," he says. "Why not?"

I hand Carl a Tupperware of cubed honeydew and sit next to him. The cement sidewalk is cold. He tells me about these kids who keep taking his stuff: his pillow, his book, his hat. Just yesterday, they taunted him and threw his belongings back and forth over his head, calling to each other, "Go out for a pass." Messing with him, they took his food too: a hot dog, a pack of Starburst, a Coke. Carl tells me he urinated in an empty bottle of Gatorade, knowing the boys would steal it.

"Carl, they could hurt you. They could have a knife or a gun."

I think of my father's gun, still on the top shelf of his Brooklyn closet, and its easy access.

"I can manage the streets," Carl says, unflustered. "Don't you worry about me."

Next to what Carl has to deal with, my marriage problems seem so stupid.

○ ○ ○

Around lunchtime, I linger outside Michael's store, spying like an undercover cop on television. In a beige overcoat, I look more like Colombo than one of Charlie's Angels. When I see Michael, I duck behind a parked car and watch him march down Fifth Avenue. I follow him as he walks past Tiffany's, Saks, and the New York Public Library. When he enters Republic National Bank, I hide behind scaffolding. Ten minutes later, he circles through the revolving door and steps outside into the sunshine. He folds an envelope and slips it into his pocket.

That night, in our bedroom, I take the envelope from his pants pocket and see a check made out to Betty Betesh for $2,000. It's difficult to catch my breath. I've heard rumors about Syrian men who support second families. I find Michael making hot cocoa in the kitchen, and I smack the check down on the counter.

"Why are you going through my things?" Michael says, looking at it.

"I was cleaning up," I say, a hand on my hip.

Michael pours boiling water into a mug. "She's a widow. She has five kids."

"So?" I say, not understanding.

"A group of guys are paying her mortgage so she doesn't lose her house." He stirs, and the spoon clinks against the ceramic.

"Do we have that kind of money?"

"It's the right thing to do." And with mug in hand, he heads for the couch.

"Why didn't you tell me?" I ask, following him.

"To protect Betty, her dignity. And if you really want to know the truth," he says, as if he isn't delivering a brutal blow, "it's none of your business."

o   o   o

It turns out there are other things that are none of my business. One night in bed, I learn that a Syrian man would never tell his wife about another Syrian man's philandering. It's a guy thing, their moral code.

"So, the alliance, the bond," I question when Michael admits he would never tell me if Rick or Eric were unfaithful, "is between you and the guy, not between you and your wife?"

"I didn't say that."

"It's exactly what you said."

"It's *lashon hara*, Casey. A big sin. Saying anything about somebody else, even a good thing, is not advised because someone could disagree, and it would be your fault for bringing it up."

"How boring." I roll over, moving to my side of the bed.

o o o

Carl's beard grows out of control. White curls cascade from his chin. The hair is matted, a developing web. I take a mental note to buy him a comb. Maybe some toothpaste and deodorant too. Handing him a tin of broiled chicken, I sit down next to him.

"Michael's still insisting the phone call was a wrong number," I say. "I followed him yesterday."

"And?"

"And nothing."

Carl lifts up the wishbone. "You need friends, Casey. Where are your friends?"

I grip one end of the chicken bone, and he holds the other. *Ready, set, go.*

"Looks like your wish is going to come true," I say to Carl.

o o o

Michael won't carry a key. Usually, I don't mind opening the door for him, but he is late again and I'm angry, so when he knocks on the door, I stroll to our bathroom, run the shower, and sit on our bed. I listen as Michael knocks softly at first, and then he bangs. He rings the bell. And then he rings it again. And again. After a while, I take my clothes off and wrap a towel around my body. I shut off the shower water and make my way to the door with a second towel on my head.

"What took you so long?"

"I was in the shower."

"You know what time I get home."

"I actually don't."

Michael rolls his eyes and walks past me. He grabs a beer from the refrigerator. "What's with all the eggs?" he asks, twisting off the cap.

"They were on sale," I say, coming up behind him. I shut the refrigerator door so fast it's lucky his hand isn't still inside it. The lie, like so many others, rolls off my tongue. The eggs weren't on sale. I promised Carl *ejje* and *spanek b'jiben*. Both recipes call for a lot of eggs.

"You bought eggs on sale? Ha! Good for you. Your grandfather would be proud." Michael relaxes on the couch, his legs propped on the coffee table. He turns on the television and drinks his beer.

"I'm going to change," I say, heading to our bedroom. "Then I'll set the table."

o o o

During a commercial, Michael places his empty beer bottle down on the coffee table and stands. "I'm going to wash up before dinner."

"Okay. It's almost ready."

As Michael walks toward our room, he points at the window and says, "That orchid has seen better days."

I take a deep breath and, even though I feel his comment viscerally, ignore him.

He shouts to me from our room. "Hey, Casey, have you seen my Rolling Stones sweatshirt?"

I enter our bedroom and see him rummaging through his drawers.

"No, I haven't seen it," I say. But it's not true. I gave it to Carl, along with vegetable lasagna. I turn and head back to the kitchen, fast.

"Hey," he says, over his bare shoulder, "you didn't make the bed again."

"Oh, yeah, sorry," I say. "I'll do it now."

"That's sort of beside the point, Casey. I don't think it's too much to ask. I don't want to come home and see it like this."

o o o

After dinner, I change into a tee shirt and pull back the comforter on our made bed. "Meaningless work," I mumble.

"What?"

"It's pointless," I say, slipping under the covers. "I make the bed, just to mess it up again."

"I disagree. I think it matters."

We are face-to-face, our heads on our pillows, and I'm tired. I'm tired of fighting and feeling so alone. Not wanting to argue, I curl up close to Michael. He puts his arm around me, and we lie there for a moment in quiet harmony.

"That bookcase isn't going to make it," Michael says, breaking the silence.

I built the unit when we first moved in, and I didn't read the directions. Something went wrong and Michael's right; the shelving isn't sturdy.

He points to *War and Peace* on the top shelf. "There's too much weight. And you keep adding more books. It's going to collapse."

I get out of bed and place the 1,225-page novel on my nightstand.

"Oh, that ought to fix things."

"I'm not trying to fix things," I say, turning from him. I lift my sketch book and a can of pencils from the shelf. Sitting against the headboard, I raise my knees, creating an easel, and rest the pad against my legs. With my hand already in motion, I say, "I'm going to draw."

Michael falls asleep, and as I doodle, I recall how not all that long ago, Michael brought home a wok from Macy's. I stir-fried snow peas and broccoli in soy sauce and drizzled in some sesame oil. Kissing me hard, Michael pressed me against the kitchen cabinets, the sizzling vegetables music to our ears. When he dabbed soy sauce on my nose with a finger, I brushed his cheek with a stalk of hot, wet broccoli. He let the brown liquid drip like sepia down his unshaven face, before reaching into the wok and gathering a handful of vegetables. He threw them at me, and snow peas clung like barrettes in my hair. We wrestled, pushing against each other, laughing so hard we couldn't breathe, thinking our lives would always be as playful as a food fight.

New York City, 1985

"I'm leaving," Carl says, the next day. "I have to get out of here before it gets cold."

"Where are you going?" I hand him a Tupperware steaming with oatmeal, maple syrup, pecans, and bananas.

"Thank you, darling," he says, saluting with the plastic spoon. "I'm headed for California."

"How are you going to get there?"

"Hitch," he says, the sun in his eyes.

"Carl, nobody's going to stop for you."

"I've made it all over this country by sticking out my thumb."

"Carl, you need a shower. Nobody's going to let you in their car. No offense."

"None taken, but I'm not going to a shelter. I'll do what I usually do. Wash up in the park. There are bathrooms there."

"Carl," I say, without stopping to think, "come with me."

"Where are we going?" he asks, shoveling in the last bite of oatmeal.

o   o   o

We cross Second Avenue, and just in case I see someone I know, I walk two steps ahead of Carl. At first, I thought that if I lived in New York City, away from the community in Brooklyn,

I'd be anonymous—a nameless, faceless individual—but that's not true. Once, my first week in the city, a Syrian woman dressed in a full-length fur coat and heels stopped me on the street and asked if I was Steven and Sharon's daughter. I told her I was, and she said she knew it because I looked just like my father. She went on to say that she'd gone to school with him, a hundred years ago, and I should tell him Esther sends her regards.

It's a huge disadvantage not knowing anything about anyone, because the Syrians know everything about each other—who is dating who; what a woman gets on her anniversary; who is, and who is not, invited to the Bar Mitzvah party at Radio City Music Hall; which designers everybody is wearing; and how much each outfit costs. They watch and report. And even though Michael claims *lashon hara* is a big sin, gossip is power.

Carl waits outside my building while I ask my doorman if I have a dry-cleaning delivery. While he checks in the back room, I wave Carl on, reckless as ever. The only difference is this is not high school. My heart races knowing that besides delivering drugs with Hawkeye, this is probably one of the most dangerous things I've ever done. *What if Michael finds out? What if I've misread Carl?*

The elevator doors close, and alone with Carl in a tight space, I begin to panic. I watch the numbers on the elevator light up, and neither one of us says a word.

When the elevator doors open, my hands shake as I jiggle my key into the lock. Doubting myself and my choices, because after all, I don't have a good track record, I wonder what others—Michael, my parents, my brother, Rochelle, Colette—would say if they saw what I was doing.

"Take off your shoes," I say to Carl. "I'll be right back." I get a garbage bag and a towel and hand them to him in the hallway. "Put your things in here. Hurry before anybody sees you."

I go back inside my apartment and wait for him to change. When he knocks, I open the door. Our white Bloomingdale's towel is wrapped around his waist.

Barefooted, he steps over the clothes I've left spewed across the carpet and heads straight to the window, gravitating toward the river. "Look at this view," he says. "It's entirely different from up here." I stand next to him. His chest is muscular and covered in white hair like snow on wide-ranging mountains, but his arms are hairless and smooth.

"I have more hair on my arms than you do," I say.

While Carl showers, I dump the garbage bag down the shoot in the hallway. Carl is in the bathroom for over thirty minutes, and the whole time I'm nervous, sitting on my bed, tapping my feet, wondering if this is the stupidest thing I've ever done.

"Carl?" I say, knocking on the bathroom door.

"I'll be out in a minute," he says.

When Carl finally comes out of the bathroom dressed in Michael's clothes, he looks like an entirely new person.

I put newspaper on the bathroom floor, and in the tiny room, we stand close. Carl smells like soap, and I trim his beard as if this is the most natural thing in the world for me to do. White hair falls from his chin like feathers. With a towel, I wipe moisture off the bathroom mirror. When Carl sees himself, he cries.

o   o   o

"So, this is where you do your magic," Carl says, standing next to me in the kitchen.

I take a bottle of white wine from the refrigerator. "How about a glass?" I say.

"I don't drink."

"Really? That's funny."

"Why is that funny?"

"No reason," I shrug, thinking about Michael and how he insists the homeless use the money people give them to buy alcohol. "Mind if I do?" I pop the cork and pour myself some, wondering what Michael would do if he saw this scene. Since we've been married, he's come home early only twice, but it could happen again, and my heart skips a beat thinking about it. Regardless, I let Carl stay. Maybe I'm desperate for company, happy not to be alone again, or maybe it's because I'm finally just doing what I want to. I take a sip of wine.

"Drinking in the middle of the day?" Carl asks.

"I'm from New Orleans. Getting wasted is a prerequisite."

"Is that a fact?" Carl sits next to me on the couch, one cushion between us. "That's not why you're drinking."

"Well, maybe not. But I can't talk to you about it."

"Why not?"

"Carl, you don't have any money, a place to live, or clothes on your back. Well, actually, you have Michael's clothes." And I laugh the kind of laugh that happens when the first few sips of alcohol reach your brain and your fingertips at the same time.

Carl looks into my eyes. "Loneliness hurts."

"Thanks, Carl."

"Just remember, you have choices. When it gets cold here, I leave. When it's warm, I come back."

"That's not how things work in my family."

Carl walks to the black lacquer wall unit across the room and lifts my sterling silver frame, a *swanee* present. In it is a picture of Michael and me on our honeymoon. We are tan and smiling.

"I used to have a wife," Carl says.

Just then, there's a knock on the door. I jump up fast. It's probably just a regular knock, but it sounds to me like an explosion—the loudest, most intrusive noise I've ever heard. Carl gets scared too and drops the frame. Glass shatters.

"It could be Michael," I say. "He doesn't carry a key. Hide."

Carl locks himself in the bathroom, and I take a deep breath. A million versions of what could go down play in my mind, because the doorman didn't buzz, and so I'm convinced it's Michael. I cross the living room and look through the peephole, grateful to see it's our doorman. He brought up our dry-cleaning.

After the doorman leaves, Carl apologizes for dropping my frame. While I pick up shards of glass, he strolls to the parson's table behind our couch, lifts Michael's velvet tefillin bag, and runs a hand over the embroidered gold Hebrew letters. He touches my sterling silver Shabbat candlesticks, one at a time, and puts Michael's black velvet yarmulke on his head. Nothing about what Carl does feels intrusive or judgmental. In fact, it feels like Carl wants to know me. He wants to understand my life. Picking up a book of matches, he asks, "May I?"

I nod and he lights both candles.

"They're beautiful," he says, mesmerized by the two tiny flames.

"They are," I say, seeing them through Carl's eyes.

I take the vacuum out of the front closet. Over the hum, I ask Carl, "So, do you really think I have choices?" Bits of glass clank inside the vacuum.

"Everyone has choices."

"Maybe I'll go with you, Carl. Travel some." I shut off the vacuum. "See, that's the problem. I can't go anywhere. I'm stuck."

"According to who?"

"According to me. And my parents. And the entire Syrian community." I reach for my glass of wine.

"You have choices, Casey."

"It doesn't feel like I do."

"Do you love Michael?"

"I don't know."

"Do you want to stay married?"

"In the world I live in, divorce is out of the question. You're committed for life. No matter what."

Carl drifts to the window. "Those are the most incredible clouds."

"Cumulus clouds," I say, joining him, remembering sixth grade at Franklin Prep and my sixth-grade science teacher, who had long, wild hair and allegedly smoked pot. Everything about him screamed free spirit.

"So, where's your wife, Carl?"

Carl presses his forehead to the window. "She's gone. Left a long time ago. She used to say, *Carl, you're not all there. You know that don't you, Carl?*" He shakes his head as if to erase the memory and places his beautiful hands on the window-pane. I make a mental note to clean the glass so Michael doesn't see Carl's giant prints.

"Trust yourself, Casey. Deep down, you know."

I turn to him. "Want something to eat?"

In the kitchen, I open the refrigerator. A jar of pickles, a bottle of soy sauce, and a few cans of club soda rattle on the door. I know the contents of the refrigerator exactly because just that morning I stared into it, unmoving, for a long time, cold air hitting my face, thinking, *What should I do?* as if the solution rested next to the orange juice, or in between the milk and eggs.

Electric tape covers the light button, keeping the refrigerator dark.

Carl is at my side. "What's with the tape?"

I rip it off, and the light in the refrigerator shines. "Don't ask. It's a long story," I say, glad I invited Carl over.

The phone rings, startling me. I pick up fast and put a finger to my lips.

"What are you doing?" Rochelle asks.

"Nothing," I say into the phone.

"You sound weird."

"I'm fine."

"Want to hang out? The baby's asleep. Want to go for lunch or something?"

Rochelle has grown on me. We are different in so many ways, but she is kind.

"I can't."

"Why not?"

"I just can't."

"You okay? You don't sound like yourself. Should I come over?"

"No," I answer a little too quickly.

"There's no traffic now. I'll take the tunnel. I can be there in thirty minutes."

"Rochelle, don't come over. Really. We'll do something next week."

"Okay," she says.

Hanging up, I take a deep breath and try to calm down. It's time for Carl to go.

I take leftover egg salad from the refrigerator and scoop some into a mound on a plate. I decorate the mound as if it's a face—carrot peels for hair, black olives for eyes, a slice of cucumber as a nose, and a tomato as a smiling mouth. I place white bread on the counter.

"Are you going to be okay, Carl?"

"Oh, don't you worry about me," Carl says. "I'll be fine. And listen here, you. Don't go selling yourself short; you're one tough cookie. There aren't many people who would let a guy like me into their apartment."

He makes himself a sandwich and cuts the bread like I have for him so many times before, from corner to corner into triangles.

New York City, 1985

Without Carl around I don't feel like cooking or doing much of anything, but on the Sunday after he takes off, Michael suggests we rent bikes and go for a ride in Central Park. He knows how disappointed I've been in our relationship lately, and I believe his invitation to be a peace offering.

"Have you seen my black sweatshirt?" Michael asks as we get ready to go. "The one we got in Soho?"

"Nope," I lie, feeling a pang of guilt.

Michael has been asking more questions lately, wanting to know where his ski jacket is, why our grocery bill is so high, and what happened to the glass on our honeymoon photograph.

I didn't set out to keep Carl a secret from Michael, but every time I started to tell him about Carl, I stopped, knowing he'd ruin it. I could hear Michael pontificating about how Carl was a man and how he only wanted one thing from me. Or possibly, he'd minimize our friendship, saying, "Of course he likes you. You cook for him and give him free clothes, my clothes." Or he'd insist that Carl was dangerous and crazy and that he could hurt me. If all else failed, he'd try a different tactic, making fun of me, saying how pathetic I was for having an old man as a close friend. It wasn't worth it.

Michael squats near his closet, digging through a pile of shoes on the floor. "I don't understand. I only see my gray sneakers. I can't find my blue ones."

I leave the room.

o   o   o

On our bikes in Central Park, it's hard to keep up with Michael. I ride behind him, lost in thought, remembering how in the beginning of our marriage, we'd lie in bed, talking. He'd say, "We're going to be together forever." And I'd say, "Yep, day after day." And Michael would add, *Week after week.* And I'd continue, *Decade after decade.* It was playful, our joined wish—prophecy. The memory makes me smile, and feeling hopeful, as we cycle past Belvedere Castle, I catch up to Michael. "You know, I was thinking, I want to apply to NYU."

"You don't need college, Casey."

"It's not about *need.*" I pedal faster. "I *want* to go."

Michael doesn't say anything for the longest time. He rides ahead, the distance between us significant, and I know I'm being punished. As I pedal, my anger builds. Michael has all the power. He decides everything—where we go, what we do, how we live. He doesn't see me as an individual with my own needs and wants.

We ride to the West Side, past the reservoir, and on the way back, near Turtle Pond, Michael takes a sharp right, cutting me off. "What are you doing?" I call out before falling and hitting the ground. Both knees bleed.

"Sorry, I didn't realize you were there," Michael says, lifting me up.

o   o   o

At home, in our apartment, I let Michael nurse my scraped knees. He soaks cotton balls in hydrogen peroxide, gently pats my wounds, and covers them with Band-Aids.

For dinner, we order Chinese food and eat out of the cartons, sitting cross-legged on the rug next to the coffee table.

"This is great," I say. "I like ordering in."

Michael swirls vegetable lo mein around chopsticks. "Don't get used to it."

"It's nice for a change."

"Change isn't all it's cracked up to be," Michael says, standing. He walks to our black lacquer wall unit and places our Stevie Wonder *Hotter than July* album on the record player. "Master Blaster" plays.

Michael jams to the music, strutting back to me. He sits down and strokes my hair. "You look pretty," he says.

"Thanks," I say, feeling happy. Shimmying my shoulders, dancing in place to the music, I dip an eggroll into sweet and sour sauce and take a bite.

Michael clamps a pea pod between chopsticks, offering it to me, and I lean in to eat it, smiling because things haven't felt this nice between us in a long time.

o   o   o

In bed, Michael holds me close and stares into my eyes. "Let's have a baby," he says.

"What?" I say, shocked by his proposal.

"You don't need to go to college, Casey. You're smart enough."

"Oh, you think so?"

"I know so. And our baby will be smart too. What could be more important than having a child?"

I'm speechless. I'm too young to be someone's mother. And a baby will change everything. College will be out of the question, and we'll have to leave Manhattan and move to

Brooklyn. I kick the sheets from my body, and they wrap around my ankles like chains. "I don't know, Michael. It feels too soon. I need time."

"Time? Time is the enemy. You plan and God laughs. Who says you'll conceive right away? As a matter of fact, you probably won't, and then what?"

When Michael wants something, he's relentless; I don't sleep all night.

o o o

In the morning, Colette calls. I'm still in bed. "Hey, I have a glamour question for you," she says.

I am both shocked and flattered. I can't believe Colette is turning to me for fashion advice.

"I got a birthday gift and I'm writing a thank-you note," she says. "Thank you for your generous gift. Is it *Y-O-U-R* or *Y-O-U-apostrophe-R-E?*"

"Oh," I say, a bit disappointed. "A *grammar* question. I thought you said a *glamour* question."

Colette laughs, and I do too. Despite our differences, we are developing some sort of relationship. Mostly, she fills me in on community gossip and gives me the lowdown on upcoming events. She knows things I don't, and it gives her an authority she likes. I don't mind.

"Colette," I try, wanting to open up to somebody, or needing approval, or both. "I know school isn't your thing, but it's really important to me. I'm thinking about applying to NYU."

"Casey, really I don't get you. You're married to a great guy who can take care of you. You've got the life. Why can't you just sit back and enjoy the ride?"

"I want a degree."

"Why? I mean, really. Why? It's a piece of paper. You're smart. Case closed."

"I want to be an artist. I've been drawing."

"So draw. Why do you have to go to college? Draw if you want."

"Colette, school opens your world, gives you choices."

"Blah, blah, blah, who says that's a good thing?"

"Most people," I say, flatly.

"Most *American* people."

"We're American."

"Not really," she says.

I exhale, exasperated. "And the patriarchy. I can't take it."

"What the hell. Seriously, Casey? What does that even mean?"

"Knowledge is power," I try.

"Well, I don't know what you have to prove, Casey. You're married to someone who likes to be in charge. He doesn't want his wife, or anyone else, coming up against him. Being too smart isn't always a good thing."

"Colette, you can't mean that."

"Well, I do." She pauses and takes a deep breath. "Okay, I'll give you this. I did whatever Michael asked, and when push came to shove, he didn't want that. He wanted you."

"Thanks, Colette," I say, shocked by her admission.

"I can't believe you thought I had a *glamour* question for you. That's really funny."

o   o   o

When Colette and I hang up, I get out of bed and take my NYU application from my bookcase. I stare at it for a long time, reading the essay choices: *Do you have a story that is essential to who you are? If you could change one day of your life, which would you change? What do you want people to know about you, but are afraid to tell them?* Not able to think about those subjects, much less write about them, I chicken out and put the application back, hiding it, once again, between my books.

Next to our albums, in the black lacquer wall unit in the living room, I stack our old issues of *Time* magazine. I use them for collages and other art projects. One *Time* cover says, "America's Message: Keep On Course—But Trim the Sails." It seems that the characteristic that took Reagan to the top, his ability to act and be the face of absolute certainty and strength, is pissing off our country. Nothing flusters him, and he's named the Teflon president. As I flip through magazines, it occurs to me that the traits people fall in love with are the ones they ultimately find intolerable. I was drawn to Michael's mannish bravado and his unwavering confidence, and now that's working against me.

I rip an image from a magazine and turn it upside down, following an exercise I read about in an art book. The point is to draw exactly what you see without looking at your paper, concentrating on process and trusting it, not attached to an outcome. The inverted image blocks your brain's natural tendency to focus on the final product, releasing you from perfectionism. According to the book, in order to draw, or at least draw well, you have to take risks, make mistakes. The good stuff is buried in the blunders.

o o o

The month of November is full of obligations: engagement parties, Bar Mitzvahs, weddings, brisses, *swanees*, *Sebets*, and charity events. Each one of these occasions requires tremendous effort in hair, nails, jewelry, and clothes. Even matching pocketbooks. I can't keep up, but mostly, I don't want to. Every time I ask Michael if we can skip one of these occasions, he says it wouldn't be nice and that we have to go. After each event, I check off the affair on my calendar, thrilled it's done, only to find a new invitation in the mail the next day, duped as a first grader who's mastered addition, only to discover she needs to learn subtraction.

"Sounds like hell with cocktails," Tracey says. "Don't they ever chill? Everything's so ramped up there. Ultra-Orthodox, ultra-skinny, ultra-rich. Isn't anybody just regular?"

o o o

With each passing day, Michael becomes more unrecognizable. Party after party, he flirts—sometimes with the bartender, sometimes with the coat-check girl, sometimes with our friends. When I complain, he denies he's doing anything wrong, says we live together, get to spend lots of time together, and the point of a party, after all, is to socialize and hang out with different people. "I can talk to you at home," he says.

Again, and again, he insists I'm overreacting and keeps telling me I'm the best thing that ever happened to him, but after one miserable evening of watching him talk in a darkened corner with a big-busted woman, I crack. I recognize his body language, the look in his eyes, and I go wild.

"I won't live like this," I scream when we get home.

"Like what?" Michael yells back. "I didn't do anything."

Drunk and hungry, I take leftovers from the refrigerator and wolf down mashed potatoes and breaded chicken, attempting to numb, or to fill, or to *something*. And as I chew and swallow, I notice Michael eyeing my orchid plant. Before he can say anything, I lift the plant high above my head and, in a rage, smash it into the garbage can.

"Are you happy now?" I scream. "It's gone."

"Finally" is all he says.

o o o

Michael sleeps soundly as I roam our apartment. Loneliness isn't a passing cloud; it is solid and inescapable. Thoughts spiral in my head, gaining momentum, taking on a power of their own, the thinking like poison. Snapshots of women cross my mind—the one with bronze skin and a British accent we met on our honeymoon, the one with green eyes who looked like a cat, and the one who felt perfectly comfortable resting her head on Michael's shoulder, laughing every time he told a joke—all of them splattered across my mind, forming a collage of legs, and smiles, and cleavage.

o   o   o

In the morning, Tracey calls. She is in New Orleans, home for winter break.

"Guess what? I bumped into Hawkeye last night."

I sit up in bed. "What, where?" My heart beats fast.

"Fat Harry's."

"How is he? How did he look? What did he say? Did he ask about me?"

"Whoa. Slow down."

"Well?"

"He was away serving in the Army, but now he's back. He looks great. And yeah, he asked about you."

"What'd you tell him?"

"That you're happily married."

"Really?"

"No."

"Well, what did you tell him?"

"I told him you're married. He couldn't believe it. He said you were a good one."

"A good one?"

"Yeah, a good one."

"Like a lobster? What does that mean, a good one?"

"I don't know. That's what he said."

"Hmm."

"Hmm, what?"

"Nothing," I say, but my mind races with memories of Hawkeye.

"How are you holding up over there, anyway?" Tracey asks.

Tracey suggested I mark my calendar, good days and bad, but I never got around to it. "I'm okay," I say.

"Any improvement?"

"Not really."

"Casey, why don't you just leave him?"

"I can't. I just can't," I say.

It's getting harder and harder to share with Tracey. She doesn't understand. And it's complex, difficult to explain because I'm not even exactly sure what I think. Am I staying because I love Michael or because I've made my bed, and now I have to lie in it, which is an unfair expectation since girls my age change their minds every day, every minute, every second. I could buy a red sweater on Monday and by Wednesday think I'd made a huge mistake, wishing I'd gotten it in black instead. At my age, time is measured in how long it takes for bangs to grow out or a pimple to go away, and with no concept of *till death do us part*, we aren't meant to make lifelong decisions. But every time I allow myself to consider a divorce, or a life without Michael, my stomach flips, and I feel like I'm going to throw up with the idea of losing him.

"You know what's really ridiculous?" I tell Tracey. "I can't leave Michael because I know he'd think it was the stupidest thing I ever did."

o o o

It's the middle of the night, and once again, I can't sleep. While I lie in bed next to Michael, sirens sound through our New York City high-rise window and memories spin around in my head as if on a Wheel of Fortune. I'm hoping that when the whirling stops and the needle lands on a specific moment in time, everything will be evident, because right now—my future isn't clear. I pull the comforter we got from Blooming-dale's to my chin.

When we got married almost three years ago, General Hospital's Luke and Laura and the royal family's Prince Charles and Princess Diana had fairytale weddings—televised and watched by millions. Maybe all the hype and promise got to me. I don't know; I mean, what motivates anyone to do anything? I keep going back to my wedding night, and so many others, looking for clues.

Outside more sirens blare. And the noise rips through me. I look over at Michael sleeping. Nothing wakes him, and there is no lonelier feeling in the world. I roll onto my side, trying to get comfortable and hug a pillow. Memories keep coming in waves. I shake my head to stop them, and when I can't, I throw the covers off and get out of bed, leaving him there.

Wearing my Madonna "Like a Virgin" tee shirt and boy shorts, I head out of our room. The telephone cord catches my ankle, and I trip. I stop myself from falling, but the phone crashes from my nightstand to the carpet with a thud. The dial tone is piercing. I place the receiver back on its cradle and check Michael. He's still asleep.

Loneliness follows me into the living room, clinging like a dark shadow.

I place an album on the record player, and my voice duets with Madonna's—*You just keep on pushing my love over the borderline.*

Sitting on the couch, I lift our wedding photograph and run my finger along the Lalique frame, a bridal gift. I stare at our image. *Are we still us?* The in-love couple who, during our first year of marriage, devoted an entire weekend in Paris to look-ing for the perfect ice bucket? I don't know why we were so eager, but we spent our whole vacation hand in hand roaming up and down quaint streets, maneuvering through crowded, dusty Parisian antique stores, asking the price of every single ice bucket we found. We never did buy one. Although it wasn't for lack of trying.

On our last night in Paris, we decided to stay in. We ordered room service—dinner plus a bottle of champagne. The champagne arrived on ice in the picture-perfect bucket, the one we'd wanted all along. It was elegant and silver and engraved with the words *Plaza Athénée*.

We had to have it.

So, we devised a plan, and the next morning, while Michael was in the lobby checking us out of the hotel, I packed the silver ice bucket in my suitcase, hiding it under a pile of clothes. We were a team—Bonnie and Clyde.

I remember my heart pounding against my chest. And as I zipped my suitcase shut, I felt the sensation of something fizzing through my veins like Coke through a straw.

O O O

I see Michael's black corduroys in a heap on the carpet. I think to check the pockets but don't. I don't want to be that person, that wife. What I want is for him to wake up and see I'm gone. I want him to come find me in our living room— wrap his arms around me and hold me tight.

I put our wedding photo down on the coffee table and consider my options. Michael and I want different things. I want to go to college and pursue my art, and he doesn't want me to. But to leave our marriage—to go against everyone and everything I've come to know—is unthinkable. Drawn to the window, I stand in front of it and look out. Night in New York City is both dark and bright—tiny, shimmering lights everywhere. I press my forehead against the glass and take a deep breath.

The album skips—*Borderline. Borderline. Borderline.* I lift the needle on the record player, stopping the music.

New York City, 1985

The pattern is becoming clear. After a few days of hard-core fighting, Michael lightens up and things settle down.

"Let's go out tonight," Michael says, bolting out of bed early in the morning. He flips through Zagat and finds Trio, a new restaurant in Soho. He calls for a reservation. "Table for six," he says into the phone.

"Table for six?" I say when he hangs up.

"Yeah, we'll tell Rick and Eric to come."

"Let's go alone."

"It's not that kind of place."

"Okay," I say, not wanting to argue.

Michael stares deep into my eyes and pulls me in close. "I'm lucky to have you," he says.

I push away the image of my orchid plant—broken terra-cotta and loose soil at the bottom of my kitchen garbage can. I try to stop the movie of Michael's top misdemeanors from playing in my head. "Thanks," I say.

There is dead silence. And then more silence. Quiet piles up like dirty laundry, and when I turn to walk away, Michael says, "Hey, aren't you lucky to have me too?"

o o o

When Michael leaves for work, I dial Tracey.

"He's got the Honey Gorgeous syndrome," she says.

"What's that?"

"He's a narcissist," she says, applying what she's learned in her psychology classes. "Unless you're calling him *Honey* or *Gorgeous*, he's not interested."

o   o   o

Red velvet ropes block the entrance at Trio. Michael gives our name to the bouncer at the door. The bouncer flips through pages on a clipboard, unfastens a rope, and lets us in.

Oversized posters of supermodels Cindy Crawford, Elle Macpherson, and Christie Brinkley grid sleek walls, and Madonna's "Into the Groove" blares. The bar spans the length of the restaurant, and people crowd in front of it, four rows deep. Colette read an article about Trio. It suggested the best way to fit in at this exclusive hot spot: black leather. I'm wearing electric-blue cotton.

The hostess wears a tiny black leather dress and, bare-legged, towers over us in red stilettos. She informs us that nobody in our party has arrived yet.

Michael makes his way to the front of the bar, and I follow, ordering my first martini. I'm wearing makeup, high heels, and my wedding band, which always works as proof of age. I never get carded. Two barstools become available, and Michael snatches them. We sit side by side and talk eye to eye like a couple on their first date.

"Who knew?" I say, eating the last olive and throwing back the rest of my martini. "This drink is perfect. Liquid heroin."

Michael laughs. "Have another," he offers.

"Really? I don't think I can handle it."

"If you can handle me, you can handle anything." He grins and signals the bartender to give us another round. "Are you hungry?" he asks.

"Starving."

o o o

When Rochelle and Rick and Eric and Colette arrive, the hostess shows us to our round table in the center of the restaurant. A stunning waitress wearing a black leather bustier approaches and takes our drink order. Just as she comes back with our cocktails, a woman carrying a shopping bag walks by wearing a knee-length skirt, a navy blazer, and sneakers.

"I hate that look," Rochelle says, pointing at the woman. "And this glass," she says, eyeing her drink. "I hate this glass. I want a stem glass. Honey, can you please get me a stem glass and six limes."

"That's not a look," I say, bold from vodka. "She's coming from work and probably just got off a subway."

"Yes," Rick chimes in, raising his single malt scotch, "she rides the subway, unlike any of you. And she probably came straight from work. Something you girls would know nothing about. Here's to coming back in my next life as a Syrian girl."

Michael lifts his glass. "I'll drink to that."

I don't like how Rick is talking. On Friday night at my parents' house, just before Shabbat dinner while Michael was at synagogue, my father called my brother, a student at NYU, into the den because he wanted to discuss a business idea. I was sitting on the couch and was eager to listen, but my mother appeared at the door. "Help me in the kitchen, will you, Casey?"

"Oh, I see," I said, joining her. "Sam is supposed to make millions. I'm supposed to make dinner."

"Casey, please," my mother said.

"Or babies. Maybe I should just make babies."

o o o

"You can poke fun all you want," Rochelle says. "But I'm proud to be a mother, and happy I don't have to drive through the Brooklyn Battery Tunnel every morning during rush hour."

"But you give something up," I say.

"Yes, I know. Traffic."

The waitress hands Rochelle a stem glass, and Rochelle pours vodka from her tumbler into it. Her long nails are polished, a perfect French manicure. Colette's are done too. Ten red talons.

Sometimes when I rebel, when I don't do what's expected, I feel like I've made a mistake. I examine my unpolished nails, wishing I'd bothered to go the extra mile.

"I know Syrian men look down on our lives, thinking we're somehow 'less than,' but I don't," Rochelle says. "Women are *not* the basement; we're the foundation."

"Behind every good man," Colette says.

"*Behind*. That's the operative word," I add.

"Your point, Casey?" Michael's Adam's apple bulges as he finishes off his drink. He puts the glass down. "I'll have another," he says to the waitress.

"Me too," I say, emptying my glass and handing it to her.

"My point is," I say, turning to Michael, "that Colette told me there is a nineteen-year-old Syrian girl who traded with her husband: sex for a three-hundred-dollar haircut."

"It's the Syrian Deal," Michael says, as if he's a great orator explaining basic economics.

"What do Syrian men want? Do you really want us barefoot and pregnant?"

"It's a privilege to be pregnant," Rochelle says, putting her glass down. "I want to have six kids."

"Six kids?" Colette says. "Are you crazy, Rochelle? Relax, will you."

I'm glad I'm not the only one having a strong reaction to Rochelle's statement. I mean, I want to have children one day too, but Syrian girls get pregnant with as much forethought as a burp, while still babies themselves, and their husbands treat them as if they are merely Fed Ex.

"That's my purpose," Rochelle says as the waitress hands her a drink in a stem glass. Six cut limes rim the edge. "To be fruitful and multiply."

"Simple math," Rick says.

Colette jumps in. "Rochelle, you don't know what you're saying. First of all, four kids is plenty. Five tops. Do you know what six kids will do to your boobs?"

"The last thing we need," Eric says, "is to hang out with a group of girls with bad boobs. Gravity does enough damage."

Thankfully, the waitress sets a basket of bread in the center of our table, interrupting our conversation. Eric dips focaccia in olive oil and starts to talk about an article he read in *The New York Times* that morning, but before he can make his point, Colette interjects. "Reading the newspaper is a ridiculous waste of time," she says, spinning the ice in her glass with a straw. "The news changes every day. And the articles are about stuff that has nothing to do with us and about things that are happening far away in countries I've never heard of. What's the point?"

"Well, of course there's a point," I say.

"Yeah, what is it?"

"You read *Vogue*, don't you?"

"Yeah."

"Well, fashion changes, but you still read to get informed."

Colette picks up her glass and leans forward, both elbows on the table, and she eyes my electric-blue Betsy Johnson dress. Smiling, she says, "You don't read *Vogue*, do you?"

While Colette's one-liner is meant to be a put-down, I don't get insulted and instead laugh because I don't care about fashion or expensive clothes. I want to look cool. And like other kids my age. Not rich. Or like other New York City girls who wear the Upper East Side uniform: Prada—black pants, boots, blazer—looking like carbon copies of one another in order to go back to Prada to shop for more of the same.

I started dressing like Madonna, wearing black lace bras, giant bows, and hot-pink lipstick, because I like an artsy, downtown vibe. I like color. And patterns. And as I shake my head, still laughing, the silver earrings I bought off the street on West Broadway jingle.

Rochelle and Colette wear chic solids: black, beige, gray.

The waitress brings us menus. Trio is the hottest restaurant in New York City, and the menu lists grilled cheese, chicken pot pie, and macaroni and cheese. Their motto: Trendy Comfort Food with a Twist. In a Changing World, Some Things Never Change.

"The grilled cheese is on white bread," Rick says. "White bread. Are they kidding? Where's the twist? Drizzled pesto? Couldn't they at least use exotic bread? Then I wouldn't feel like a sucker paying twelve dollars for an appetizer that's really a kid's meal."

"I like white bread," I say, thinking about Carl and how we always ate our sandwiches on white bread.

Michael rolls his eyes. "She does."

"What's that supposed to mean?" I ask, using a spoon to fish out the lone olive in my glass.

Rick flips through the breadbasket. "It's plain Jane. Mass production. McDonald's."

"We couldn't get pita in New Orleans when I was a kid, and my mother used to come back from her trips to New York with bags of it. At school, I was embarrassed to unwrap my lunch knowing a half-moon shaped sandwich was inside. I wanted white bread like all the other kids in my class. I wanted Oreos and Pop-Tarts and everything else boxed in red, white, and blue."

Syrians didn't need to fit in with American kids. They had each other. They ate pita chips with hummus before it was stylish to do so, and American ethos didn't guide them. It was Middle Eastern culture and the Bible they adhered to. In regard to women's rights and the gay movement, Michael would say, "Those are American issues. Everything we need to know is in the Torah."

"The Torah can't answer everything," I'd fight back.

"Oh, yes it can. It's like rain. Go a couple of weeks without it and see what happens. God knows what he's doing. Look at something as simple as a peanut. It's miraculous. Comes protected in its own corrugated box."

"White bread is like cherry pie," Rick says. "Nobody wants cherry pie."

"I do," I say, remembering Morgan coming to my house while my parents were at a Saints game. He ate an entire cherry pie, picking it up from our kitchen counter and biting into it like a sandwich. My parents were mortified when they got home. "What kind of person eats a whole pie?" my father said.

"I made the best grilled cheese the other day," Michael says. "On sourdough bread, not white bread, of course."

"How'd you make it?" Colette asks, leaning in.

"I used these great pans. Drizzled a little truffle oil. So good."

"I bought the pans," I say, aware I sound like a baby. "And it's my recipe."

I'm tired of Michael making himself the protagonist, the hero, and eliminating me from every story. If I'd said I'd made a grilled cheese sandwich, nobody would've cared. And I'm tired of feeling alone, not due to the absence of other people, but because I'm not sharing anything that seems to matter. When Michael speaks, even about the most trivial things, his words take on some kind of magical importance.

"Can we order?" I ask, putting my menu down. "I'm hungry."

o o o

When the waitress sets our main courses on the table, Michael checks out a girl walking by. She wears black leather jeans, tight as if they'd been painted on her skeletal body.

I tap Michael's arm. "Hey, remember me?"

Eric looks at Michael. "You're going to hurt your neck like that, buddy." He blows on mashed potatoes.

"What? I appreciate beauty," Michael says, unapologetically.

"That has nothing to do with appreciation, my friend. That is lust," Rick says, smirking and downing his scotch.

Michael leans in, chewing. "Our forefathers had it going on. They didn't get all caught up about sex back then."

"A lot of things were different back then. You could have more than one wife. You want another wife?" Colette asks Michael. "You can't even handle the one you've got now." Colette eyes her husband. "But, Eric, I'm down for that. And you can let your second wife make you dinner every night."

"Back then," Rick says, "men could sleep with other women and it wasn't a whole big deal like the world was coming to an end or something. Men had needs. Women understood that. And couples didn't get divorced over stupidity."

"Hold on," Rochelle says. "Obviously, there were problems. That's why the rabbis, thousands of years ago, changed things and said no more. Infidelity is a sin. Not allowed."

With more hostility than intended, I say, "Apparently men are slow learners, because it's taken a long time for the message to trickle down."

"Relax," Michael says, nudging me.

I'm amazed at how a single word, *relax*, can take me down. Like a bullet.

"We're joking around," Michael says.

Getting close to Michael's face, I look into his eyes. "Well, it's not funny." I blow on hot macaroni and cheese and take a bite, burning my tongue.

"What's the matter?" Michael whispers.

"Nothing."

"Did you drink too much? Are you drunk?"

"It's like the song says, 'All you touch and all you see is all your life will ever be.'" I don't think Roger Waters meant that as an insult, but I did.

"Oh, you're definitely drunk."

"No. I'm just talking. I like to talk. You know I like to talk."

"*Fishelbee*," Rick says, swigging scotch.

"Fish what?" I ask.

"It's Arabic," Eric explains.

"I figured, but what does it mean?"

"Verbal throw-up. Women are masters," Rick says.

The waitress sets our desserts down, and drunk, it's hard to concentrate. I stick a finger into the white candle in the center of our table, coating my nail with wax. I dip my other nine fingers into the wax one by one. "Look. A French manicure," I say, lifting my empty martini glass, pinky extended.

○   ○   ○

"Let's play a game," Colette says.

"What do you want to play?" Michael asks, swirling ice around in his drink.

"Fuck, Marry, Kill."

"No way," Rick says. "That game is trouble."

"How do you play?" I ask.

"We name three people," Eric says, "and you have to pick one to fuck, one to marry, and one to kill."

"That's gross," I say.

"Loosen up, Casey, will you?" Michael throws his head back and finishes his drink.

"You go first," Colette says to Michael. She licks chocolate from her spoon. "Do me, Rochelle, and Casey."

"Oh no. You're not supposed to play with people who are here," Eric says.

"Rules. Rules. Rules." Colette holds her glass near her mouth. "Michael, just go."

"That's an easy one," Michael says. "I'd marry Casey. Rochelle, I'm sorry to say, it's nothing personal, but you've got to go."

"No problem, Michael. I'd kill you too," Rochelle says, reaching for a strawberry.

"And Fuck? Who would you fuck?" Colette asks, scooping up crème fraîche with an elegant, polished finger.

"I think that's pretty obvious," Eric says.

o o o

Michael wants to *marry* me. That shouldn't have made me feel bad, but it does, mostly because he wants to fuck Colette. All ten fingers, coated with candle wax, feel numb.

Rick lights a cigar. Eric lights a cigarette. Michael disappears.

A few minutes later, I stand and say, "Excuse me. I'm going to the bathroom."

Rochelle picks berries off a tart. "It's in the basement," she tells me.

Drunk, I hold on to the banister and head down the stairs. I find the bathroom at the end of the hall and stumble my way into a stall.

Martinis. I hadn't meant to get so drunk.

Hawkeye. I hadn't meant to get so drunk that night either.

o o o

Two girls enter the bathroom. I hear them fighting, and their screaming is not helping my headache. Back at the sink, I see one of the girls has pink Cindy Lauper hair and she's jabbing a single finger on the other girl's chest, right on her heart, pushing her into the electric hand dryer. The dryer sounds and blows hot air. The girl who is getting pushed around runs out of the bathroom. The one with Cindy Lauper hair joins me in the mirror and sings out loud, "Girls just wanna have fun."

I wash my hands and exit the bathroom. Looking for the stairwell, I make a wrong turn and wander down a long, dark corridor. There is a silhouette of a man, a shadow, with one foot in the men's room and one foot out. He leans against the doorframe, talking to a girl. They stand maybe an inch apart. As I come upon them, I see it's Michael and the girl from upstairs. He's smiling, and there's a glimmer in his eyes. I put my face in his, getting close, as if I have to get this close to see. "He's married," I scream, facing the girl. I jab a finger into Michael's heart. "You. Are. Married!"

I run from the club, not stopping for my coat or purse. I head to the street and jump into a cab. As the driver pulls away from the curb, I glance out the window and see Michael leap over the red rope in front of the restaurant, frantic, looking all around and calling my name.

Without my coat, I shiver, realizing winter has arrived.

Brooklyn, 1985

My mother comes to the door in a robe and slippers.

"Casey, what are you doing here? Come in," she says, holding the storm door open. "You're going to freeze to death out there."

She gives me money to pay the cab driver, and then she puts her arm around my waist, leading me to the living room. We sit side by side on the couch. She strokes my back with an open hand. "What's going on?" she asks, her forehead creased.

I tell her about Michael's mystery phone calls and his flirting.

"Men," she says.

"What?"

"Men. That's a man for you."

"It's not okay, Mom."

"That's the way it is, sweetie." She says this as if there is nothing to be done, no choice to be made.

"But, Mom, it hurts."

She nods.

"It's not enough," I continue.

My mother sighs. "Nothing was ever enough for you."

"What do you mean?"

"You always wanted more. You were premature, barely five pounds, and at six months the doctor instructed me to put you on skim milk."

"Skim milk's like water. I was probably starving."

"Don't be ridiculous. You were fine," she says, waving her hand dismissively. My mother takes a deep breath and looks into my eyes as if she has the most important thing in the world to tell me. "Once, when you were four, I fed you a hot dog for dinner. That should've been enough, but you wanted another one. I couldn't believe it. As long as I kept cutting, you kept eating. You had four hot dogs. That's unheard of."

"Mom, what are you trying to say?"

"Accept what is. Make the best of it. There is good and bad in everything." I see pain in her eyes, her own disappointments palpable. "Anyway," she moves on, because she isn't one to stay in a raw place for very long, "what's good for the goose is good for the gander."

"What are you saying, Mom?"

"It's a game, Casey. Cat and Mouse. Come on. You've been drinking. I'll make us some tea."

She loops her arm around my back like how she did when I was small and woke in the middle of the night with an earache. In our New Orleans den, a single lamp lit the dark room. My mother sat on the ottoman that matched my father's black leather chair, and I lay across her lap. She stroked my head, moving loose hair out of the way, and squirted drops into my ear, which journeyed through the canal with precision and weight. The pain, excruciating and deep, shocked me, but soothed by my mother's warm lap, I understood that agony could be lessened by love.

The phone rings, and my mother answers it in the kitchen. She holds the phone with one hand and, with her other, puts water on to boil. She tells Michael I'm fine and that I'll be home soon.

I motion *no way* with my hands and mouth, "I'm not going back."

"Of course you're going back," she says when she hangs up. "After you calm down and have some tea." She walks to the hook by the side door. "I want you to take this when you go," she says, handing me her coat. "It's cold outside. You can't walk around without a jacket in the middle of winter."

The coat is Givenchy. It's faux leopard with big shoulder pads. It's a Grandma Rose hand-me-down, and even though I don't care about designer clothes, I think this coat is cool. I slip it on as my mother pours hot water into two mugs. She rips open tea bags and says, "You make a marriage work, Casey. Everything will be fine." She hands me a mug. "Sometimes we can't see the bigger picture. When people turn forty, their eyesight begins to go and they think it's the worst thing in the world, but it happens just as the wrinkles and cellulite appear. Things work out. Just as everything on your body goes to pot, your eyesight goes too."

I take a sip of tea and burn my tongue. "Ow," I say. "This is hot."

"Oh, Casey, stop it now."

"What?"

She shakes her head. "Always negative."

"I'm not negative."

"Tea's supposed to be hot."

"I know that, Mom." I sigh as I stand. "Where's Dad?"

"Upstairs. Watching TV."

"I'm going to say hi. I'll be back."

o   o   o

I can see from the hallway my parents' bedroom is dark, the only light coming from the television. "Hi, Dad," I say, knocking.

o   o   o

"Hi, sweetheart. Come in," he says, pulling the covers to his waist. He sits up against his headboard. "What's going on?"

"Nothing," I shrug. "Can I just stay here with you for a while?"

"Sure can," he says, patting his mattress. Lights flicker from the TV screen. I lie down next to him, wrapping myself in my grandmother's coat, and close my eyes, allowing the drone of TV voices to wash over me, a wave. After a few minutes, my father says, "Casey?"

"Yeah?"

"Everyone has problems. Everyone wants a divorce."

I lift my head to look at him.

"But you don't get one," he says, making eye contact.

My father is a rule breaker. But he won't break this one. Not getting a divorce is the *gold star* of rules.

My mother calls up to us, "Casey, your tea is getting cold."

"We'll be right down," my father says.

In the cab, on the way to their house, I thought that if I explained what was going on, my parents would come to my rescue; they'd understand and be on my side. It hits me hard and all at once that regardless of my circumstances, they'll always expect me to go back to Michael.

When my father heads downstairs, I say, "I'm right behind you. I need a minute."

Feeling cocooned in my grandmother's coat, I curl up on my parents' bed, wanting to stay there forever. Resting my pounding head on my father's feathery pillow, my mind races, searching for answers. It didn't strike me as unusual that the bookcase in our New Orleans den didn't house books; instead, it was lined with trophies: engraved silver plaques, vases, and bowls; First Place Men's Singles, First Place Men's Doubles, and Golf Club Champion. And I remember how one night my father came home with an orange bag. He set it near the trophies and fished out a couple of flashlights and three plastic guns. The guns shot discs: yellow, red, blue, and green. My father turned to Sam and me. "Let's play hide-and-seek," he said. "Let's play in the dark."

"Go hide," my father told me, and as I walked away, he jeered, "No place is safe. No matter where you go, I'll find you."

I slinked down the hall like a criminal. As scared as I was, I never considered quitting. I climbed a tower of drawers and crawled inside a cabinet to silence, waiting in the dark, a sitting duck.

"Shhhhhh," my father said to Sam as they entered my room. "She's got to be in here."

I heard them sneaking around and my heartbeat quickened, whacking against my chest like a slap.

"Hee hee hee," my father cackled, and I held my breath, tolerating the intolerable. He flung the cabinet door open. "Got you," he said. He flashed a devilish smile and pulled the trigger.

As the memory fades, I feel strangely lucid, armed with direction and purpose. Done with feeling defenseless, I think about Carl and how he told me I have choices and that I'm a tough cookie. If Carl could take matters into his own hands, so can I. Even though I know I'm probably drunk, I go to my father's closet and once again steal his gun.

Self-righteous indignation has a mind of its own.

New York City, 1985

On the way to Manhattan, as the taxi turns onto Ocean Parkway, I slip my hand into my grandmother's leopard coat pocket and cup my father's gun. I stare out the window, considering my options, which seem as bleak and bare as Brooklyn trees. The anticipation of going home and facing Michael is excruciating, and it's not until we cross the Brooklyn Bridge that I remember a Fourth of July, years ago, in New Orleans. Tracey and I, taking matters into our own juvenile hands, stealing *Deep Throat* from the top shelf of my parents' closet and hiding it in a brown paper bag. We rode our bikes to Aunt Susie's house, the red tassels on our handlebars blowing in the wind. We slipped *Deep Throat* into Aunt Susie's VCR, took one of her videos—*Someone Else's Husband*—and rode back to my house. As if we were dutiful parents punishing our out-of-control children for inappropriate behavior, Tracey and I put *Someone Else's Husband* into my parents' VCR. Later that night, Tracey and I watched through my bedroom window as firecrackers burst into color against a black sky, and we got a kick out of imagining our parents' confused faces when they turned on their video machines. Giggling under the covers, we reveled in the idea that they could never ask us about it.

"It's not nice to keep secrets," Tracey said.

"Your secrets are safe with us," I added.

And we laughed until we couldn't breathe.

o   o   o

As the taxi approaches the FDR, it starts to snow.

"I hear we're going to get hit hard tonight," the taxi driver says. At first tiny flurries sprinkle light as powdered sugar, but then the flakes begin to stick. "Freewill" plays on the radio. *If you choose not to decide, you still have made a choice.*

At Sixtieth Street, the cab driver makes a sharp turn onto First Avenue, and because I'm feeling hungover, my stomach churns. When he slams on the brakes at a red light, I feel like I'm going to throw up. Putting my face close to the partition, I ask him to pull over.

"But you said Seventieth Street."

"Pull over," I say, holding my stomach with one hand, covering my mouth with the other. Before the car can completely stop, I open the door, lean out, and throw up on the sidewalk.

When I shut the car door, the driver looks at me through his rearview mirror. "Too much drinking for one night, huh?"

"I guess," I say, a bad taste in my mouth.

"You young people, you never know when to call it quits."

o   o   o

The door is unlocked and Michael is waiting for me when I get home. Bare-chested, he's lying in bed, watching television. "Where were you?"

I'm done playing games. "You know where I was."

"Oh, still cranky, I see."

"No, I don't think you do see."

Michael's eyes narrow. "I see you making a big deal out of nothing."

"What happened tonight *was* a big deal."

"Stop it, Casey."

"I will not stop."

"Oh, you wanna go a few rounds?" Michael says, his nostrils flaring. "Do it with someone else." He waves his hand as if he's swatting a fly. "Move, please. I can't see the television."

From the corner of my eye I see *War and Peace*, and furious, I lift the 1,225-page book from my nightstand and fling it across our room. It flies—soars—in the air, arching like a learning curve, hitting the ceiling, before it comes crashing down on my wobbly bookcase. The shelves and my books collapse to the ground with a crack, fully, and all at once, heaped like a pile of firewood.

"Have you gone insane? Look at this mess," Michael yells.

I storm out of our room.

Michael jumps out of bed and follows me. He grabs the sleeve of my grandmother's coat. "Where do you think you're going?"

"I'm leaving you, Michael," I say, opening our apartment door.

He slams it shut.

I open it again.

"Fine," he says. "Go."

In the hallway, I push the elevator button, my heart racing, my mind spinning. By the time I get to the lobby, I've lived a lifetime inside my head, playing out all kinds of scenarios and ways of being. I'm angry and hurt, but I'm not ready to go. I have more to say, more to do. I get back in the elevator.

When I open the door to our apartment, I find Michael fast asleep on the couch. Seeing him asleep, able to rest at all, feels like a smack across my face, and something inside me snaps. He can sleep through anything. Nothing fazes him, and I've had enough.

I drape my grandmother's leopard coat across the carpet near the door and get the roll of electrical tape and scissors from our kitchen drawer. Michael snores as I bind his ankles and wrists with the silver tape. I retrieve the gun from the leopard coat pocket and sit on the coffee table facing him.

"Michael!" I tap his shoulder.

"What?" he mutters.

"Wake up. You're sleeping."

"I'm not sleeping."

"Well, it looks like you're sleeping."

He opens his eyes and stares into the barrel of the gun. "What are you doing?"

"Kill," I say.

"What?" He tries to sit up, but the tape around his ankles and wrists makes it difficult for him to move.

"Don't know who I'd marry. Or who I'd fuck. But I do know who I'd kill."

"That's not loaded," he says, still struggling.

"Maybe it is. Maybe it isn't. Can't be too sure. About anything." I twirl the gun around a finger. "You wanted me to loosen up, right? Well, I'm loose now. How wild do you want me?"

"I thought you learned your lesson after the card game."

"You thought a lot of things."

"What does that mean?"

"We have to talk, Michael. You know I like to talk. I suggest you don't fall asleep."

"That isn't funny." Tape digs into his skin as he fights to break free, and the vein in his forehead swells like a wild blue river.

"No, it's definitely not funny. In fact, it's sad. You had to have me. Relentlessly, you pursued. And then once you got me, you didn't want me anymore."

"That's not true."

"Well, it feels true. This isn't enough, Michael. This marriage of ours isn't enough. I need more."

"More what?"

"More everything. No more crumbs."

"You need too much. I'm suffocating."

"Suffocating? I barely see you."

"It's a feeling, Casey. Like you're gobbling me up whole or something."

"Well then, maybe you shouldn't be married. You're like living with a Ken doll. There's Businessman Michael. Playboy Michael. Rabbi Michael. Philanthropist Michael." And imitating a commercial voiceover, I say, "Porsche not included."

"What's gotten into you?" He thrashes his body, but he's hardly able to move.

My head spins, dizzy from vodka. Instead of cautiously considering my next move, I act, or react, without considering the consequences, as I have so many times before. I have what I want: Michael's undivided attention.

"You don't know me, Michael."

"Apparently," he says.

"You don't want to know me."

"Don't tell me what I want."   ·

"I have something to tell you. It's finally time to tell you."

"What?"

"I wasn't a virgin when we got married."

"I know that."

"You know that? Why didn't you say anything?"

"It wasn't important."

"You. Mr. Syrian, didn't think that was important?"

"Was it?"

"Do you want to know how it happened?"

"No."

And there it was. I'd need to know, but he didn't.

"It was a mistake. I acted without thinking because I was angry and hurt."

"Seems to be a pattern," Michael says.

"I'm revengeful. Did you know that, Michael?"

"I know it now."

"I need to be able to tell you things."

"You've told me enough for one night, don't you think?"

The lines in his forehead form deep grooves.

"No more secrets," I say, speaking slowly, enunciating every syllable. "No. More. Secrets."

"What are you going to do, Casey? Shoot me?"

"Maybe."

"This is unforgivable, you know?"

"So many things are unforgivable, Michael."

"What do you want, Casey?" he asks.

In that moment, I believe his question is sincere. We've had iffy role models, generations of marriages that followed a particular prescription, and in patriarchy there is no mutuality; there is no love. I want to change things, live differently.

"I want a partner."

"I am your partner."

I pick up the gun and extend my arms into a long triangle, holding him at gunpoint. "Only me, Michael. No more flirting. No more phone calls."

"Put that damn gun down, will you? You're drunk."

"Kill. Kill. Kill. Fuck. Marry. Kill. Classy."

"I get it, Casey. I do."

I don't say anything.

"You're absolutely crazy, but it's always been you. Only you."

I feel myself weakening.

"I see how much I've hurt you and I'm sorry," he says.

"A lot. You hurt me a lot."

"I know that now."

"You're still awake."

"I'm stupid, but I'm not that stupid."

As a child, my mother called me Tinkerbell because of an undying wish that like a fairytale, all would be well in the world. I dreamed at night I had wings, that I could fly and spread, like pixie dust, sheer love.

I place the gun on the coffee table. "I'm going to take the tape off now."

"Good idea."

I cut the tape off his ankles and then his wrists. As soon as Michael is free, he pins me on the couch and brings his face close to mine. "You're out of your mind. You know that?"

He stays there, breathing heavily, and then with fervor kisses me on my mouth. I feel something new, and my breath quickens, matching his. Our eyes are open, wide open. Overwhelmed with emotion, and in my own skin—a sensation I haven't felt in too long, if ever—we switch places, and I get on top. For the first time, I don't hold back, I don't hide, and I lift my shirt over my head and drop it to the floor. My stomach is bare and I touch my scar, owning it. I place Michael's hand on it too.

"How come you never asked me about this?"

"I thought you didn't want me to."

"Feel it," I say.

He moves his fingers along my skin as if he's learning Braille.

New York City, 1985

Michael's alarm clock rings at seven as usual. He prays and perks coffee. We don't talk, and it's like the night before—my shattered bookcase, Fuck, Marry Kill, Michael touching my scar—never happened.

I stand at the stove, in a white tee shirt and matching panties, melting butter in a pan, and Michael says, "Think fast," and he throws me an egg. I catch it. "Go for it," he says. "Apply to NYU."

"I did."

"You did?"

I brace myself, thinking he's going to be mad, but instead he takes a deep breath and says, "Okay, just so long as nothing changes around here."

It's the small things sometimes that crystalize everything, and even as Michael and I are made up and getting along, making eggs in our kitchen, Michael feeling conciliatory and trying to give me what I want, it hits me.

Michael leaves for work, and that's it. I finally have a clear vision of my future: me—living in Brooklyn, the mother of four, or more; checking Michael's pockets; and forever asking him for permission.

Michael isn't a bad person. We just see the world differently. Shaped by our pasts and all the people we have met and known, their stories and spirits pump through our veins like blood, hold us up like bone.

Michael is entitled to have what he wants, but so am I. If we stay together, one of us will certainly suffer, and I can see it will always be me. Needing to belong to myself first, I can no longer make others happy if it won't make me happy too. I've been trying to hold on to everything—my beliefs, my desires, my power, but also my marital status—and those things will never all go together. Inherent in choosing is loss.

Scrubbing dried eggs from the bottom of the pan, I clean the skillet. I do the dishes and pick up all my clothes from the floor. I strip off my tee shirt and stop to touch my scar, finally accepting it. It's part of me and always will be. It's my connection to Big Sam and Hawkeye, a reminder to never be that powerless again.

Dressing quickly, I pack my suitcase and tuck my father's gun safely in between my clothes. My plan is to take it to a place I read about in *Time*, a new initiative that turns guns into shovels and rakes. It's called Guns to Gardens, and I skim for its address in the white pages.

I pour hot coffee into a mug and sit at our black marble dining room table, looking out the window where my orchid plant used to live. My parents are going to be totally disappointed. I'll have to stand up for myself, remind them that *this is my life*, and when they try to scare me and warn me that I'm making a big mistake, I'll have to say: *I've made them before.*

All Tracey will say is *Finally.*

I stand, and needing air, open the window. The sky is a glorious blue, and the world smells of daylight—vast as hope. Last night's snow barely covers the ground, and looking down at the street corner where I used to meet Carl, I see a little girl riding her bike, carving tracks in the light snow. I remember my own childhood bike and how I'd ride around my Lakefront neighborhood, taking left after left, and then a right, no set path, just pedaling and ringing the bell. And there was the smell of kumquats and the humid breeze on my skin.

I close my apartment window and decide that while I wait to hear from NYU, I'll apply to BU and Tulane. I'll go to New Orleans, see Hawkeye, find closure. Maybe I'll run into Carl.

I pack my *Like a Virgin* album, sketchpad, and set of colored pencils and carry my suitcase to the door. It's heavy, filled with books—*Gone with the Wind*, *Lolita*, *Little Women*, *The Scarlet Letter*. Wearing my grandmother's leopard coat, I look around one last time before I walk out, leaving the bed unmade.

THE END

Author's Note

It took me twenty years to write *The Marriage Box*, twenty years to get the tone just right. And what allowed me to tell this story at all was my ability to laugh at myself and not take myself so seriously. This book is a work of fiction, but it touches on my real world, and the Syrian Jewish community— my community—and so I want to make some things clear.

The Syrian Jewish community is many things, and as time goes on, we grow. Over the decades, since our arrival in this country, we have changed. Today we go to college and get PhDs, women work more often than not, and while traditionally we were merchants, we are now writers, artists, teachers, nurses, therapists, florists, party planners, caterers, and clothing, jewelry, and home designers. We run businesses—big and small. Today we are religiously observant and not, affluent and not; we get married at eighteen and not.

I'm writing this note to let my readers know that it took me so long to finish this book because it was essential for me to tell this story using all the ingredients of good fiction while maintaining the utmost respect. Sure, I make fun and take some liberties for the purpose of successful storytelling. But the essential truth is that this warm, hardworking, charitable community is mine—it is where I chose to live and raise my family.

Syrian Jews have been in America for five generations now. Like every community around the globe, we have our beauty and our flaws. In many ways the community that exists today doesn't look anything like the one depicted in *The Marriage Box*. And in some ways, it's exactly the same.

It is my hope that this novel be a catalyst for endless questions and conversations—for some change, but also for some doubling-down. *The Marriage Box* is for the generations to come. It's just a bit of our story. You write the rest.

Acknowledgments

Alison Espach—I thank my lucky stars for you. Once you read this manuscript and texted back, "I loved it!" I knew *The Marriage Box* was ready for publication, and the world. I treasure your feedback, as I admire and respect you as a teacher, a writer, and an all-around lovely person.

Lisa Ellison, you are a wise and gentle teacher, a kind, generous person, and a good friend. Your guidance led me to discovering the heart of this story. Thank you for believing in me and my writing.

Many thanks to Brooke Warner and the entire She Writes Press Team. It's a gift to be supported by an editor and an editorial team that believe in you and your talent. I waited a long time to find the right match. She Writes Press feels like home.

Marilyn Fallack (A' H), you were my cheerleader. When nobody understood my need to isolate and my desire to write this book, you backed me up. A friendship based on honesty, mutual respect, and devotion is priceless. I miss you.

To Susie Sutton and Nicole Dweck Goletka, thank you for reading everything I wrote way before publication. And for encouraging me every step of the way. Your involvement and support has meant so much to me.

Esther Djmal, when you were overworked and exhausted, you stepped up and made time for this project. Your keen eye, editorial skills, and dedication are much appreciated.

Thank you to all my friends, family, and fellow authors who supported me throughout my writing journey. You bought *Life and Other Shortcomings* and reviewed it; you sold copies in your retail stores; held book clubs in your homes; purchased multiple copies as gifts; and helped me to network, secure engagements, get blurbs, and celebrate. You stood by me and encouraged me! You know who you are and how much your love, generosity, and friendship mean to me. Thank you from the bottom of my heart.

I want to thank my mother and father for all the stories they told me while I was growing up: Susa Belle, Dommie, and my father as a little boy. Those moments left impressions, and I feel blessed that I get to do the storytelling now. Nothing transcends like a good story, and one day at the height of the pandemic, I was editing *The Marriage Box* and thought my parents would get a kick out of a section I was working on. They were quarantining in Florida and I was in New York City. The days were long and scary then, but hoping to lift all of our spirits, I called and asked them if they'd like to hear a portion of my book. Their enthusiasm was everything, and for the next month, every day at four on FaceTime, I read them a single chapter. We were separated by 1,100 miles, yet during a very lonely time, we were intimate. Thank you, Mom and Dad, for listening. And for laughing. I'm so grateful for that time we got to spend together.

Thank you, Mark, for never holding me back. It's true, I used some parts of our personal story, but from the beginning, you understood deeply that this book was a work of fiction. More importantly, you valued my creativity and my need to bring this book to life. My gratitude to you for that is huge. I am so proud of our real-life story, and also this made-up one. They are certainly different, but they are also intertwined. Thank you for trusting me.

About the Author

Corie Adjmi is the author of *Life and Other Shortcomings*, a collection of short stories, which won an International Book Award, an IBPA Benjamin Franklin Award, and an American Fiction Award. Her prize-winning short stories and essays have appeared in dozens of journals and magazines, including *North American Review*, *Indiana Review*, HuffPost, *Medium*, *Motherwell*, and *Kveller*. *The Marriage Box* is Corie's first novel. She is a mother and grandmother and lives and works in New York City.

Author photo © Alberto Vasari

SELECTED TITLES FROM SHE WRITES PRESS

She Writes Press is an independent publishing company founded to serve women writers everywhere. Visit us at www.shewritespress.com.

Bess and Frima by Alice Rosenthal. $16.95, 978-1-63152-439-4. Bess and Frima, best friends from the Bronx, find romance at their summer jobs at Jewish vacation hotels in the Catskills—and as love mixes with war, politics, creative ambitions, and the mysteries of personality, they leave girlhood behind them.

Closer to Fine by Jodi S. Rosenfeld. $16.95, 978-1-64742-059-8. Bisexual and Jewish, Rachel Levine must battle the homophobia and misogyny of her own community, and even her own family, while falling in love, coming of age, and developing personally and professionally into the woman she was meant to become.

Stitching a Life: An Immigration Story by Mary Helen Fein. $16.95, 978-1-63152-677-0. After sixteen-year-old Helen, a Jewish girl from Russia, comes alone across the Atlantic to the Lower East Side of New York in the year 1900, she devotes herself to bringing the rest of her family to safety and opportunity in the new world—and finds love along the way.

Wishful Thinking by Kamy Wicoff. $16.95, 978-1-63152-976-4. A divorced mother of two gets an app on her phone that lets her be in more than one place at the same time, and quickly goes from zero to hero in her personal and professional life—but at what cost?

A Marriage in Four Seasons: A Novel by Kathryn K. Abdul-baki. $16.95, 978-1-63152-427-1. When New York couple Joy and Richard experience a devastating stillbirth, the must navigate the repercussions of their loss—including infidelity, divorce, and an illegitimate child—before finally reconciling.

Unreasonable Doubts by Reyna Marder Gentin. $16.95, 978-1-63152-413-4. Approaching thirty and questioning both her career path and her future with her long-time boyfriend, jaded New York City Public Defender Liana Cohen gets a new client—magnetic, articulate, earnest Danny Shea. When she finds herself slipping beyond the professional with him, she is forced to confront fundamental questions about truth, faith, and love.